VOTE MATTIE FOR MARRIAGE

"You didn't have to ask Tami about that," she said. "I never would have known I could be a write-in candidate."

"I wanted you to be happy."

She seemed to lose her ability to breathe too. "You did?"

"I do." The firelight reflected in her eyes, and he thought that maybe she'd never looked so beautiful. The desire to kiss her seized him by the throat and nearly choked him.

He took a half step away from her and tried to think about anything but Mattie's lips . . .

The Amish Quiltmaker's Unconventional Niece

JENNIFER BECKSTRAND

ZEBRA BOOKS
Kensington Publishing Corp.
www.kensingtonbooks.com

ZEBRA BOOKS are published by

Kensington Publishing Corp.
119 West 40th Street
New York, NY 10018

All Kensington titles, imprints, and distributed lines are available at special quantity discounts for bulk purchases for sales promotion, premiums, fund-raising, educational, or institutional use.

Special book excerpts or customized printings can also be created to fit specific needs. For details, write or phone the office of the Kensington Sales Manager: Attn.: Sales Department. Kensington Publishing Corp., 119 West 40th Street, New York, NY 10018. Phone: 1-800-221-2647.

First Printing: November 2022
ISBN-13: 978-1-4201-5203-6
ISBN-13: 978-1-4201-5204-3 (eBook)

10 9 8 7 6 5 4 3 2 1

Printed in the United States of America

Chapter 1

Mattie Zook was a little ashamed, sort of resentful, and very irritated.

But hopefully, none of these emotions showed on her face as she serenely stared up at the minister, pretending to listen to him and getting madder and madder by the minute.

It was unfortunate that the sermon was on Matthew 5:22—the verse about it being a sin to be angry. By feeling so mad, Mattie was sinning even while she sat right there in church. That probably counted as a double sin.

How could she be anything but angry when her *dat* had sent her to this dry, barren place in the middle of nowhere—so remote that even the trees looked like they didn't want to be there? As soon as she'd stepped off the bus in Monte Vista, Colorado, her skin had dried up like an overtoasted piece of overbaked bread, and her lips had cracked in three places, even while plastered with a coat of Vaseline. Her head hadn't stopped throbbing since yesterday, a condition that Aunt Esther called "altitude sickness." Who in the world wanted to live in a place where you could get altitude sickness? It sounded like a dread disease with no cure.

Mattie sighed inwardly and tried not to be mad at Aunt

Esther. It wasn't Aunt Esther's fault that Mattie's *dat* had sent her to Colorado. It wasn't Aunt Esther's fault that Mattie would probably shrivel up like a prune and drop dead from dehydration—if the altitude sickness didn't get her first.

There was a possibility that it was Mattie's own fault, but she couldn't see it in her heart to regret what she'd done, so she opted to blame the person who had insisted she come to Colorado—her *dat*.

Sometimes it was wonderful hard to honor her *fater* and *mater*. Then again, the commandment didn't say you couldn't be irritated with them.

Church services were being held in the Eichers' barn this morning, a barn three times smaller than any barn in Pennsylvania Amish country. The doors were open to let in the cool air, but Mattie was still sweating—probably another symptom of altitude sickness. There was a smattering of laughter when a Plymouth Rock hen wandered into the barn and pecked at the ground near the minister's foot. The minister obviously wasn't about to interrupt his sermon and didn't even acknowledge the chicken clucking softly at his feet. A young man who looked to be about Mattie's age rose from his seat, scooped up the chicken in one fluid movement, and took it outside. More laughter. The minister didn't even pause.

Mattie turned her head slightly to get another look at the men and boys sitting across the way. If the dry air and the altitude weren't bad enough, the selection of eligible boys in the *gmayna* was even worse. Byler, Colorado, had a very small Amish population, and Mattie could count on one hand the number of unmarried boys who looked like they were even close to her age. Among them, there was only one who was even slightly good-looking—the boy who had dispatched with the chicken and returned with a feather stuck to his shirt. He had dirty blond hair and bright blue eyes, but Mattie had no desire to get to know him because he sang too loudly and acted as if he was truly concentrating on what the minister had to say. Mattie hated pretenders.

Not that it mattered. Mattie wouldn't be getting acquainted with any boys, because she wasn't planning on being here for more than a month. It wouldn't take Mamm but a few days to miss Mattie's help with the cooking and the cleaning and *die kinner*. For sure and certain Mamm would insist that Dat send for Mattie after a week of hanging laundry by herself.

In the meantime, Mattie just had to hold on and figure out how to keep herself from drying up and blowing away with the wind.

Aunt Esther stood, shuffled past the women in her row, and led Winnie out behind the barn to the outhouse. Winnie was potty training, and at that age, the bathroom waited for no minister. Most Colorado Amish had indoor bathrooms, thank Derr Herr, but the outhouse was a convenient addition for church services. *Gmay* was always held at the house of one of the members, and the bathrooms got a lot of use.

Mattie really liked Aunt Esther, even if she was the reason Mattie was no longer in Leola, Pennsylvania, with her friends. Aunt Esther had moved to Colorado two years ago, adopted Aunt Ivy's baby, and gotten married. No doubt Dat had sent Mattie to Colorado because he thought Aunt Esther would be a *gute* influence on Mattie. And because there wasn't anybody in Colorado for Mattie to sue.

Yet.

Aunt Esther was going to have a baby, and though Mattie wasn't planning to be here long, she hoped she could be some help to her *aendi*. Aunt Esther made beautiful quilts that sold for hundreds of dollars at a shop in one of the ski towns. Mattie didn't quilt, but she could do dishes and laundry so that Aunt Esther had more time to quilt. Aunt Esther was sweet and quirky, and Mattie wouldn't mind getting to know her better. Esther always had a needle or quilting clips attached to her dress and a piece of chalk tucked behind her ear. *Ach*, *vell*, a piece of chalk or a straw or something else that might come in handy. This morning, Aunt Esther had a pencil behind her ear. Did she even realize it? Should Mattie tell her?

After the sermon and the hymn and a very long, very dull, and ineloquent prayer, the reverent group of members became a beehive of activity. Two men whisked the bench out from under Mattie almost before she stood up. Men and boys took the benches to the lawn and configured them into tables for the fellowship supper. The women set bowls of church spread and bread on the table, along with big pitchers of ice-cold lemonade.

Mattie backed up to the barn wall and leaned against it. She didn't know anybody and didn't have an assignment, so she didn't really know how to be of help. She swallowed past the lump in her throat and tried to ignore the lonely ache in the pit of her stomach. She didn't know anybody here except Aunt Esther, Winnie, and Uncle Levi. She had no friends, hardly any family, and her dry lips were going to fall off her face. She couldn't remember ever feeling so forsaken.

She closed her eyes and mustered all her anger so she wouldn't burst into tears. She'd never forgive her *dat*, even though as a Christian she was supposed to forgive everybody. Surely even Gotte would make an exception for a *dat* who had banished her for the sin of trying to help him out.

Someone tapped on her elbow. She opened her eyes.

Two nearly identical girls, maybe a few years younger than herself, stood in front of her, smiling widely. "*Hallo*," said one of them. "You're Esther's niece, aren't you?"

Mattie pursed her lips and nodded. What had they heard? She tried to relax. Maybe they hadn't heard a single thing.

One of the girls pressed her hand to her chest. "I'm Sarah Sensenig. This is my *schwester* Sadie. You probably won't be able to tell us apart for several weeks."

Mattie's lips curled involuntarily. "You do look very much alike."

Sarah pulled at the sleeve of Sadie's burgundy dress, the perfect match to Sarah's own. "Mamm thinks it's so cute. She told us we have to dress alike until we turn eighteen."

Sadie's grin widened. "That's next week. I'm making a pink dress for myself for our birthday."

"And I'm going to wear yellow," Sarah said. "We're sick of dressing alike, but we did it for Mamm because we love her and because she gets a divot between her eyebrows when she's angry." Sarah rolled her eyes. "The things our parents make us do sometimes!"

Mattie couldn't disagree with that. Dat had made her come all the way across the country out of spite. She pushed her annoyance from her mind. "Sadie has more freckles than you do."

Sarah nodded vigorously. "Most people don't notice that the first time."

Sadie giggled. "I still don't think Freeman has noticed. Sometimes I get the feeling our *bruder* can't tell us apart."

Sarah huffed in protest. "Of course he can, Sadie. What a terrible thing to say about your very own flesh and blood." Sarah grinned at Mattie. "Freeman is our *bruder*. He is also a twin."

Mattie widened her eyes. "You have two sets of twins in your family?"

"*Jah*. But Freeman's twin is a girl, so no one has trouble telling them apart. Suvie got married last October and moved to Montana. That made Freeman wonderful sad. And us too." Sadie's eyes sparkled with mischief. "Freeman needs a *fraa*. Do you have a boyfriend, Mattie?"

Mattie nearly choked on the question. "Um, *nae*. No boyfriend, but I'm not really interested in having one."

"Wait until you meet Freeman," Sadie said. "Believe me. You'll be interested."

Sarah gave her sister the stink eye. "Sadie, quit trying to find a *fraa* for Freeman. He doesn't like it. He's already told you he can find a *fraa* for himself."

Sadie didn't seem discouraged or less enthusiastic. "Freeman is a boy. He couldn't find a *fraa* for himself even if the girl had a sign around her neck."

Sarah pursed her lips in disgust. "*Jah*, he can. And he doesn't appreciate you meddling in his love life."

"Well, someone has to meddle, or he'll end up a bachelor, and then you and I will have to take care of him when he's old. Think long and hard about that before you scold me for trying to get rid of him."

Chicken Boy passed right behind Sarah. She turned, caught a handful of his sleeve in her fist, and yanked him toward her. "This is our *bruder*, Freeman." The relationship was obvious. They all had the same intelligent blue eyes.

Freeman's apparent annoyance at being interrupted by his sister gave way to a brilliant smile when he looked at Mattie. Okay. Maybe it didn't matter that he sang too loud. He was wonderful handsome. "You're Esther's niece. She said you were coming from Ohio."

Sarah cuffed him on the shoulder. "Pennsylvania, Freeman. She's got a Pennsylvania Amish *kapp*."

Mattie fingered her *kapp* strings. That was another thing she liked about Pennsylvania. Their prayer coverings were much prettier. They were still white and covered their heads, but they were made of sheerer fabric and had a pretty heart-shaped design at the crown. She almost felt sorry for any girl who didn't wear the Pennsylvania *kapp*.

Freeman held up his hands. "Okay. Okay. Pennsylvania. I didn't notice her *kapp*."

Sadie leaned forward and whispered loudly, "He doesn't notice anything. That's why I don't think he can tell us apart."

Freeman wrapped his arm around Sadie's shoulders and pulled her close to his side. "Of course I can tell you apart, *Sarah*. You're my favorite *schwester*." Sadie elbowed her *bruder* in the ribs. He grunted and grimaced in mock pain. "*Ach*, that really hurts, Sarah. I'm changing favorite *schwesteren*."

Mattie couldn't help but grin at the playful teasing between *bruder* and *schwester*. There was nothing playful about the stern way her *fater* ran their family.

"Oh, stop," Sadie said. "Our new friend is going to think you're a *dummkoff*, and we want her to like you."

New friend. Mattie liked the sound of that.

Freeman glanced behind him. "I'd better go help, or I'll be accused of being an idler." He nodded to Mattie. "Nice to meet you . . . I didn't catch your name."

Sadie rolled her eyes. "See, he doesn't notice stuff. He's never going to get a *fraa*."

"It's not Freeman's fault," Sarah scolded. "She didn't tell us her name yet."

Mattie laughed. "I guess I didn't. I'm Mattie Zook."

Freeman held up his thumb and showed Mattie the inch-long scar on the pad. "Esther gave me five stitches when I split my thumb open. She's wonderful nice like that."

Sarah not-so-gently nudged Freeman out of the way. "*Ach*, *bruder*, Mattie doesn't want to see that. It's rude."

Sadie eyed Mattie curiously. "Our *mamm* says you got in some sort of trouble in Pennsylvania, and your *dat* sent you out here as punishment."

Mattie coughed on Sadie's bluntness. "She said that?"

Sarah yanked on Sadie's sleeve. "Sadie, that's not polite."

Mattie did her best to smile. It didn't go very well. "For sure and certain Colorado is punishment enough."

Sadie frowned. "What do you mean?"

Where to begin? The reasons seemed so obvious. "We're in the middle of nowhere. The wind blows, and it's so dry, the dust gets in your teeth, and there are like three trees in the whole town. Your district is tiny, and there's hardly anybody my age. Our district in Leola is three times bigger, and there are hundreds of young people and fun youth groups and dozens and dozens of boys to choose from. And the ministers preach interesting sermons instead of boring ones. How can you bear to live here?"

She realized she'd maybe gone too far when the only response she got was wide-eyed silence. Had she offended them? She was always eager to tell the truth, but maybe she didn't have to spread the truth around in such a wide swath. She should have mentioned how beautiful the mountains were and stopped at that.

"We have a gathering almost every week," Sadie said weakly. "Lots and lots of *die youngie* come. One time we had twenty."

Mattie clamped her mouth shut before she said something to make it worse, like *My youth group has more than fifty*.

Freeman lost any hint of good humor on his face. "We're not rich like the Amish in Lancaster County. My *dat* had to find a place where the land didn't cost an arm and a leg."

"We're not rich," Mattie snapped, as if Freeman had accused her of some horrible sin. And to be sure, to the Amish, being rich was a sin. Since the love of money was the root of all evil, the more someone had, the easier it was to be tempted. The truth was, the Lancaster County Amish were rich—rich in land, even if their bank accounts were just as modest as any Amish man in Colorado. It was a generalization that made Mattie furious.

Freeman drew his brows together and folded his arms across his broad chest. "I apologize for making assumptions about you. Maybe you're not rich, but for sure and certain you're a snob."

Mattie clenched her teeth and glared in Freeman's direction. "No need to beat around the bush. Why don't you tell me exactly how you feel? You have a very high opinion of your own opinion."

Freeman gave her a withering stare. "Scorn is a very unattractive look on you, Mattie Zook." He turned on his heels and strode out of the barn, not once looking back to see Mattie seething in her own juices.

Chapter 2

Freeman was the last to climb into the buggy after church. Mamm and the twins were arguing about pink and yellow dresses while Dat sat quietly at the reins, no doubt eager to get home and away from the bickering. It was good-natured bickering, the kind people engage in when they disagree but still love each other, but Dat had heard the same argument for years. He was understandably tired of it. Freeman folded himself into the back with his two *schwesters* who were talking at once, as if attacking Mamm from both sides would be more effective. "Mamm," Sadie whined, "you said we could wear different colors on our birthday."

Mamm straightened her bonnet. "I know what I said, and you can wear different colors. It's just that I don't approve of your choice of colors. That pink dress you're making is a peacock dress, and I don't like the look of it."

"It is not a peacock dress. All the girls are wearing bright colors. Mattie Zook was in baby blue at *gmay*."

Sarah nodded. "If the Pennsylvania Amish are wearing it, it must be okay."

"If all the Pennsylvania Amish jumped off a cliff, would you?" Mamm said.

Freeman turned his face to hide a grin from his *schwester*.

If all Pennsylvania Amish were like Mattie Zook, even he might be tempted to jump off a cliff.

He sighed and shifted in his seat. Freeman didn't like it when he lost his temper, and he liked it even less when he lost his temper over some snobby girl who wasn't worth the effort or the frustration. Unfortunately, he'd been too distracted by Mattie's good looks to consider that she might be hiding a sharp tongue. *Ach*, *vell*, now that he knew what she was like, he could avoid her and look elsewhere for the girl Gotte had in mind for him.

Freeman liked living in Byler—he really did—but part of losing his temper was because Mattie's words had some truth to them. There were maybe three girls in the *gmayna* whom Freeman could date without robbing the cradle or settling for someone fifteen years older than himself. An older girl might work. Esther Kiem was six or seven years older than her husband, Levi, and they seemed a perfect match. But older, single women in Byler were scarce, as scarce as younger single women. Freeman had tried, sincerely tried, with every girl of marriageable age in the district, but he just hadn't been able to force himself to love any of them. He'd come close with Linda Eicher, but when it became obvious she loved Ben Kiem, there had been nothing to do but get out of the way.

Maybe he should spend a year in Ohio or Indiana looking for a wife. After today, he definitely didn't want to go to Pennsylvania. Mamm's *schwester* lived in Wisconsin. He could go stay with her for a few months and bring a *fraa* back with him. The thought gave him no pleasure. Even if he found someone he wanted to marry, she certainly wouldn't want to live in Byler. He probably shouldn't have been so quick to chastise Mattie Zook. How could he blame her for not immediately seeing how *wunderbarr* Byler really was?

Sadie pinched her lips together. "At least the Pennsylvania Amish have exciting lives. I just sit around all day waiting for a boy to notice me, and there are only two my age."

"Be patient, Sadie lady," Dat said. "In his time, Gotte will bring the right boy to you."

Sarah nudged Sadie with her arm. "It was very rude what you said to Mattie."

Dat turned around and looked at Sadie. "What did you say?"

Sadie narrowed her eyes at Sarah. "I just told her we once had twenty young people show up to a gathering. What's rude about that?"

"Not that," Sarah said, rolling her eyes. "You pried into her personal business when you asked her why her *dat* sent her to Colorado."

Mattie had said something about her *dat* punishing her. She must have done something very bad to be sent to Colorado. All the more reason to steer clear of her.

Sadie squeaked in protest. "That wasn't prying. I was just making friendly conversation."

Sarah rolled her eyes again. "Friendly conversation is '*Hallo,* Mattie. How was the train ride from Pennsylvania?' not 'We heard you got in trouble in Leola.'"

Freeman chuckled. "It depends on your tone of voice."

Sarah reached across Sadie and punched Freeman in the arm. "It does not."

Freeman flinched when a siren blasted. He peered out the back window. Close behind, a police car followed them with the lights flashing and the siren wailing. Dat pulled to the side of the road, and the police car followed him. What in the world? They certainly couldn't have been breaking any speed limits.

Sadie hooked her elbow around Freeman's arm and squeezed tight. "Are we in trouble?"

Freeman shrugged. "I don't know." He wasn't particularly concerned. Sometimes the police stopped them if a buggy light was broken or if they thought their horse was breaking some town ordinance.

The policeman was a woman, with her black hair pulled back into a severe bun. Freeman watched her through the window as she talked to Dat. "I'm sorry, sir, but there is a new town ordinance, effective today, June first. Your vehicle is not in compliance with the ordinance, and I'm going to issue you a warning."

"I'm afraid I don't know what you mean," Dat said. "All those big words strung together make my head hurt."

The policewoman suddenly looked embarrassed, as if she didn't even know what she was talking about. "I'm sorry. The town council just passed a new rule. Buggies and horses are no longer allowed on the main streets." She handed Dat what looked like a map. "Buggies and horses are prohibited on streets colored red."

Dat studied the map. Freeman leaned forward and looked over Dat's shoulder. "But," Dat said, "if we can't drive on these roads, it will take much longer to get anywhere. A ten-minute drive to church will take an hour."

Freeman stared at the red lines crisscrossing the paper. "This doesn't seem fair to the Amish."

The policewoman's face turned a darker shade of red. "I'm sorry. I just enforce the law. I don't make it." She handed Dat another piece of paper. "Here is your official warning. I'm afraid that next time I'll have to write you a ticket."

The silent shock in the buggy lasted until the police

officer got into her car and drove away. "Well, how do you like that?" Mamm said.

Dat sat frozen with the map in front of his face. "Why would they pass a law like that?"

Freeman felt his temper simmering for the second time today. This had to be some sort of a record. "This is Bill Isom's doing. He's on the town council."

Mamm grunted. "I must be a wicked woman indeed that Derr Herr has seen fit to afflict our family with Bill Isom."

"We haven't done anything wrong, Mamm," Freeman said.

Dat shook his head. "Maybe it's not because we're wicked, but because Gotte wants to see if we will act like Christians in the face of adversity."

By "acting like Christians," Dat meant they would pretend nothing had happened and adjust to the new rule. Freeman would go along with what Dat said. There was nothing else he could do about it if he wanted to be a *gute* Christian. Freeman tamped down his anger and thought of today's sermon. *Whosoever is angry with his brother without a cause shall be in danger of the judgment.* Sometimes it was wonderful hard to be a pacifist, especially when men like Bill Isom took advantage of all that good will.

At least Freeman would get his chores done earlier tonight. He always worked faster when he was mad.

Mattie marched into the house and tore off her bonnet. "This isn't right, Aunt Esther. We have to do something."

Uncle Levi didn't seem all that upset that some policewoman had pulled them over in their buggy and told them that all Amish people had to stay off the main roads from now on. Esther seemed mildly irritated, but Mattie was livid. She'd just gotten into town and didn't know how things worked around here, but even she knew that a rule keeping buggies and horses off the roads was completely unfair.

Mattie followed Aunt Esther into the kitchen, and Esther buckled Winnie into her booster seat for an afternoon snack. "For sure and certain it's upsetting," Esther said, pulling the pencil from behind her ear and replacing it with a plastic toddler spoon she was probably going to use to feed Winnie.

Mattie threw up her hands. "Upsetting? It's tyranny, like we're living in a dictatorship."

"I don't even know what those words mean," Esther said, handing Winnie half a banana. "But I know we can't change anything. If we're mad, nothing will change. If we're not mad, nothing will change."

Uncle Levi chuckled, put his arm around Esther, and gave her a squeeze. "Don't take this the wrong way, but I half expected you to go outside and start throwing apricots."

Esther gave her husband the stink eye. "The minister's sermon got to me."

Levi winked at her. "It was a powerful sermon." He sat down at the table and peered at Mattie. "There's nothing for us to do except study that map and try to obey the law. And if we can't, then we'll just have to pay the fine."

Mattie sighed. It was the dilemma of being Amish. The Amish weren't politically active and they didn't vote, so they rarely concerned themselves in politics or legal disputes. If there was a law or a rule that they felt went against their religion, they simply ignored it. Several years ago, the government went so far as to throw Amish men in jail for not sending their children to public high school, or others for not being willing to fight in the army. It was good-hearted Englischers who finally helped change laws that the Amish refused to follow.

Well, Mattie couldn't just sit idly by and let her aunt and uncle be treated like this.

Someone gave three short raps on the front door. Mattie went into the entryway to answer it, but before she got to the door, an elderly Englisch woman let herself in. Her short, curly gray hair stuck out from underneath the sky-blue visor she wore. Her tennis shoes glistened sparkly white, and her jumpsuit was a pretty shade of lavender. She carried a purse the size of a small country. Eyeing Mattie from head to toe with a pleasantly neutral look on her face, she said, "You must be the niece."

Mattie had never seen anything quite like this woman before. Even her glasses were out of the ordinary. They dangled from her neck from a chain of chunky beads. "Um, if you mean Esther's niece, yes, I am."

"I'm Cathy Larsen, and while it's nice to meet you, I don't really have time to make small talk. I have something very important to discuss with Esther. Is she home?"

"In here," Esther called from the kitchen.

Cathy half walked, half shuffled into the kitchen. Mattie followed behind her, wildly curious about this Englischer who was apparently Aunt Esther's friend—at least enough of a friend to walk into the house without waiting for someone to invite her in. Cathy turned to Mattie. "I'm a little slow today. My bunions are acting up, even though I had them removed in October. Those doctors charge all this money, and the surgery doesn't work, but they don't give your money back. It's a racket if you ask me."

"Cathy!" Winnie squealed, throwing up her hands in welcome.

Cathy's lips curled upward in what could probably have passed for a smile. "Hello, my little pumpkin. You get bigger every time I see you." She tapped Winnie on the nose, sat next to her, and set her giant purse on the table.

"Is everything okay?" Esther asked, pulling out a chair and sitting down.

Cathy motioned for Mattie to sit too. "You might as well hear this. It's a travesty of justice, that's what I say."

Levi sat and leaned back in his chair. "What happened?"

"Dorothy Manfield told Jeri Williams that the town council passed a new ordinance. The police are going to start writing tickets to anyone driving a buggy or a horse on the main roads in town."

Levi propped his elbow on the table and rested his chin in his hand. "Technically you ride a horse and drive a buggy."

Cathy cocked her eyebrow in Levi's direction. "Do I look like I care?"

He laughed. "Not really."

"This isn't funny, Levi Kiem. The town is picking on you Amish people. Something needs to be done."

Mattie tapped her hand on the table. "I agree."

Cathy studied Mattie's face. "I like you already, Esther's niece. I'm sorry. I can't remember your name."

"It's Mattie. And we got stopped by the police on the way home from church. She gave Uncle Levi a warning and a map and said he had to stay off the main roads. It isn't fair."

"Darn tootin' it isn't fair," Cathy said. She glanced at Esther. "Aren't you mad about this? You get mad when the mail doesn't come on time."

Aunt Esther blushed. "I do not. I mean, not lately."

"Well? Aren't you mad?"

Esther huffed out a breath and handed Winnie a piece of cheese. "Of course I'm mad, but being mad won't help anything, and it's not good for my apricot tree."

Cathy held out her hand. "Let me see the map the officer gave you."

Levi pulled the map from his pocket and unfolded it. "Red is where we can't drive."

Cathy put on her glasses, and her wrinkles bunched on top of each other. "This is ridiculous. How are you supposed to get anywhere in this town?"

Mattie nodded. "That's what I said."

Uncle Levi heaved a great sigh. "There's nothing we can do."

Cathy looked over the top of her glasses. "I think I know why you're not more upset about this, Levi. You Amish don't really feel right with God unless you're being persecuted."

Uncle Levi burst into laughter. "That's not true."

Mattie had never considered that, but regardless of what Uncle Levi said, Cathy may have been right.

Cathy focused her attention on Aunt Esther, as if she'd had enough of Uncle Levi for one day. "I've been expecting this for three years. Bill Isom always has his knickers in a knot about something. He says the horses and buggies tear up the pavement and cost the town money in road repairs and manure cleanup. And he claims buggies are a safety hazard." Cathy shook her finger at Esther. "We all know he doesn't like the Amish, and we all know he likes to get his own way. That's the real issue."

Mattie frowned. "Who is Bill Isom?" And could she sue him?

Cathy tossed the map on the table. "He's on the town council. There are only three of them, and they make all the decisions for the town. Bill and Fred always vote together, and Tami always votes against Bill and Fred. It's eternally two against one."

"So they voted to keep the buggies off the main roads?" Mattie asked.

"Yes, two against one."

Mattie was glad that at least this Tami person was on their side. "Why does Bill Isom hate the Amish?"

"He's an old-timer. When the Amish started moving in, he said it ruined the quaint charm of our little town. He's been out to get you ever since."

Mattie had already made the mistake of insulting the town once today, so she kept her mouth shut, but Byler, Colorado, and "quaint charm" had nothing to do with each other.

Cathy glanced at Levi. "Remember what he tried to do to David Sensenig?"

"Freeman Sensenig's father?" *Ach*, with all the other stuff that had happened, Mattie had almost forgotten her unpleasant encounter with Freeman Sensenig. Oy, anyhow, that boy was rude.

Cathy nodded. "Bill tried a sneaky legal trick to get all of David's water shares. And since he did the same thing to Lon and me, we hired a lawyer for all of us. Bill eventually backed down but not before we spent three thousand dollars in legal fees. Those lawyers are worse than doctors when it comes to bleeding you dry. But I don't blame the lawyers. If Bill hadn't stirred up trouble in the first place, my great-grandson would still have a college fund."

"Oh, that's too bad," Aunt Esther said.

Cathy waved her concern away. "Don't worry about it. He's four years old. Our bank account will recover before he actually gets to college. I like to think that maybe he'll go off to Europe to find himself and decide he doesn't want to attend college at all. Then I can use that money for a cruise or a really expensive TV."

Mattie couldn't contain a small smile. She had no idea

what Cathy was talking about, but she liked her attitude. "So Bill Isom is behind this new ordinance. Can we talk to him, maybe convince him to change it?"

Cathy shook her head. "Not a snowball's chance. Bill likes to get his way. Once he's made up his mind, he's like a block of cement."

Mattie wasn't about to give up, even if moving a block of cement was hard. "I think we should at least let them know that we think the new ordinance is wrong. If nobody complains, then Bill won't understand how it hurts us."

"Oh, I'm sure Bill knows exactly how it hurts the Amish. He just doesn't care. He's a bully, and like I said, he enjoys being right."

Mattie drew her brows together. "We have to do something." She could always try to sue somebody. She wasn't completely unfamiliar with that process. Of course, if she sued Bill Isom, Dat would have her back in Leola before the ink dried on the legal documents. She wanted to go back to Pennsylvania wonderful bad, but she also wanted to help the Amish here in Byler. If she didn't do something, they'd be forced to take the back roads for eternity. She couldn't let that happen, no matter how badly she wanted to get back home. Besides, if she couldn't find a kindly attorney willing to take her case for free, she wouldn't be able to sue anybody.

Cathy eyed Mattie, as if trying to determine how serious she really was about putting up a fight. "I like you, Mandy."

"Mattie."

"I like you, Mattie. Bill Isom can make a grown man cry like a baby, but don't tell Lon I said anything."

Mattie frowned. "That's why a person like him can get away with being a bully. Nobody dares stand up to him."

"Yep. That's about the size of it," Cathy said. "I agree that somebody needs to do something. But an eighty-four-year-old woman with two new hips might not be the Amish's best hope."

Levi popped a piece of Winnie's cheese into his mouth. "It's not worth the fight. That's why we're not going to do anything about it. We'll get by without driving on the main roads. The Lord said to turn the other cheek."

Cathy fingered the beads on her chain. "At some point you'll run out of cheeks."

Mattie wasn't going to sit idly by, no matter what Uncle Levi thought. "Will you take me to the next town council meeting? They need to know how bad this is for the Amish."

Cathy pulled her shoulders back. "If you have the guts to go, I have the guts to take you."

Aunt Esther shot a concerned look in Uncle Levi's direction. "I don't think that's a good idea, Mattie. Your *dat* wouldn't approve, and it's not the Amish way."

"Dat doesn't need to find out."

Aunt Esther's features darkened like a storm cloud. "I couldn't keep this from your *dat*."

Ach, she shouldn't have said that. Aunt Esther would never want to feel like she had to choose sides between Mattie and her *dat*. Mattie had to be smarter than that. "You're right, Aunt Esther. I would never put you in the middle of me and my *dat*, and it's too much to ask of you to keep secrets for me. I will write to Dat tonight and tell him that I am planning on attending the town council meeting. If he gets mad, I'll tell him you didn't want me to go. You don't have any responsibility for my behavior."

"I feel responsible anyway."

Cathy grunted. "Kids nowadays don't have respect for their elders."

Mattie glanced at Cathy, puzzled by her apparent change of opinion. "He might even be glad I'm going."

"Somebody needs to speak up for the downtrodden," Cathy said.

Esther gave Cathy the same puzzled look that Mattie no doubt had on her face. "Whose side are you on, Cathy?"

Cathy pursed her lips. "I don't know what you're so huffy about. I'm always on the side of truth and justice."

"Aunt Esther," Mattie said, "I know you're worried about me, and my *dat* might not approve, but I'm still in *rumschpringe*." Not even the strictest Amish parent could argue with *rumschpringe*. It was how Amish teenagers had gotten away with some very bad behavior for hundreds of years. "You and Dat need to allow me some freedom. That's what *rumschpringe* is all about. Just be grateful I don't want to go out drinking or kissing Englisch boys. Of all the terrible choices I could make, going to a town council meeting doesn't seem that bad, does it?"

Aunt Esther couldn't argue with that logic, though she tried. "But it isn't the Amish way. We believe in being separate from the world. The town council knows we don't vote. They're not going to listen to you."

"I think they will," Cathy said. "If they see that they've ticked off even the Amish people, maybe they'll realize they've gone too far."

Cathy was right. Now Mattie *had* to go to the town council meeting. "I won't be breaking any rules, not even the Ordnung. I'm just going to share my opinion. They'll see that even though we love peace, we also want to be treated fairly. We demand to be treated fairly. Maybe Bill Isom will change his mind."

Aunt Esther eyed Mattie doubtfully. "But you're going to be polite, aren't you?"

"Of course. I'll be so sweet, they'll feel like throwing up."

Esther heaved a sigh. "That's not exactly what I had in mind."

Chapter 3

Mattie hadn't been to a town council meeting before, and it wasn't as grand as she'd imagined it would be. The town of Byler held council meetings in the small lunchroom of the elementary school, which was the only school in town, except for the even smaller one-room Amish school. The elementary lunchroom smelled like sour milk and ketchup, and instead of folding chairs, people had to sit at the collapsible lunch tables on the small round seats that were only big enough for half an adult's bottom. Mattie didn't mind the seating. She sat on a backless bench every other Sunday for *gmay*. Discomfort was part of being Amish.

The town council and mayor sat at a table on the stage that was part of the lunchroom. The American flag, the Colorado flag, and three huge gray rolling garbage cans stood behind them. The mayor sat at one end of the long folding table, and the town council sat at the other. The woman on the council, whom Cathy said always voted against Bill Isom and the other man, was young and pretty, with a good-natured air about her that made Mattie like her even more than she already did. One of the men had big, round glasses and sparse hair on his head. He wore jeans and a bolo tie. The other man had to be at least sixty, but he had a full head of chestnut brown hair. He wore a fancy suit with a yellow tie, and his beady eyes darted back and forth as if he were waiting for a robber to sneak up behind him.

Since Mattie was inclined to dislike both men, she had to admit to herself that the man's eyes might not have been as beady as she imagined them.

Cathy set her giant purse on the lunch table and pointed to the man with the impressive hair. "That's Bill Isom. And that's not his real hair. He's got plugs."

Mattie didn't know what plugs were, but Cathy acted as if they were a disgrace, so Mattie went with that.

Cathy growled under her breath. "They obviously don't like spectators. Who wants to sit on these tiny platters?" She shuffled to the back of the room, pulled a folding chair from against the wall, and dragged it next to Mattie. "I'd like my whole bottom to fit on the seat, thank you very much."

The meeting was scheduled to start in five minutes, and Mattie and Cathy were the only two people in the audience. A short, plump woman poured each council member and the mayor a glass of water then sat down behind the mayor and pulled out a notepad. Four more people trickled in before six-thirty. Mattie didn't know whether to be relieved or irritated. She was glad the room wasn't packed with people because she was a little nervous to speak, but she was also irritated that more people wouldn't hear her talk about why the new town ordinance needed to be repealed. Of course, the most important people in the room were the ones on the stage, and if she could convince them, she didn't need to convince anybody else.

Shortly before six-thirty, Freeman Sensenig strolled into the room looking somber and determined. Even though Mattie didn't like him all that much, broody was a good look on him. His thick, dark eyebrows were pressed tightly together, and his blue eyes flashed like a gathering storm.

Her throat constricted until she could barely breathe. Speaking in front of strangers was one thing, but getting up in front of grumpy acquaintances was quite another. Freeman thought she was a snob. What would he think about her trying to "fix" the town? Mattie swallowed hard. She had come for Aunt Esther and Uncle Levi. She didn't care what Freeman thought or why he was here. Too bad she couldn't ignore her pounding heart or the feeling that she might throw up.

Freeman also pulled a folding chair from against the wall and set it up behind the lunch tables. He glanced in her direction, and she quickly looked away, though she didn't know why she should be embarrassed to see Freeman Sensenig. He was the one who had been rude. He should be embarrassed to be seen by her. He should be embarrassed to be seen anywhere. A boy like that should be home working on his manners.

The mayor called the meeting to order, and Tami Moore, the councilwoman, led the twelve people in the room in the Pledge of Allegiance. The Amish didn't say the Pledge of Allegiance because Jesus said, "Swear not at all," and because their only allegiance was to Gotte. Mattie stood out of respect, and Freeman probably did the same, though Mattie couldn't see him from where she sat. Bill Isom's booming voice drowned out everyone else in the room, and the glare he directed at Mattie was meant to make her feel small. What it really did was make her madder. Anger might have been a sin, but it gave her courage and a large dose of righteous indignation.

After the pledge, there was a prayer and a thought given by the other councilman. Cathy leaned close to her ear. "That's Fred Evans. He thinks everybody who disagrees with him is a fascist."

Mattie didn't know what a fascist was, but the way Cathy said it made her think it was something bad.

The mayor, wearing overalls over a dress shirt, announced that they would now open the meeting to public comment. Mattie's heart leaped into her throat. She had thought she'd have to wait until the very end of the meeting. She didn't feel completely ready.

Ach, *vell*, ready or not.

A podium with a microphone sat off to the right facing the stage. Cathy nudged Mattie and pointed at it. "You're up, Molly."

"It's Mattie."

"Sorry. I was thinking of Molly Hatchet, the rock group. I can't seem to keep Mattie in my head. I'll think of a bath mat. That should help me remember."

Six audience members made their way to the podium. That was the entire audience except for Cathy, who said she didn't trust herself not to lose her temper with Bill Isom. Mattie couldn't seem to catch her breath as she followed Freeman and stood behind him in the line of people waiting to speak. What was Freeman going to say? Was he here for the same reason Mattie was?

The first woman spent her minute lecturing the council about the dead tree in front of her house. Since it touched the road, she thought the town should pay to have it removed. It became apparent that the woman was somehow related to Bill Isom, and he was especially sympathetic.

The next two men complained about the house near Gunbarrel Road that had never been finished or occupied. The wood was rotting, and the whole property was an eyesore. Mattie knew exactly the property they were talking about. They'd passed it on the way to Aunt Esther's house from the bus station. Aunt Esther said someone had started building the house ten years ago, run out of money, and abandoned the whole thing. It appeared that Bill Isom wasn't related to either of the men who complained because he stared at his phone while they talked.

The next woman in line wore a yellow skirt with matching yellow shoes. She looked to be in her sixties, but her hair was jet-black without a streak of gray. It was a beautiful color. "Mr. Mayor and town council," she said. "I just want to speak in support of the new ordinance prohibiting buggies and horses on our streets. I can actually drive without getting manure on my tires, and I don't have to wait behind a dozen buggies to drive down my own street. I haven't been late to a hair appointment since the new rule went into effect."

How many hair appointments had she gone to? According to the police officer, the rule had started two days ago. Mattie narrowed her eyes. Something seemed fishy.

Bill Isom beamed like a propane lantern. "Thank you for coming out tonight and voicing your opinion. As a council, we felt very strongly that we needed to take action to make our roads safer for everyone."

Tami leaned into her microphone. "Margaret, will you make a note that I voted against the new ordinance?"

The short woman taking notes drew her brows together and jotted something down on her notepad.

Bill Isom pretended Tami wasn't even in the room. He smiled sweetly at the woman in yellow—her skirt a perfect match for his tie. "I'm sure you represent the majority of Byler citizens who have found driving in town much more pleasant without the buggies crowding up our roads."

Tami leaned into her microphone. "Margaret, will you make a note that the woman speaking is Mr. Isom's wife?"

If she hadn't been so nervous, Mattie would have

laughed. Tami Moore had spunk. Mattie liked her more and more. And Bill Isom less and less. But how nice of his wife to come out and support him.

It was Freeman's turn at the microphone. Freeman was tall and well-built, obviously a hard worker. A man didn't get muscles like that by sitting around all day. Mattie liked how he stood up straight, as if he wasn't ashamed or embarrassed or nervous to speak. Mattie had a soft spot for *gute* posture.

"My name is Freeman Sensenig."

Bill folded his arms and leaned back. "I know who you are."

Mattie didn't like the look Bill gave Freeman, as if Bill were a cat ready to pounce on a mouse. But Freeman didn't look much like a mouse, and Bill seemed a little over-confident.

"I'm here to speak against the new town ordinance," Freeman said, his voice strong and determined. "It is not fair to the Amish. We try to be good neighbors and responsible citizens, and this ordinance discriminates against us."

"Thank you for coming today," Tami said. "Can you help my fellow council members understand the hardship this ordinance places on the Amish in our community?"

Freeman nodded, and Fred pulled out a pocketknife and started cleaning his fingernails. "A trip to the bishop's house that used to take ten minutes now takes an hour. In some cases, we can't get to where we want to go without using one of the main roads. If church is at the Yoders' house, I can't get there in my buggy without breaking the ordinance."

Bill wasn't moved. "You can walk."

Freeman stiffened. "It takes an hour and a half to walk to Yoders from my house, unless I take a shortcut through one of your pastures."

Someone in the audience laughed. Mattie's lips curled upward.

Fred shoved his pocketknife into his pocket. "I don't see why you Amish don't just buy cars. It would make everything so much easier."

Tami pressed her lips into a hard line. Apparently, Mattie wasn't the only one trying to keep her temper.

"Our faith directs us to stay separate from the world," Freeman said. "We do not buy cars because rejecting worldly possessions keeps us from being proud. The ordinance is a great burden on the Amish."

Bill Isom glanced at his phone. "I'm afraid your time is up."

Mattie felt Freeman's anger more than saw it. She sensed it in his steely eyes and his mouth pulled into a tight line. It was there in the way he squared his shoulders and walked back to his seat without another word.

Her heart did flip-flops in her chest when she realized it was her turn. But whether she was bullied or ignored or dismissed, she was determined to stand up for Aunt Esther and Uncle Levi and all the other Amish people in town, because except for Freeman, they wouldn't stand up for themselves.

"My name is Mattie Zook. I'm here to speak against the new town ordinance."

Bill sighed. "You have one minute."

"I'm from Leola, Pennsylvania, and I'm visiting my aunt and uncle here in town."

She could almost see Bill Isom's ears perk up. "So you're not even a resident of Byler?"

Mattie's heart sank. Did she have to be a resident? "No."

"Then technically you aren't allowed to speak during the public comment section. We are only interested in hearing from people who actually live here. The way we conduct town business is none of your concern."

Tami rolled her eyes. "That's not true, Bill. Your brother-in-law came last month to comment on curbside recycling, and he lives in Monte Vista."

"At least he's a Coloradan," Bill said. "I, for one, am not willing to waste the council's precious time on someone who doesn't even live here."

Tami tilted her head to one side, as if trying to see Bill more clearly. "It's one minute, Bill. I dare say we can spend one minute hearing what Mattie has to say. Besides, even if she's only here for a visit, she lives in Byler right now. I'd say she technically counts as a resident."

Bill looked at his phone. "Well, it's a moot point because her time is up."

Tami's face turned a shade redder, but she kept her temper. That kind of self-control was probably a requirement for being on any town council. "We've spent Mattie's minute debating about whether she could speak. So we need to start her time over again."

Bill set his phone on the table, as if he needed to prepare to do battle with both hands. "We'll have to vote on it."

A voice from behind Mattie pierced the void of the school lunchroom. "Let her talk, you Communist!" That was Cathy.

Tami clasped her hands together, and her knuckles turned white. "Do we really have to take three more minutes to vote on it?"

Bill pulled a yellow booklet from the bag at his feet and held it up for everyone to see. "I believe in strictly following Robert's Rules of Order. If we don't have procedure, we're just a sham of a government."

The mayor still hadn't said a word, but he seemed to be enjoying himself immensely watching the town council bicker. He clasped a bag of trail mix in his fist and popped nuts into his mouth while his eyes grew as wide as saucers, much as if he were watching an exciting movie.

Tami's sigh came out sounding suspiciously like a groan. "Okay. Fine. I make a motion to give Mattie Zook one minute to speak, plus up to five minutes for question and answer." She eyed Fred, who was now picking his teeth with his pocketknife. "Fred, I need a second."

"Let her talk, you Fascist!" Cathy again. Mattie had no idea what a Communist or a Fascist was, but the title seemed to deeply offend Fred. His face turned beet-red, and he ran his fingers through the comb-over on top of his head. Unfortunately, this upset the delicate balance of his hair, and several long strands that were supposed to lie across the top of his head fell down over his ear. He quickly remedied the situation by pulling out the comb attachment of his pocketknife and smoothing his hair back in place.

Bill glared at Cathy. "If you can't keep quiet, I'm going to have Margaret remove you from the meeting."

Margaret looked up from her notes as if some loud noise had startled her. Her face turned a pale shade of green.

Mattie bit down hard on her tongue to keep from laughing. Margaret was obviously not prepared to throw anybody out of the lunchroom. And Mattie was pretty sure that Cathy would put up a fight. Even though Mattie was still annoyed about the no-buggy ordinance, town council meeting was turning out to be quite entertaining.

The mayor broke his silence. "I second the motion."

Bill leafed through his book. "I don't think you're allowed to second a motion, Mayor."

Tami pressed her fingers to her forehead as if a headache was coming on. "He's right, Lyman. It has to be a council member." She folded her arms and stared at Fred. "Well, do you believe in free speech or not?"

Fred squirmed in his chair for a few seconds, glanced at Bill—who was also staring at him—and looked out into the audience at Cathy, as if he was afraid she'd call him more names. He cleared his throat. "I don't think it will hurt to let the girl speak her peace, Bill. I second it."

"We have a motion and a second," the mayor said, obviously a little put out he hadn't been able to second Tami's motion. "All in favor of letting Miss Mattie Zook speak for another minute with five minutes for Q&A, say aye."

"Aye," Tami said.

Bill's "nay" was almost deafening.

Fred pressed his lips together. "Aye." He turned to Bill, who was frowning as if Fred had betrayed the whole town. "It won't hurt to hear her opinion."

"Three cheers for democracy," Tami said, and Mattie detected only a slight hint of sarcasm in her voice. Tami softened her expression and smiled at Mattie. "Please go ahead and speak, Miss Zook. You have one minute."

"The Amish of Byler pay their fair share of taxes for road maintenance. It is not fair that they are not allowed to drive on most of the roads in town. In Leola, we try to get along by sharing the road."

Tami nodded. "I'm guessing there are many buggies in Leola, Pennsylvania. I'd love to hear how the Amish and Englisch compromise about the roads."

Fred frowned. "Pennsylvania is in the United States, Tami. There aren't any English people there."

Tami smiled sweetly at her companions. "The Amish call non-Amish people Englisch. Isn't that right, Mattie?"

"Yes," Mattie said, her confidence growing. It was nice to know that at least one person on the stage wanted to hear what she had to say. "Some people don't like all the buggies on the roads in Leola and Bird-in-Hand and other towns, but most people can see the benefits. Drivers are forced to slow down and watch for buggies, so buggies actually make roads safer, especially in town. People can't just speed down the streets. They have to make way for the buggies. And most local Englischers like the tourism that Amish businesses bring to the area. The buggies add to the charm."

Fred clicked the tiny light on his pocketknife on and off. "Nobody comes to Byler to see the Amish."

Bill tapped his knuckles on the table. "We wouldn't want them to. An increase in tourism leads to an increase in traffic. And then the roads would really be clogged."

One of the men who had complained about the unfinished house chimed in. "Hannah Kiem's quilts are famous. We could start a museum right on the spot where that old house is."

"Too expensive," Bill said. "And I'll have you know, young lady, that most of our road maintenance is taken from the gas tax. You Amish don't buy much gas."

Mattie decided the best strategy was to appeal to the council's sense of fairness. "But you can see how it places a great burden on the Amish who live here, can't you?"

Bill shook his head. "No, I can't see how it does." *Ach.* Bill probably didn't even know what fairness meant. "The Amish know how to adjust to life in the modern world. They've been adjusting for hundreds of years. When we invented cars, they kept driving buggies. When we built good schools, they kept their children away. When we had wars, they refused to fight."

Tami frowned. "Bill, the Amish haven't adjusted at all. They've stayed the same while the world adjusted to them."

"Exactly," Bill said. "And we're not going to adjust anymore. We have to put our feet down, or they'll walk all over us."

Mattie's righteous indignation nearly spilled out. With

great effort, she kept her temper. "We don't want to walk over anybody. We just want to drive on the roads."

Bill refused to be convinced. "There are plenty of roads you can drive on. Haven't you seen the map?"

Mattie bit down on her tongue. Hard. No wonder Cathy didn't have a nice thing to say about Bill Isom. There wasn't anything nice about him. "I've seen the map, and it's a really mean thing to do to your own citizens."

Bill rolled his eyes. "If it's mean to care about the safety of our roads, then I guess it's mean."

"Show some humility, you bureaucrat." That was Cathy again. Margaret buried her face in her notes, probably hoping Bill would forget that he'd asked her to throw Cathy out.

Bill pretended not to hear and looked at his phone. "Your time is up."

Tami sighed in resignation, obviously unwilling to fight for more time for Mattie. What was left to say anyway?

Bill suddenly found a sweet disposition. He smiled indulgently at Mattie. "We haven't changed our minds about the ordinance, but we truly appreciate your faith in the democratic process in bringing this difficulty to our attention. You Amish are of sturdy stock. We know you will be good citizens and obey our town rules."

Mattie seethed as she marched back to her seat. Something had to be done about Councilman Bill Isom and his little red map.

Bill lost his smile and pointed at Freeman. "And don't cut across my pasture, or the police will be called."

Freeman stood and walked out of the lunchroom, obviously not about to listen to another word from Bill. Cathy grabbed her colossal purse, motioned for Mattie, and followed Freeman out the door. Mattie met them in the hall.

Cathy huffed her displeasure. "Bill Isom is in sore need

of a cleansing enema. That would unplug him, for sure and certain. You'd think since he's up for reelection in November he'd at least pretend to have some compassion."

Mattie growled. "What else can we do? That ordinance is unfair, and they all know it."

Freeman folded his arms across his chest. "There's nothing to be done. You can't reason with an unreasonable man."

Mattie's heart flipped all over itself as she thought of a horrible, *wunderbarr* idea. And now that she'd thought of it, there was nothing she could do but plow ahead. She squared her shoulders and balled her hands into fists. "There is something I can do. I'm going to run for town council."

Chapter 4

"You'll do no such thing," Aunt Esther said, looking up from her quilting long enough to frown sternly at Mattie. "Your *dat* would never forgive me if I let you run for town council." She pulled the chalk from behind her ear and made a mark on her quilt.

Mattie was ready for every objection Aunt Esther could throw at her. "I will write to Dat tonight and tell him what I am up to. You bear no responsibility."

"Do you think saying that makes me feel better?"

It would probably save time if she just laid out her arguments all at once. She counted on her fingers. "I haven't been baptized yet, it's not a sin, the ordinance is unfair, and I want to help. Besides, I'm in *rumschpringe*."

"Mandy has a point," Cathy said.

"It's Mattie."

Cathy frowned. "The memory is definitely going." She sat down on a chair opposite Esther, picked up a needle, and started quilting. "Mattie wants to help. What's wrong with letting her run for office? The campaign will keep her from doing drugs or getting pregnant."

Esther squinted at Cathy. "Are those the only alternatives?"

"Right, Aunt Esther. The campaign will keep me out of trouble."

"But why in the world do you want to run for town council? I don't mean to be rude, but it sounds a little insane, especially for an Amish girl."

Cathy shrugged. "Maybe it's just a phase she's going through."

Mattie eyed Cathy with exasperation. "Whose side are you on?"

Cathy shrugged again. "I already told you. I'm on the side of truth and justice."

Esther completely abandoned her needle and leaned back in her chair. "It's so rash. Have you thought about how hard it might be? You don't know anything about running for office and even less about being in office."

"I can be Mattie's driver," Cathy said. "The first priority of every politician is to be able to go places. And I know a few people who might be willing to help on the campaign."

Mattie sighed. "I don't know anything about government, but I want to run. I want to show Bill Isom that he can't get away with being a bully."

"If this is about teaching Bill Isom a lesson, then it's not worth it. Revenge is not a good reason to run for office."

Mattie smoothed her hand along Aunt Esther's quilt. "The buggy ordinance is unfair, Aunt Esther, and the only way to get rid of it is to get Bill off the town council. I know Tami would vote for our side. Then it would be two against one."

Cathy nodded in satisfaction. "You're talking like a politician already." She looked at Esther. "This girl's a natural."

"But I'm afraid you'll get your feelings hurt or your

heart broken or your dignity squashed. I'm also thinking about your protection."

"None of those things scare me. I'm stronger than you think. I'm probably the only Amish girl you know who has filed a lawsuit."

Aunt Esther deflated like a leaky balloon. "But it's not the Amish way."

"I know," Mattie said, "but it's *for* the Amish here in Byler. I want to help, and who better than a Pennsylvania Amish girl who nobody knows or cares about."

Aunt Esther shook her head. "I care."

"I just mean that it won't ruin my prospects of finding a husband because I'm not staying here, and the *gmayna* can't be mad at you and Uncle Levi because I don't belong here anyway."

Esther seemed to be wavering. "I'll have to talk to Levi."

"Much as I respect and love Uncle Levi, it's not his decision," Mattie said.

"It is if you're living in our house."

Ach. Could she learn to show some humility? "You're right. I'm sorry."

"You could come live with me," Cathy said. "But Lon's CPAP machine is loud. You'll have a hard time sleeping, and you need to be sharp for the campaign trail."

Mattie couldn't imagine that the campaign trail would be very cumbersome. Byler had a population of about two thousand people.

Esther didn't seem to like that suggestion. "No, no, we promised your *dat* we would take care of you. You're not living with anybody but us, no matter what." She glanced at Cathy. "No offense."

"None taken. It was a symbolic gesture. I don't like houseguests."

Mattie had gone a long way to convincing Aunt Esther,

and that was the most important thing. Uncle Levi was like a calm, unhurried river. If Mattie could get Aunt Esther to say yes, Uncle Levi would readily agree. He didn't like contention, and he'd do anything for Aunt Esther.

Now she just needed to find someone who knew how to make posters.

Freeman clanged his wrench against the metal pipe in hopes that brute force would fix the clog. This new sprinkler machine had given him nothing but trouble since they'd bought it. It plugged up so much, it felt like it might be faster to shut down the system and use a bucket to water the fields.

Freeman read page twenty-five of the user's manual one more time. What was he doing wrong? He needed to concentrate, but concentration was completely impossible today. Bill Isom seemed determined to make Freeman and his whole family miserable. First there was the battle about the fence, then it was the battle over water rights, and now it was the battle over Byler roads. Freeman didn't have time to take the back roads everywhere he went, and he didn't have time to fight the new ordinance. What were any of them going to do?

Mattie Zook was just arrogant enough to think about running for office. But arrogant or not, Freeman had to admire her courage and her impudence for daring to pick a fight with Bill Isom. There was no chance for her to win, but at least she was willing to try something. Freeman couldn't even fix his sprinkler. And it was getting too dark to see much of anything.

An old K-car pulled off the road next to the field and stopped. Cathy Larsen slowly eased herself out of the car, but for being well into her eighties, Cathy moved surprisingly well. She put her head down and started across the pasture toward Freeman with that huge purse of hers slung over her arm. Thousands of dirt clods and many deep furrows lay between them, and Cathy wouldn't get very far, no matter how well she moved. She was going to trip and hurt herself.

Freeman sprinted in her direction. "Cathy, stop," he called. "Let me come to you."

Cathy lifted her head and squinted as if trying to figure out who was yelling at her. She stopped in her tracks and peered at Freeman running like a madman toward her. "It's not urgent," she said, when he finally got to her. "But thanks for coming so quickly."

"Is everything all right?" Cathy was Freeman's next-door neighbor, "next-door" meaning a quarter mile down the road with two fields between them. Sometimes Cathy came to Freeman and his *dat* when she needed something done around her house. Her husband, Lon, didn't get around very well, and Freeman helped with odd jobs that were too hard for Cathy to do herself. He cleaned the leaves from her rain gutters every spring and shoveled the snow off her driveway every winter. Last week, he'd changed a tire on her K-car.

Cathy waved her hand in the air. "No need to panic. I'm fine. I've come to ask you a favor."

"Okay. What can I do for you?"

"Do you remember Mandy Zook?"

Freeman drew his brows together. "Do you mean Mattie Zook from Pennsylvania?"

Cathy made a face. "I don't know why I keep calling her Mandy. I can't get that Barry Manilow song out of my head." She sighed. "Yes. Mattie Zook from Pennsylvania. She seems like a good sort of girl, don't you think?"

A butterfly or two came to life in Freeman's stomach be-cause even though Mattie was vain and proud and a bit of a snob, she was still the prettiest unattached girl in Byler. Freeman wasn't blind, and neither were the butterflies in his stomach. She'd bravely stood up and faced the town council. But she'd also turned up her nose at Byler and thought she was better than the Colorado Amish simply because she came from Pennsylvania. "She's a little intense."

"The perfect quality for a politician," Cathy said. "She's running for town council."

"We all say crazy things when we're angry."

Cathy shook her head. "Nope. It's not just talk. She paid the fee and filed for the election this morning. I drove her there. The first thing every politician needs is a car or a willing driver."

Freeman fingered the stubble on his jaw. "She's really going to do it?"

"Bill Isom made her pretty mad."

The butterflies in his stomach turned to heavy stones. "That's a very bad idea. Bill won't be nice, even to an Amish girl, and I can't imagine Mattie knows the first thing about running for office."

"She's determined to do it."

Freeman felt sick for Mattie, and he didn't even like her. "You've got to talk her out of it. You know better than anybody how spiteful Bill is. He doesn't like it when people get in his way."

Cathy clutched her purse tighter. "I don't think I could talk her out of it. I don't want to talk her out of it. Somebody needs to teach Bill a lesson."

"It shouldn't be Mattie."

"Who better than Mattie? She's Amish, so she's a novelty. She'll get the sympathy vote from the old-timers, and she's young so the Millennials will like her. No one else dares to run against Bill, and we all know he needs to be off the town council. Byler is getting a reputation for bad government."

Freeman couldn't imagine that a tiny town like Byler had a reputation for anything. "She's going to get hurt." Mattie wasn't exactly Freeman's favorite person, but she didn't deserve what was coming if she ran for office.

"I'm glad you feel so protective."

"Not especially protective. It's just that I can see what's going to happen, and I feel sorry for her."

Cathy's mouth twitched with irritation. "I was counting on you feeling protective."

"I don't see why."

"Because you need to help Mattie in her campaign."

Freeman's eyes nearly popped out of his head. "Absolutely not."

Cathy didn't seem to hear him. Either that, or she was purposefully choosing to ignore his refusal. She pulled a piece of paper from her purse. "I'm assigning you to be her campaign manager."

Freeman spoke louder, just in case she hadn't heard him, which was just wishful thinking. "Cathy, I am not going to help Mattie with her campaign. I don't know the first thing about voting or government or anything."

She reached in her purse and pulled out a piece of paper. "Here is Tami Moore's phone number. I told her you'd be calling to ask about Mattie's campaign."

"I don't want to."

"You've got to help her, or Bill Isom is going to chew her up and spit her out."

Freeman shook his head so adamantly, he could have fanned up a breeze. "I won't do it. There are plenty of Englischers who can help, including you."

Cathy seemed genuinely surprised that he would suggest she could help. "I can't be her campaign manager. I'm the driver *and* her chief of staff. Besides, I have pickleball twice a week, quilting group, and a weekly lunch with my sister. And I'm certainly not going to miss the *Great British Baking Show*. I've got plenty on my plate. You've got to step up."

"I have to work the farm and take care of the animals. I have less time than you do."

Cathy was unmoved. "My motto is: If you want something done, ask a busy person."

Freeman took off his hat and scrubbed his fingers through his hair. "It doesn't matter, because I've been baptized. I couldn't help if I wanted to, and I don't want to."

"Of course you can help. The Amish don't vote, but according to Esther, there's nothing in the Ordnung that says they can't help someone get elected."

This conversation was getting ridiculous. Cathy refused to see reason. "It's not the Amish way."

Cathy blew a puff of air from between her lips. "That's just an excuse and a pretty lame one, if you ask me. Mattie needs your help."

Maybe it was time for brutal honesty. "I don't like her."

"You don't have to like her. You just have to feel sorry for her. Bill is not going to be nice."

That was true enough. "But why me? She lives with Esther and Levi. Can't they help her?"

"Esther and Levi have a toddler and a baby on the way. They don't want to make trouble for themselves in the *gmayna*."

"But you don't care if I get in trouble with the *gmayna*?"

"You're young and impetuous. The elders won't be so touchy about you."

A single burst of laughter escaped Freeman's lips. "I am not impetuous. I'm one of the most cautious men you know."

Cathy nodded. "And that's why I'm asking for your help. You and Mattie are the only Amish people who cared enough to come to the town council meeting. You are the only ones who are brave enough to fight Bill Isom. You want to help all the Amish people in town, don't you? If Mattie gets elected, she'll vote to repeal the buggy ordinance, and that's reason enough to help her."

That was probably true, but what would the bishop say?

Cathy pinned him with a serious look. To anyone who didn't know her well, it would have looked like a scowl. Cathy was pretty stingy with her show of affection. "When somebody in town needs help, you are the first person they call. You're not afraid of hard work, and you're not afraid of Bill Isom. I trust you to protect Mattie's feelings when Bill gets mean. Mattie needs you. But don't let it go to your head."

Every impulse told him to run away as fast as he could, but then Cathy would probably try to catch him, trip on a rock, and break a hip or something. "Okay. Okay. I'll help her, but only because you asked so nicely and you helped my *dat* with that water dispute."

"Yeah. You owe me big-time." Cathy handed him the paper she'd pulled from her purse. "Here is the list of dates you'll need to know about. Meet the Candidates night is the second Tuesday in September. Election day is November first."

Almost six months away. There was still time to talk Mattie out of running.

"One more thing. Mattie is quite proud."

"For sure and certain," Freeman muttered.

"She would never ask for help, even if she needed it, especially not from you."

Freeman furrowed his brow. "Why not from me?"

"She thinks you're rude."

"I am not rude. The first day I met her, she insulted the whole town and the whole state. She's a snob, and I told her so."

Cathy cocked an eyebrow and looked as if she was about to scold him. "I'm sure your righteous indignation knows no bounds, but I can't imagine that Colorado needs you to come to its defense. Colorado is the country's best kept secret, and I just as soon people stay away. Except for Mattie, of course, because she's brave enough to try to change the ordinance. Since Mattie is proud—in the best possible way, of course—she doesn't think she needs your help. You have to pretend this is your idea. You might have to beg."

"Beg?"

"Beg her to let you help."

"I refuse to beg. If she doesn't want my help, I'm not going to bother."

"She doesn't think she needs help," Cathy said, "but we both know how far that will get her."

Freeman clenched his teeth. Life would be almost impossible for the Amish if they couldn't drive on their own roads. On the other hand, he hated the thought that snobby Mattie Zook would think she was doing *him* a favor.

He swallowed past the lump in his throat. Mattie was the best chance the Amish had. Changing the ordinance would be worth eating two helpings of humble pie. Probably.

Chapter 5

On Mattie's first day in church, everyone had been friendly. It seemed the whole *gmayna* had wanted to meet the new girl who was staying with Esther and Levi. Freeman had been a *dummkoff*, but his sisters were nice and so were the rest of *die youngie*. What they lacked in numbers, they had made up for in friendliness.

No one was quite so friendly today. Teenage girls glanced at her then whispered behind their hands. The ministers and even the *Vorsinger* gave her stern and disapproving looks during the service, and she overheard two *fraaen* talking about her while they prepared church spread for the fellowship supper. "*Ach*," one woman said, "did you hear about Esther's niece from Pennsylvania?"

"*Jah*. Been here two weeks and already stirring up trouble."

"She should go back to Pennsylvania. We don't do that sort of thing here in Colorado. She'll give the Amish a bad name."

Mattie pressed her lips together and slipped out of the kitchen, her ears burning and her blood boiling. Didn't these people appreciate what she was trying to do for them? Nobody liked the new town ordinance, but nobody else had the nerve to do anything about it. They should at least show some gratitude.

Mattie jumped when Sadie hooked her arm around Mattie's elbow and pulled her outside to the wide wrap-around porch. Sarah followed close behind, shaking her head and rolling her eyes at Sadie. Sadie wore a navy blue dress, while Sarah looked very sweet in dark red. Mattie smiled. It seemed that the twins didn't mind that Mattie was trying to give the Amish a bad name. The three of them sat on the porch swing, which was wide enough for five or six girls. "You must be wonderful happy to not have to dress alike anymore," she said.

Sadie giggled. "We are, but it takes me ten extra minutes to decide what to wear every day."

Sarah groaned. "You only have four dresses, Sadie. It doesn't take you that long."

"It does too. I lie in bed for ten minutes before we have to get up, planning what I want to wear. I'm glad I'm not Englisch or it would take even longer. Kirsten Greene owns eight pairs of shoes. Can you imagine trying to decide what to put on your feet every day?" Sadie nudged the porch slats with her toe and made the swing move back and forth. "We heard the most exciting gossip about you, Mattie. Is it true you're running for mayor of Byler?"

"Sadie," Sarah scolded, "it's not nice to ask such things."

"It's all right, Sarah. It's a perfectly nice question, and it's not a secret. I'm not running for mayor. I'm running for the town council."

Sadie stared at Mattie wide-eyed. "*Ach, du lieva.* We aren't even supposed to vote. Do you think you'll get shunned? I don't think Freeman can marry you if you're shunned."

Sarah nudged Sadie hard with her elbow. "She won't get shunned. She hasn't been baptized yet."

"Well, I don't know how they do it in Pennsylvania," Sadie said. "And I'll bet Freeman doesn't know either. How can he date her if he doesn't know?"

Mattie eyed them doubtfully. "I hope you're not mad at me."

Sadie's mouth fell open. "Mad at you? I think it's *wunderbarr*. You're the bravest person I know. Even braver than Freeman who killed three rattlesnakes in one day." She pinned her gaze to Mattie's. "With. His. Shovel."

Mattie looked at Sarah, who hadn't said very much. "Do you think I'm wicked for running for office?"

Sarah drew her brows together. "I don't think it's wicked, especially since you're still in *rumschpringe*. We're supposed to be able to do anything while we're in *rumschpringe*, even though Mamm won't let us get cell phones. It's just so different from what any of us have ever done. Do the Amish in Pennsylvania run for office?"

"*Nae*. They wouldn't dream of such a thing. Very much like it is here."

Sarah wrapped her fingers around Mattie's fist. "Sadie is right. You're very brave."

Sadie nodded. "I would die of terror just standing up in front of people and having to think of something to say. I'd probably faint."

Mattie's pulse raced. Was she excited or nervous about getting up in front of people? The pounding in her heart felt more like resolve than anything else. Maybe fighting for her family and neighbors was exactly what Gotte wanted her to do. She hoped so, because she refused to turn back now.

"You can probably tell that the *gmayna* isn't happy about it," Sarah said. "But under all that disapproval, we know you're doing us a huge favor. Nobody but me and Sadie will tell you how grateful we are, but just know that everybody is secretly hoping for you to win. I, for one, am tired of walking everywhere."

Mattie laughed. "And Cathy has already informed me she's not going to allow more than eleven people in her van at a time. She only has twelve seat belts."

Freeman stomped up the porch steps and sat next to Sadie on the swing. Mattie's heart did a little skip, but surely it was a leftover skip from the thought of getting up in front of people. Then again, maybe her heart skipped because Freeman was so handsome yet so unaware of it. When he was around, Mattie couldn't pry her gaze from him. Too bad he was as prickly as he was good-looking.

Sadie scooted closer to Sarah to make room for Freeman. "Freeman, you don't think Mattie is wicked, do you?"

Sarah huffed out a breath. "Sadie, that's not polite."

Sadie frowned. "I don't see why not. Mattie asked us the same thing, and I want to know what Freeman thinks."

Freeman grinned at his sister. Mattie was wildly jealous of that grin. After her first day at *gmay*, Freeman had barely acknowledged her existence. "I don't think Mattie is wicked."

Mattie thought she might melt into a puddle. Freeman Sensenig had actually said something nice about her . . . well, not exactly nice, but not mean either. For some reason, Freeman's good opinion was important to her. He seemed like a man who tried to be honest in everything he said.

Sadie rocked back and forth on the swing. "Aren't you proud of her for running for office? We are."

Freeman pressed his lips together. "I'm not proud of her exactly. Honestly, I think she's a little foolish."

It felt as if a small bird had flown directly into Mattie's face. She blinked back her disbelief and gasped for air. To think she had harbored a charitable thought for Freeman only moments ago.

"'Foolish'!" Sadie giggled. "*Ach*, Freeman, what a thing to say." She swallowed her laughter. "But you'd still date someone like Mattie, wouldn't you?"

Freeman cocked an eyebrow at Sadie. "Quit trying to find me a *fraa*, Sarah, or *Sadie* will be my favorite sister from now on."

"Oh, *sis yuscht*, Freeman! I'm Sadie."

How could Mattie have ever thought Freeman was good-looking? He was a grumpy, judgmental, irritated young man who found fault with other people so he wouldn't have to examine his own shortcomings. She stared at the road that ran in front of Miller's house. "I don't really care what you think."

Sarah nudged Mattie with her shoulder. "Oh, Mattie. He didn't mean it. He's just teasing."

Mattie glanced in his direction. "He doesn't look like he's teasing."

Sarah punched Freeman in the shoulder. "Freeman, tell her you're teasing."

Freeman shook his head. "I'm not teasing. She shouldn't run."

Sarah's mouth fell open. "How can you be so rude?"

"I'm not rude. I'm being honest."

Sarah slugged him again. "It's rude."

Freeman rubbed his arm and laughed. "Ouch. You're going to give me a bruise."

"I hope so," Sarah said. So did Mattie.

Freeman stood, took his *schwesteren*'s hands, and pulled them off the swing. "You two go help with the fellowship supper. I need to talk to Mattie."

Mattie nearly choked on her own spit. What did Freeman

think he had to say to her? Why didn't he just go away and leave her alone? Forever.

Sarah folded her arms and sat back down. "They don't need more help, and what do you want to talk to Mattie about?"

Freeman gave his *schwester* a dirty look. "Go."

"You can't boss us around," Sadie said, sitting down next to Sarah.

"Yes, I can. Now leave us alone, or I'll tell Mamm what really happened to her bird clock."

Sadie glared at Freeman. "That was four years ago."

Freeman nodded. "And I'm so petty, I'm still using it against you."

Sarah growled and stood, taking Sadie's hand and pulling her up. "*Cum.* Freeman wants to kiss Mattie in private."

Mattie nearly jumped out of her seat, and Sadie laughed so hard, she snorted.

"Ha, ha," Freeman said, his lips twitching upward slightly. "You're not as funny as you think you are."

Sarah grinned wryly. "I'm very funny. Sadie laughs at all my jokes." She pulled Sadie halfway down the porch steps then came back up again. Pointing her finger in Freeman's face, she said, "Don't be rude."

Mattie was tempted to sneak into the house while Freeman's back was turned, but no matter how unpleasant Freeman was, she was not a coward. Let him say what he wanted to say and get it out of his system.

And kissing was out of the question. Sarah *had* to know that.

Mattie held her breath. Kissing would not even cross her mind. It certainly hadn't crossed Freeman's. Sarah had just been trying to get under his skin. There would most certainly not be any kissing, any hint of kissing, any thoughts of kissing, or any desire to kiss Freeman Sensenig. She couldn't stand him.

Freeman looked anywhere but at her as he sat on the far end of the swing. "I thought you wanted to get out of Colorado. If you win the election, you'll be here in the middle of nowhere for four years."

Mattie felt her face get warm. "I'm sorry I insulted your beloved Colorado, but you have to admit there's more water in a bathtub."

Freeman swiped his hand across his mouth—perhaps to hide a smile? "It's arid here, for sure and certain, but the clothes on the line dry three times as fast, and we never get mold. And who doesn't prefer crisp toilet paper to that damp stuff in more humid climates?"

Mattie pursed her lips so she wouldn't smile. "I do like crispy toilet paper."

"It's the best reason to live in Colorado."

She cracked a smile. "I don't think they'll put that on the travel posters, and I don't mean to argue, but my skin feels like it's been crammed into a toaster, and the trees don't even try to look happy. I expect they're too thirsty."

"Can trees look happy?"

"They do in Leola." She twisted her *kapp* string around her finger. "But the mountains truly are beautiful, and there's lots of fresh air. Dry fresh air. I didn't mean to sound like a snob. I was mad at my *dat* for sending me here, and I blamed the whole state."

"I guess I shouldn't have gotten so defensive."

She shook her head. "I was boastful about our district and our ministers and our abundance of water. But you've really got to stop making yourself so unpleasant."

"Me? Unpleasant?"

"I barely know you, and you've already accused me of

being proud, snobby, and foolish. You don't have a very endearing personality."

Freeman shrugged as if he didn't especially care what she thought. "If you go ahead with this election, Bill Isom will make your life miserable."

"And that's why you think I'm foolish?"

He sighed. "I shouldn't have said it quite like that, but yes. You've been in town two weeks, so you don't know. Bill Isom has a reputation. Most people around here shake in their boots when they hear Bill's name."

"It's true that I don't really understand, but is Bill really that frightening? I think Cathy would have told me if I'm in danger."

"*Nae*, nothing like that. But he's going to hurt your feelings, and I think you'll regret running."

Mattie blew a puff of air from between her lips. "Hurt my feelings? Is that all? I'm not afraid of that."

"Well, you did get offended when I called you snobby. I'm afraid Bill is going to call you a lot worse. It doesn't seem that terrible now, but Bill is clever. He knows how to hit you right where it hurts."

Freeman looked genuinely worried, and Mattie was actually quite touched by his concern. "Cathy said he tried to take your *dat*'s water rights."

"Remember what you said about the bathtub?"

She smiled. "You mean how there's not much water in Colorado?"

"*Jah*. Water shares are a big source of contention. We don't get enough rain, and we use irrigation to water our crops. Bill claimed about a half acre of our land. He tore down our fence and put one of his own around his new property line. Then he tried to take my *dat*'s water shares to go along with the land. If Cathy and Lon hadn't helped us, we would have lost half our water. Our farm couldn't have survived. Bill called the sheriff twice to complain we were trespassing on his property. It wasn't true, but it sure got my *dat* all worked up. He had to go on blood pressure medication. The judge told Bill to stop using the police to harass us. But now he's found another way to make us miserable."

"If he weren't on the town council, he wouldn't be able to make laws like this. I've got to stop him."

"I admire your courage, but I don't think you should run. We will adjust to the buggy ordinance. It's not worth breaking your heart." There it was again, a glow of deep concern in his eyes. Maybe he wasn't such a grumpy, judgmental person after all.

"It's worth it to me," Mattie said. "I've got to fight for what I believe is right, and when I make up my mind, nobody can talk me out of it."

A grin played at his mouth. "*Jah*. I can see that." He exhaled deeply and pinned her with a serious look. "I don't think you should run, but if you're determined to do it, you can't do this on your own. You're going to need my help."

Mattie eyed him skeptically. "Don't you think I'm smart enough to run my own campaign?"

"I didn't say that."

"You didn't have to. Amish men always think they're smarter than women."

Freeman practically growled his reply. "Maybe you should get off your high horse, Mattie Zook. You don't know what I think or how I feel."

She folded her arms. "I can run my campaign just fine without your help. I tie my shoes by myself every morning, and I know how to milk a cow."

Freeman threw up his hands. "Oh, *sis yuscht*. Do you want to win or not? Because if you want to win, you need to swallow your pride and let me help."

"*Ach*, because you're so much smarter?"

"*Nae*, because no matter how smart or righteously indignant you are, you cannot do this on your own." He was practically yelling now. He glanced across the lawn to where the men and women were setting up the fellowship supper and lowered his voice. "You don't know anybody in town. Who are you going to ask to donate money? Who will print signs for you, and where are you going to put them? You've got to get permission from the neighbors to put up election signs. What is your platform? How are you going to get out the vote?"

Mattie's stomach dropped to the ground. "What is a platform?"

"Exactly. Look, you need my help, not because I'm smarter than you or know more, but because every candidate needs lots of support." He cleared his throat. "Please let me help."

"*Ach*, *vell*," Mattie said, eating a bit of crow. She'd overreacted. Freeman was right. She needed all sorts of assistance, and she had no idea where to begin. "You really want to help that badly?"

"Well. Yes. And, no. To tell the truth, Cathy asked me to help you, and even though I'd rather get a root canal, I owe Cathy a lot."

Mattie gave him the stink eye. "How nice to know you'd rather get a root canal."

"Who cares about why I want to help? Believe it or not, I sincerely don't want Bill Isom to hang you out to dry."

Mattie straightened her spine. This was no time to be proud or snobby or foolish, but she couldn't help but be a little stubborn. "I don't want your help, and you obviously don't want to give it, but if Cathy thinks I'll have a better chance of winning with your help, then I guess I don't mind.

Cathy would be irritated if I didn't let you help me, and she's not fun to be around when she's testy."

Freeman nodded, and Mattie gritted her teeth at the smugly satisfied expression on his face. He looked around as if checking for spies or other eavesdroppers. "Look, I don't want you to think I'm chicken or anything, but nobody can know about this. I've been baptized, and while I don't believe it is going against the Ordnung to help you, I don't want to upset my *dat*. He's upset enough as it is about the buggy ordinance. When he heard you were going to run against Bill Isom, he clutched his chest and started sweating."

"He's upset that an Amish girl is running for town council?"

"*Nae*," Freeman said. "He's worried about you. We all are."

He probably had no idea how his gaze warmed her heart. "Some of the *fraaen* say I'm making the Amish look bad."

Freeman shook his head. "That's what the gossips say, but my family, at least, thinks it's brave and *wunderbarr* and wildly reckless."

Mattie's lips curled involuntarily. "*Ach*, *vell*. *You* think it's wildly reckless."

"*Jah*, I do. But I also think it's a wonderful unselfish thing to do. You don't even live here."

"It's probably the only reason I can run for town council. I'm an outsider, and if I lose, I can just go home and nobody in Leola will know or care. They won't have a reason to be mad at me."

He peered at her doubtfully. "And if you win? You'd be stuck here for four years." He emphasized the word *stuck*.

Mattie rolled her eyes. "Contrary to what you might think, I don't hate it here. I imagine prison would be worse."

He laughed. "Here or prison?" When you put it that way, Byler doesn't seem so bad." His piercing gaze made her stomach feel like it was doing loop-de-loops. "Don't think that I don't understand what a sacrifice this is for you. *Denki* for caring about a group of people you don't really know and for being brave enough to do something about it."

Mattie raised her eyebrows. "I'm not brave. I'm just angry."

"A lot of us are angry. You are the only one who has the courage to try to make it right."

Mattie wasn't sure if it was courage or foolishness.

A certain young man had accused her of both.

Chapter 6

Mattie used the ladder, working on one side of the tree while Aunt Esther stood on the ground getting what apricots she could reach without a ladder. Neither Levi nor Mattie wanted Esther to get on a ladder, not in her condition. She would thin what apricots she could and leave the rest to Mattie. Winnie ran around and around the tree singing, "I go potty. I go potty."

Aunt Esther laughed. "I wish she did it as well as she said it."

"I guess that's the first step," Mattie said.

"At least it's June so she can play outside." Aunt Esther broke a leafy twig off the tree and tucked it behind her ear. "Accidents are so much easier to clean up."

Thinning apricots wasn't hard, but it was important that you didn't touch your face or anything else or the apricot fuzz would make you itchy.

"*Denki* for helping, even though you don't like apricots," Aunt Esther said. "The crop is going to be *gute* this year. We might even be able to sell some."

Mattie smiled. "You can sell my share, for sure and certain."

"I can't believe you don't like apricots. They're Levi's

favorite. I'm planning to make dozens of apricot pies for him when the apricots get ripe."

Mattie wrinkled her nose. "I don't know that I'll volunteer to help with that."

Esther took her bucket and dumped the little green apricots into the compost pile on the edge of the yard. She came back to the tree and held out her hand to Mattie. "Here. Do you want me to dump your bucket?"

"*Denki.*"

Esther handed Mattie her empty bucket and waddled over to the compost pile with Mattie's bucket. "You're a wonderful cute pregnant lady," Mattie called.

Esther grunted and patted her stomach. "Only if you think a baby whale is cute."

Mattie laughed. "I do."

Esther came back to the tree and planted herself close to Mattie's ladder. "Mattie, Levi and I are wondering if you could do us a favor."

"Of course. Anything. You've been so kind to me." Last week, Aunt Esther and Uncle Levi had grudgingly agreed that Mattie could run for town council after her *dat* had written to give his permission. Dat's permission was in the form of a letter chastising Mattie for being proud and headstrong and for giving her *mater* an ulcer. But he'd also said that because she was in *rumschpringe*, she could do what she wanted, even though she would probably go to hell and shame the entire family. Mattie didn't care about the stinging rebuke. She'd gotten what she wanted, and for now, that was all that mattered. She tucked the hurtful words into a dark corner of her heart where she could examine them after the election was over.

Mattie was glad that she wouldn't have to sneak around her *aendi* and *onkel* for the next four months, but it was obvious they weren't happy about her running for office.

One morning she'd caught the tail end of a conversation between Esther and Levi. "You know how Ben was at that age. She's just going through a hard time. She'll lose interest soon enough."

She hated to tell them that she wasn't one to lose interest. She'd stuck with that lawsuit in Leola for over a year. Because she didn't want to upset her very kind *aendi* and *onkel*, Mattie resolved that, where possible, she'd keep her campaign activities a secret. As long as they didn't know what was going on, they wouldn't have a chance to be upset or worried.

If anything did make them upset, it was always easier to ask for forgiveness than permission. What Aunt Esther and Uncle Levi didn't know couldn't hurt them. Mattie and Freeman were planning to hold all campaign meetings and activities in an old shed on Sensenigs' farm that the family didn't use anymore. Esther and Levi would be blissfully unaware that a campaign was even going on until "Vote for Mattie" signs started popping up around town.

"What can I do for you?" Mattie said.

An apricot made a satisfying plop as it went into Esther's bucket. "It's Levi's *bruder* Caleb. We're worried about him."

In the almost four weeks Mattie had been here, she had been to Levi's parents' house twice for dinner and one night for Scrabble. Caleb was Levi's younger *bruder*, only seventeen or eighteen years old. He was still growing into himself, with gangly arms and legs and a croaky voice. His feet were so long, they arrived at church five minutes before he did. "What are you worried about?"

"Lily Eicher broke his heart something wonderful, and he's been down in the dumps ever since. We were hoping that maybe you could cheer him up."

Mattie frowned. "Me? What can I do?"

"Oh, I don't know. Let him come over and visit. Go on a drive with him, on the back roads, of course. He could hire a driver and take you to the sand dunes. That's always a fun trip."

Mattie didn't know what to say. Spending time with Levi's little *bruder* didn't sound appealing in the least. Would Freeman call her a snob for feeling that way? Mattie was twenty-two, and the idea of befriending a boy five years younger than she was made her want to yawn. Besides, she would be working on the campaign. Aunt Esther knew how busy she was going to be without any boys complicating her life.

"*Ach*, I don't know, *Aendi* Esther. Surely Caleb has other friends he could do things with."

"Of course he has other friends, but I think getting some attention from a pretty girl like you would really make him happy."

Mattie pressed her lips into a hard line. She wasn't quite sure what Aunt Esther was thinking with such a request, but it wouldn't be too hard to just avoid the issue. She wasn't going to be home all that much, and there just wouldn't be a convenient time for her and Caleb to get together. Problem solved. "Okay. I'm sure we'll be able to find a time where we can go for a drive."

"Or play a game. He loves Life on the Farm and Uno." Esther caught her breath as if she'd thought of a *wunderbarr* idea. "He loves to do puzzles. We should pull out a puzzle when he comes over."

"Okay," Mattie said, but she didn't even pretend to be excited about it. If Aunt Esther didn't see what a *dumm* idea it was, then there was no hope that Mattie could talk her out of it.

Levi opened the kitchen window. "Guess who's here," he called.

Esther swiped her hands down the front of her apron and smiled up at Mattie. Did she sense a little embarrassment in that smile? "He's here already."

Mattie narrowed her eyes and glanced in the direction of the house. "Who's here?" She knew the answer to that question before it left her mouth. *Ach, du lieva.*

Esther scooped Winnie into her arms and headed toward the house. "*Cum*, Mattie. We've done enough apricots for one day. Caleb is here for dinner and games."

Of course he was. "But, Aunt Esther, I've got other plans tonight." Mattie was supposed to meet Freeman at the shed later to talk about yard signs.

Aunt Esther stopped in her tracks. "Can you change them? Caleb came especially to see you. It would mean the world to me if you could just be with us tonight. Caleb is heartbroken, and I made stew." Mattie wasn't sure what stew and Caleb's broken heart had to do with each other. Aunt Esther was either trying to make her feel guilty or hungry. Probably both.

Mattie groaned inwardly. "I guess I can stay for a while."

"Oh, *denki*. We're all just trying to support Caleb in his time of need. He'll be thrilled to know you're staying. You can tell him all about Pennsylvania and your family and the farm."

"There's not much to tell." Unless Caleb wanted to hear Mattie's rant about how much greener Leola was than Byler or how her skin was already dry and scaly from the lack of humidity. But even Mattie was tired of that conversation. Colorado wasn't going to get any wetter, and Pennsylvania was the land of damp toilet paper.

"It doesn't matter. Caleb's just excited to get to know you. I know you won't let us down."

Esther disappeared into the house, leaving Mattie annoyed

and sweaty. Would it be possible to slip out of the house later without Esther, Levi, or Caleb noticing? She could claim she had to go to the bathroom and climb out the window, but that seemed like a mean trick to play on someone who had just gotten his heart broken. Mattie heaved a sigh. If she didn't want to hurt Caleb's feelings, she'd have to be late for the yard sign meeting.

What would Freeman say? He was irritated with her already. Would he quit the campaign altogether? After much protest, she'd agreed to let him help, but it hadn't taken Mattie long to realize that she could not win this election with only Cathy's help. She needed helpers desperately, and the realization irritated her, especially where Freeman was concerned. He could be so smug, and if he knew she needed him, he'd never let her hear the end of it.

Mattie climbed down from her ladder and peered at her bucket a third full of little green apricots. Aunt Esther threw apricots at the house when she got mad. When Mattie got mad, she didn't throw things. Sometimes she wrote a letter. Sometimes she filed a lawsuit. Sometimes she ran for office.

Tonight there was nothing to do but bite her tongue, take a deep breath, and keep her temper. Caleb wouldn't come every night. She'd get those yard signs done eventually. And if she could help Caleb along the way, well then, it was a small price to pay for another human being's happiness. She dumped all but one of her apricots in the compost pile and launched the last one at the house in honor of Aunt Esther. It made a little ping as it met with the brick and bounced harmlessly to the ground. Throwing an apricot was quite satisfying in its own way, but not nearly as satisfying as it was going to be to beat Bill Isom in the election. Mattie was looking forward to that.

Mattie strolled in the back door, down the hall, and into the kitchen. Caleb stood next to the table, hat in hand, looking very much like he was presenting himself for inspection. And he was nervous. His Adam's apple bobbed up and down and beads of sweat congregated on his upper lips. He looked exactly like Mattie imagined Levi looked ten years ago, with the same curly hair that was as thick as a mop and the same smiling brown eyes. He'd be quite handsome in five years or so, but right now he was a typical, awkward teenage boy with a mild case of acne and an unpolished sense of humor.

Caleb gave Mattie a painfully eager smile. "Um, Mattie. *Hallo.*"

"*Vie gehts?* It's nice to see you. Esther said you were coming over."

He nodded, swallowed hard, and made a valiant effort to keep his smile going. "Can you believe this weather we're having?" he said breathlessly. Lord willing, he wouldn't faint. Maybe she should encourage him to sit down.

Mattie glanced at Aunt Esther who was stirring a pot of stew on the stove. She wished Aunt Esther hadn't put her in such an awkward position. How was she supposed to help Caleb forget his broken heart? He should be spending time with boys and girls his own age. Caleb still had dark freckles, for goodness' sake! "It's very . . . dry," she said. It was always dry—nothing exceptional about that.

"It got up to eighty-five yesterday. Ben said it's the hottest day of the year so far."

"How hot does it usually get in July?" Mattie asked, because Caleb seemed to be quite impressed with the heat.

"It never gets hotter than eighty. I think we're having a heat wave, and it's still three days until July starts."

"*Ach*, that is hot." Thank goodness for the weather.

Without it, most people wouldn't know how to start a conversation.

Unfortunately, they had now run out of things to talk about. Caleb fell silent and stared at her as if he thought she might bite him.

Esther tapped her spoon against the pot. "Caleb, would you help Mattie set the table?"

Caleb jumped as if he'd been stuck with a pin. "For sure and certain. Where are the bowls?"

Glad that Caleb wouldn't be able to set the table and stare at her at the same time, Mattie pulled bowls and small plates out of the cupboard and handed them to Caleb. He took the bowls, his hands shaking slightly. Oy, anyhow, he was tense. "Esther says you're thinking of running for town council."

"I'm not thinking about it."

The relief on his face was almost comical. "That's good to know."

"I've already thought about it, and I've made up my mind. I'm running."

His countenance drooped like a fallen pudding cake. "*Ach,* I didn't know that."

"But she might change her mind," Esther said. "I hear it's a lot of work and can be wonderful contentious."

Caleb formed his lips into an O and nodded. "Bill Isom is wonderful mean. He accused me of breaking one of his sprinklers when I was just walking down the road. I didn't want to get hit by the cars going by, so I stepped on his grass. He made me pay him five dollars for the broken sprinkler head."

Mattie pressed her lips together. If Caleb meant to discourage her, he was going about it the wrong way. Caleb's story was one more reason she needed to win this election. "I'll never get over that you have to water your lawns here."

"Some people don't. The Batemans just have rocks in their front yard." Caleb squinted at the last plate in his hand then rubbed it back and forth on the leg of his trousers.

Esther gasped. "Caleb, what are you doing?"

"There was a dirty spot."

"That's not how you clean a plate. Your pants are dirtier than my whole kitchen." Esther held out her hand. "Give it to me." Caleb sheepishly held out the plate. She snatched it out of his hand. "You're going to give us all some dread disease."

Mattie hid a smile. Teenage boys didn't have enough sense to fill a teaspoon. She knew. She had a fourteen-year-old *bruder*.

"Uh, sorry, Esther. That's how I do it at home."

Mattie made a mental note never to eat at Caleb's house again unless she brought her own plate and silverware.

"Does your *mamm* know?"

Caleb furrowed his brow. "She ain't never said anything."

Esther handed him a clean plate. "Then she doesn't know." She shook her finger in his direction. "Don't do that anymore."

"I'm sorry, Esther."

"It's okay. I'm mostly upset that one of my plates was dirty. I'm very particular about washing my dishes."

Mattie grimaced. "It might be my fault, Aunt Esther. I did the dishes this morning."

Esther examined the plate Caleb had handed her. "It's all right. As long as it wasn't me. I'm afraid my mind is turning to mush with this baby."

"Being pregnant is not a disease," Mattie said. "You seem quite normal to me." Except for the twig behind her ear. But that behavior wasn't new to Esther's being pregnant.

"Are you getting stretch marks? I hear stretch marks are the worst part."

Esther shook her head. "It's the heartburn. I think the baby's foot is pressed right up against my stomach. And its head is wedged against my bladder."

Mattie giggled. "Mamm says after six babies, she can't run anymore without leaking."

Caleb froze as if his feet were nailed to the floor, and his face turned a bright shade of red. "Um, maybe I should step outside."

Esther cocked her eyebrow. "Whatever for?"

"You're talking about private things I don't think I'm meant to hear."

Ach, Caleb *was* young. A boy his age wasn't quite ready to acknowledge where babies came from or how they got here, and he certainly wasn't ready to hear two women talk about it.

Mattie stifled a grin. "*Nae*, stay here. We are done talking about babies and private things."

Caleb wiped the sweat from his forehead. "Okay." Esther handed him five spoons. "It sure is some crazy weather we're having, isn't it?" he said.

After dinner, Levi, Caleb, and Mattie did the dishes while Esther put Winnie to bed. Then Levi pulled out a thousand-piece puzzle and poured the pieces on the kitchen table. Did that mean they would have to finish the puzzle before they set the table for breakfast in the morning?

Caleb laughed nervously. "It looks like I'm going to be here for a long time."

Exactly what Mattie was thinking.

They turned over each piece, setting aside the edge pieces. The puzzle was a picture of an assortment of brightly colored candy. It was cute and challenging, but if Mattie concentrated hard enough, she might be able to rush them through putting it together. With four of them working, surely it couldn't take more than an hour.

"This is our hardest puzzle," Levi said. "Last time we did it, it took us three days."

Mattie bit her bottom lip. She didn't care what Levi said; she'd finish this puzzle in an hour or die trying.

"Mattie," Esther said, "Caleb has started working with the remodeling business. Haven't you, Caleb?"

Levi, his *bruder* Ben, and their *dat* remodeled bathrooms and kitchens as a business. Apparently, Caleb was now old enough to join them. "That's nice," Mattie said, more interested in quickly putting the puzzle together than hearing about Caleb's new job. She fit two side pieces together and connected them to three more. There was hope for quick completion.

"*Jah*," Caleb said. "They let me do all the easy stuff, but Dat says everybody has to start somewhere."

"Tell Mattie what you did today," Levi said, sitting back and clasping his hands behind his head.

Mattie did her best not to let her irritation show, but they would never get the puzzle done in time if Levi didn't even work on it.

Caleb also stopped working on the puzzle, as if he couldn't concentrate on telling her a story and doing a puzzle at the same time. What was wrong with these two? "I was pulling out plywood because we're putting in a new subfloor, and I found a nest of baby mice."

"Oh, how cute," Esther said. She also pried her eyes from the puzzle and watched Caleb as if he was telling the most interesting story she'd ever heard.

Well, Mattie wasn't going to be so easily distracted, and

now she had to do the work of four people. She wanted to stand up and loudly insist that the other three quit lolly-gagging and help her, but with astounding self-control, she silently concentrated harder on the pieces in front of her and barely listened to Caleb at all.

"Do you think I did the right thing, Mattie?"

Mattie glanced at Caleb. She had no idea what he'd been talking about except that it had something to do with a mouse and some plywood. She decided to just agree with him. "Um, *jah*, I think you did the right thing."

"They'll make their way back into the house, for sure and certain," Levi said.

Mattie took ten precious seconds to look up from the puzzle. "You let the mice go?"

Caleb hesitated, his eyes darting from Esther to Mattie and back again. "Um, *jah*. That's what I just said. I picked up the whole nest and took it outside."

"*Ach*." She should probably pay more attention to the conversation so Caleb didn't think she was rude. "If their *mater* is still in the house, they won't survive outside on their own."

"So you don't think I did the right thing? They were really cute, and I didn't want to hurt them."

Mattie gave Caleb a half smile. "I'm sure you did the right thing." It probably wasn't appropriate to mention that she really didn't care, because how callous was a girl who didn't care about baby mice? So she kept her mouth shut. What she really cared about was finishing this puzzle so she could go to Freeman's shed and work on yard signs.

Levi leaned forward, picked up a random piece, and fit it into the puzzle. How did he do that so quickly? "Caleb is really handy with a crowbar. He's going to be a big help in the business."

"I'm sure he is," Mattie said. But she didn't really care about that either. Right now, all she cared about was that Caleb was quick with puzzles.

Caleb picked up a puzzle piece, examined it for about seven days, and put it back down again. "So, Mattie, what is your favorite color?"

Ach. It might be time to consider that bathroom escape.

An hour later, Mattie looked up from the puzzle and gazed longingly at the clock. Freeman was waiting for her, and there was no way to reach him and tell him she wouldn't be coming. Eventually he'd give up and go home, but for sure and certain he'd be irritated with her for not showing up. It couldn't be helped. Esther and Levi weren't happy with her campaign to begin with, and they'd be extra unhappy if she just up and left the thousand-piece puzzle for them to do with Caleb. Climbing out the bathroom window wasn't an option. She wouldn't be able to squeeze her hips through, and she didn't want to hurt Caleb's feelings.

Mattie watched Caleb out of the corner of her eye. He didn't seem especially heartbroken about . . . what was the girl's name? He was obviously nervous, but he certainly didn't seem as forlorn as Esther seemed to think he was. He laughed at all of Levi's jokes and hummed to himself while he searched for puzzle pieces. There was a lot of humming and very little puzzling going on. Caleb probably put four pieces into the puzzle altogether. Did he really like puzzles, or had Esther just said that to be encouraging?

It was obvious that Esther liked puzzles. She concentrated almost as hard as Mattie did and had fit in at least a third of the pieces they'd done so far. Her interest made sense since she was a quilter. Every quilt she made was a beautiful puzzle of contrasting colors and shapes.

Mattie glanced at the clock one more time. It wasn't going to matter how fast she worked on this puzzle. She wasn't getting out of here before it was done, and they weren't going to finish for at least another hour. She pictured Freeman sitting in his shed, his arms folded tightly over his chest, getting madder and madder.

She'd have to take him a plate of her famous snickerdoodles to apologize. Did Freeman like cookies? Did he like apologies? Did he like Mattie, even a little bit? Or was he just putting up with her because he wanted her to beat Bill Isom in the election? And did it matter, as long as he was willing to help her?

Caleb picked up a blue piece, stared at it, and tried fitting it in with the red candy. "I sure like doing puzzles." He gave up on the piece and put it back on the table. "I sure like being here with you, Mattie."

It was a nice thing to say, but Mattie didn't especially believe him. Doing puzzles with your *bruder*, *schwester*-in-law, and some stranger from Pennsylvania was no way to nurse a broken heart. "*Denki*." She probably should have said something equally as sweet, like "I'm having a *gute* time too," but she didn't want to lie. She settled for a half-hearted smile. It was the best she could do.

Caleb smiled back and picked up another puzzle piece. "So, Mattie, which do you like better, French fries or mashed potatoes?"

The bathroom window escape was looking better and better. She could totally grease her hips.

Chapter 7

"I told her that if she wanted Andy to notice her, she should just go over there and play volleyball on his team. And she said, 'I can't do that. All the other girls have already joined his team. He's the only boy on the team.' All the girls like Andy. They won't leave him alone."

Sadie led Lucky between the rows while Freeman guided the ridge plow in a straight line, burying the weeds and shoring up the potato plants at the same time. It was hot, back-breaking work, especially at the end of June, but Freeman didn't mind it. He'd rather be outside working in solitude with his horses, breathing the fresh air and feeling the sun on his back, than cooped up indoors doing just about anything else.

Unfortunately, potato weeding required two people, one to guide the horse and the other to work the plow, and today horse guiding was Sadie's job.

Freeman loved his *schwesteren* fiercely, but Sadie was a little bit of a trial out in the fields. No matter what Freeman said, Sadie would not stop talking. How could he listen for the songs of the birds or the music of the wind when his *schwester* chattered on about boys and friend problems and her plans for a quilt for Suvie's new baby?

"And that's the problem. Andy knows all the girls like him, and he's so stuck up about it."

Freeman had already asked Sadie once to be quiet, but she took it personally that he didn't want to hear what she had to say about the gathering last week, and he truly didn't want to hurt her feelings. Besides, it seemed that the horse, Lucky, liked Sadie's stories. He strolled calmly and obediently down the furrow, rarely stepping on a potato plant and occasionally nodding in acknowledgment of what Sadie said to him. So Freeman let her talk while he wrestled with the ridge plow until her voice became part of the background noise of his work, a pleasant lilting sound that reminded him he had people to love and *schwesteren* who counted on him.

Even though they could be wonderful bothersome.

"There's only one other boy Andy's age and six girls. Of course Andy and Mervin get all the attention. It wonders me if I should go live with Mattie in Pennsylvania so I can meet more boys. There's nothing for me here."

Freeman smiled to himself. Sadie was young. She had lots of time to find a husband, but he understood her concern. He felt it all the time. And *jah*, he'd probably have to go to Ohio or Indiana to find a *fraa*. Maybe even Pennsylvania, but only if he got very desperate. Of course Mattie didn't represent all the girls in Pennsylvania, but if even half of them were as snobby and undependable as Mattie, he didn't want to set foot in Pennsylvania Dutch country.

He'd waited for over an hour last night for Mattie to show up. The shed reeked of the sharp, caustic smell of fertilizer. It stung Freeman's nose and made it hard to breathe. After ten minutes, he'd left the shed and waited for her outside, pulling weeds while watching the road for her buggy. At least the time hadn't been completely wasted. He could always pull weeds.

Had she decided she didn't need his help? Had she made other plans without bothering to tell him? She could have at least had the courtesy to let him know she wasn't going to show up. He was mad but not especially surprised. Mattie hadn't really wanted his help in the first place. And if she thought she was too good for Freeman, then she could just run this campaign all by herself. What did he care?

At the end of the row, Freeman pulled the plow from the dirt so it would be easier for Lucky to turn around. Instead of guiding the horse to the next row, Sadie stopped and pointed toward the road. "*Ach*, look, Freeman."

Mattie Zook was walking across the field holding a plate covered in tinfoil. He appreciated that she was trying to avoid flattening the potato plants as she stepped over furrows and mounds, but he wasn't especially eager to talk to her. He had a feeling she'd only say something to irritate him. But whatever was on the foil-covered plate might be worth the irritation. And she certainly looked pretty, even in that drab brown dress. Like as not, that color made her eyes sparkle like two stars on a summer night.

Freeman cleared his throat and swiped his hand across his mouth. Mattie was pretty. There was no getting around that. But it didn't mean she had any *gute* qualities or that Freeman would ever want to date her.

"You really need to date her," Sadie said. "She's pretty and wonderful brave and doesn't care when I ask her questions."

"She's kind of a snob."

Sadie rolled her eyes. "Don't be silly. Just because she doesn't fall all over you like Susie Miller, doesn't mean she's a snob. You are so full of yourself, *bruder*."

"I am not, Sarah. She's full of herself."

Sadie's mouth twitched upward. "Quit calling me Sarah. You know full well which twin I am."

He rested the plow on the ground and folded his arms. "Of course I do, but you keep telling Mattie that I can't tell my own *schwesteren* apart. She thinks I'm an idiot."

"She does not think you're an idiot. She thinks you're grumpy and rude. You called her foolish to her face."

Freeman shrugged. "She doesn't like me. I don't like her. Sounds like we both agree that we don't want to date each other."

Sadie grinned as if she had the whole dictionary memorized. "Then why is she here? For sure and certain, that plate of cookies isn't for me."

"I have no idea. She probably wants me to try her shoofly pie because she thinks Pennsylvania Amish food is so much better than anything we make in Colorado."

Sadie scrunched her lips together. "Boys are so *dumm*."

Mattie finally crossed to where Freeman was standing, her cheeks and eyes bright from walking so far. Freeman tore his gaze from those fascinating eyes and examined the handles of his ridge plow. The handles needed to be inspected regularly for cracks and such.

"*Hallo*, Mattie," Sadie said, grinning so wide, Freeman could count her teeth. "How nice of you to come and visit poor Freeman. He never gets visitors because he's so ornery." Half chuckling, half growling, Freeman lunged at Sadie, who squealed in delight and bolted down one of the furrows. "I'm just telling the truth," Sadie protested.

Mattie laughed. "I don't wonder but Freeman likes for people to leave him alone."

Freeman nodded in exaggerated agreement. "I'd be much happier if people never said another word to me."

Sadie came back and smacked him on the arm. "That's not true. You're the most popular boy at gatherings."

He raised his eyebrows. "So you're taking it back?"

"*Nae*," Sadie said. "You might be popular, but you're still ornery."

Freeman glanced at Mattie and pointed to Sadie. "You see what I have to put up with?"

Mattie's lips curled upward. "It's terrible. Just terrible." She hesitated then handed Freeman the foil-covered plate, which did turn out to be a pie tin. "I brought an apology in the form of apricot cherry tarts."

Freeman grunted and pulled back the tinfoil to reveal little square tarts drizzled with a powder sugar glaze. "You didn't have to. I'm over it already."

"Over what?" Sadie said. She pointed to the pie tin. "Could I have one? They look *appeditlich*."

"Only if Freeman says it's okay. They're his to do what he wants with." She cleared her throat. "Including throw them in the dirt."

"*Ach*, *vell*, I'm not as mad as all that." How could he be irritated when she was looking at him like that and heavenly smells drifted from the warm pie tin?

Sadie frowned. "What are you mad about?"

Freeman knew better than to answer that question. "We're always mad at each other." He distracted Sadie by offering her a tart, which she received like an eager toddler.

Sadie took a bite, closed her eyes, and moaned with pleasure. "*Ach*, Mattie, these are heavenly. Freeman, you've got to try one. They're still warm."

Mattie clasped her hands behind her back. "I don't even like apricots, but Esther convinced me to try her recipe this morning using some of the apricots she canned last year. She has about a hundred quarts of apricots. She's trying to use them up."

Freeman picked up a bar and took a bite. The flaky pie crust topped with glaze was the perfect sweet complement to the tart apricots and plump cherries. He promptly popped the rest of the bar into his mouth. "Hmm. So *gute*, Mattie."

She seemed extraordinarily pleased with his compliment. "Do you really like them?"

"They're like a little apricot pie in every bite. I love them. Make me another batch, and I'll never be mad at you again."

Mattie widened her eyes. "Is that a promise? Because I feel like you're going to have lots of opportunity to be mad at me in the next four months. I just don't want you to regret saying something you can't take back."

Sadie's gaze darted between Freeman and Mattie. "So why are you mad at Mattie? Will somebody please answer my question?"

Freeman handed Mattie the pie tin, took Sadie by the shoulders, and turned her toward home. "Sorry, sis. We have grown-up stuff we need to talk about."

Sadie glared at him. "Grown-up stuff? Of all the ridiculous things to say. May I remind you that I am eighteen years old and plenty grown-up to hear anything you and Mattie have to say to each other?"

Freeman gave her a regretful smile, as if he understood her frustration but couldn't do anything about it. "You have to go, kiddo."

Sadie huffed out a breath. "Oh, *sis yuscht*. I'll go, but if you think I'm going to come back and help you finish plowing, you are greatly mistaken, *bruder*." She patted Mattie on the arm. "No offense to you. You can't know what a pain in the neck Freeman is." She turned on her heel and stormed off, going perpendicular to the furrows so that she had to step over every row of potato plants to make it to the edge of the field.

Freeman grinned and called after her, "Come back in ten minutes."

Sadie didn't even turn around. "I won't."

"Set the timer in the kitchen. Ten minutes," Freeman said, trying wonderful hard not to laugh.

Sadie looked back and stuck out her tongue.

This time Freeman did laugh. Mattie's smile was wide, but she must have thought it best to not laugh at Sadie's expense. Mattie stepped closer to Lucky and patted his neck. "Pretty horse," she said.

Freeman nodded. "He's one of a *gute* pair of using horses. A little more steady than Louie, with a sharper eye." She seemed a little breathless. "Did you walk from Esther's house?"

"*Jah*. Walking helps me remember how mad I am that the Amish can't use the roads in their own town. It strengthens my resolve." She gazed over the field. "What kind of crops are you growing? I've never seen this plant before. It's very pretty."

"Potatoes," Freeman said. "They grow real well here in the high country."

"And they're green. I love green." She smiled at him as if sharing a private joke then bent over and fingered a potato plant. "I came by to tell you I'm sorry about not coming to work on yard signs yesterday."

Freeman knew what was coming, but she seemed to be beating around the bush. "But?"

"But what?"

"Now you're going to tell me you don't want me working on your campaign."

A deep furrow appeared between Mattie's brows. "Why would I tell you that? I really need your help, and I hope you're not too mad to still help me."

Freeman was surprised at how glad he felt that Mattie

still wanted his help. "*Ach*, when you didn't show up last night, I thought you'd changed your mind about me."

Mattie sighed. "I'm sorry about that. Levi's *bruder* Caleb came over, and Esther wanted me to cheer him up, so I felt like I couldn't leave. Levi pulled out this thousand-piece puzzle, and it all went downhill from there."

"Did you cheer him up?"

Mattie gritted her teeth. "I don't know. Esther said Caleb likes puzzles, but I'm sure he put in maybe four pieces the whole night. It was frustrating because I wanted to finish the puzzle so I could come over, but everybody else was so slow. I almost climbed out the bathroom window, but I thought that would be rude. Do you think that would have been rude?"

Freeman nodded. "Very rude."

"It would have made him more depressed, so I stayed, even though I can't stand teenage boys. *Mein bruder* is fourteen, and the nicest thing I can say about him is that he doesn't always chew his food with his mouth open."

Freeman was suddenly very glad he wasn't a teenager. "That's quite an accomplishment. Most teenage boys don't have any manners. And I don't wonder that Caleb didn't help with the puzzle. Everybody knows he's color-blind."

Mattie's mouth fell open. "He's color-blind? That explains a lot. But why did Esther say he likes doing puzzles? We spent almost four hours on that thing and still didn't finish it. We ate our cereal standing up this morning." Mattie narrowed her eyes. "Esther threatened to invite Caleb over tonight to finish the puzzle. I'd better get home and finish it so I don't have to spend another painfully awkward evening with Levi's *bruder*."

Freeman offered Mattie an apricot cherry tart then took another one for himself. "So when do you want to work on yard signs? The man at the copy center said they need at least three weeks to print them."

Mattie thought about that. "I don't think I can commit to working on it tonight, just in case Caleb comes over to finish that puzzle. I suppose I could climb out the bathroom window, though I still think that would be rude."

"Very rude."

"Okay, then. I'll come over Thursday after dinner."

Freeman's heart thumped against his chest, though he didn't know why he was so excited. Maybe just the thrill of working on a campaign and possibly defeating Bill Isom was reason enough, even though they had their work cut out for them. "Have you thought of what to put on the yard signs?"

She pressed her lips together. "I haven't been able to think of anything."

"Cathy says people just have to see your name all over town, and it has to be an exciting color. The person who has the most signs usually wins the election."

Mattie caught her bottom lip between her teeth. "Is that true? I don't think anyone in the district would let me plant a sign in their yard."

Freeman patted Lucky's neck. "We have to go to every house in town and ask if we can put a sign in their yard."

Mattie turned pale. "Every house?"

"*Ach, vell*, maybe not every house. But we're going to need a lot of help. They're the same people you need to ask for money. Cathy has donated twenty dollars to your campaign, but that will only buy us twenty signs, plus we'll have to pay someone to design them."

"Can't we find someone to just give us some signs out of the goodness of their heart? I found a lawyer in Leola willing to help me for free."

Freeman chuckled. "*Jah*. We can do that. It's called asking people for money."

Mattie cracked a smile. "*Ach*. I hate asking people for money, but I want to win, so I'll do it. Where do we start?"

Freeman pointed to the nearest house, the Weilers', a hundred yards down the road. "Right there is as good as anywhere."

Mattie huffed out a breath. "Okay. I can be brave." She gave Freeman a dazzling smile. "*Denki*, Freeman. I really do need you."

The way she said it made his knees turn to jelly and his heart bang like a drum. She probably meant *I really do need your help*, so all the heart palpitations were completely unnecessary. "It sounds like you have plenty of experience asking for money. How did you get a lawyer to help you for free? And why did you need a lawyer?"

Mattie's lips twitched sheepishly. "One of our neighbors was dumping trash onto our property. A lot of trash. Dat went and talked to him, but he refused to clean up his mess, and he knew Dat wouldn't do anything about it. You know, we're supposed to be peacemakers. Well, I didn't think our neighbor should get away with throwing junk on our farm, so I asked a lawyer to help me sue him. When Dat found out, he tried to get me to withdraw the lawsuit, but my attorney had already spent a lot of time on it, so I told him *nae*. *Ach*, he was so mad, he sent me off to Colorado as punishment."

Freeman gave her a wry smile. "You have made it very clear that Colorado is a harsh punishment."

She shook her head, a smile playing at her lips. "You are never going to let me forget that, are you?"

"Probably not."

"That man is still dumping trash on our farm, and Dat still cleans it up every week. Even though I know we are supposed to turn the other cheek, it doesn't seem right that our neighbor isn't held responsible. At the very least, someone should make him stop."

"We are commanded to love our neighbor, I guess."

Mattie squared her shoulders. "But loving our neighbor does not mean letting them mistreat us. That is why I can't let Bill Isom get away with banning us from the main roads. It's not fair."

"*Nae*, it's not. But you know why the *gmayna* is against what you're doing. They see it as starting a fight."

She nodded. "I know. 'Blessed are the peacemakers.'"

"Cathy said that the Amish like to be persecuted." He curled his lips. "She's wrong, but I think what she sees is that we are willing to suffer injustice if it is Gotte's will."

Mattie studied his face. "That's why you think I'm foolish. Because I'm going against Gotte and *Gelassenheit*."

His face got warm. He shouldn't have called her foolish. She would probably slap him with that word forever. "I said it was foolish to run against Bill Isom. I didn't say you were foolish. And *Gelassenheit* means yielding our lives to Gotte's will. If you feel that running for office is Gotte's will, then you should do it."

Mattie fell silent for a few seconds. "*Denki* for saying that. I know what I'm doing doesn't seem very Amish, but I do feel that Gotte is leading me to run for office. He can't like it when His children mistreat each other."

"You're very brave, but I think you can see why the *gmayna* doesn't want you to interfere. Your running for office is completely opposite to what they think should be done. We don't even vote. Running for office seems like the next level of wickedness."

Laughter burst from Mattie's lips. "I've gone from foolish to wicked in a matter of minutes."

"That's not what I meant."

Mattie cocked an eyebrow. "You always make me feel so *gute* about myself. I can't imagine why we don't spend more time together."

Freeman threw up his hands. "Oh, *sis yuscht!* Don't put words in my mouth. You know what I mean. I'm only being honest."

She grinned. "I know you are, but you deliver your honesty like you're throwing rocks at my head. Maybe you could aim at my feet for a change."

Her smile was like a brilliant sunrise, and it stole his breath. He looked away and brushed his hand down Lucky's neck while he gathered his wits. "I hate to be the one to point it out, but you're even more blunt than I am. You throw darts instead of rocks."

"I do not," she protested.

"Uh, *jah*, you do. Remember when you wouldn't shut up about Colorado and how your skin was going to dry up and fall off?"

She opened her mouth to say something and promptly closed it. After a pause, she said, "I'm not very *gute* at keeping my opinion to myself. I like to be right."

"And so do I. Maybe we're more alike than we want to admit."

Her eyes flashed mischievously. "I appreciate that you are willing to admit that you may be a little bit like me— foolish, wicked, and snobby."

He laughed. "Speak for yourself. I'm not any of those things."

She rolled her eyes. "I'm sure you aren't."

"And neither are you."

"I don't mind that most of the Amish in town are opposed to my campaign, including Aunt Esther and Uncle Levi. If I can get the ordinance changed, it will be worth all the suspicious looks and gossip I get."

"You're braver than I am." Freeman wasn't sure if he should feel ashamed that he wouldn't run himself or simply grateful that Mattie was willing to sacrifice for everyone.

"I'm doing this for them, even if they don't appreciate it."

"That describes many great men and women," Freeman said. "Always doing something for people who didn't really appreciate it. Like Queen Esther. Or Moses."

"*Jah*, poor Moses. His people took to complaining about bread from heaven." Mattie hooked her hand around her elbow. "I don't need to be appreciated. I just want to make it right for the Amish who live here. And if I can make Bill Isom lose his temper, all the better."

"You don't want to be on Bill's bad side, but I don't see any way around it since you're trying to defeat him in an election. It was a foolish notion to begin with."

She gave him the stink eye. "I know you think it's foolish. You can stop saying it now."

Out of the corner of his eye, Freeman saw Sadie come out the back door and start across the field toward him. He smiled to himself. She must have set the timer.

Mattie saw Sadie too. "I should go." She glanced reluctantly at the Weilers' house. "Maybe I'll stop at every house between here and Esther's and ask for money."

"Don't do that."

"But you said I needed to start knocking on doors."

Freeman pulled a piece of notebook paper from his pocket. "Before you ask for money, you need to make a flyer."

"A flyer?"

"*Jah*. A paper that tells people who you are and why you're running for town council." Freeman handed her the paper. "I've written down some things you might want to put on the flyer. Thursday night, we can talk about it. Maybe Cathy will help us design something on her computer."

"*Ach*, I wouldn't know the first thing about that."

"Cathy knows. I mean, at least she knows how to use a keyboard. Instead of the shed, let's meet at her house at six-thirty. Does that work for you?"

Mattie nodded. "I'll be there . . . unless I'm dead."

"Or you break your arm or something," Freeman said.

"You think I'm going to break my arm?"

He laughed. "*Nae*, but death shouldn't be the only reason for not showing up."

"I guess Esther could have her baby."

"Is she that close?"

"It's coming soon," Mattie said.

Freeman nodded. "Okay then. If you have an emergency, I'll understand if you're not there."

She looked at him with a teasing question in her eyes. "Will you? Because you get sort of testy about stuff like that."

"I do not."

She grinned. "We can argue about your temper later. At least you're not one of those pouty types."

"I don't have a temper. And I never pout."

Mattie gave Lucky one last pat. "Like I said, we can argue about it later. In the meantime, you should make a list of all the flaws in your personality you need to work on before Thursday night."

He folded his arms across his chest. "Very funny."

She gave him a syrupy sweet smile. "Just trying to be helpful."

Sadie came to the end of the row huffing and puffing. "Well, I'm back, but only because Mamm told me if I didn't come back out I couldn't go to the gathering next week."

Mattie hooked her arm around Sadie's shoulders and gave her a hug. "It's so nice of you to help your *bruder*. He needs all the help he can get."

Sadie rolled her eyes. "Tell me about it."

Mattie was still laughing as she turned and walked away. Freeman couldn't keep his eyes off her. She might be a snob, but she was the most fascinating girl ever to set foot in Byler, Colorado.

"Did you kiss her?" Sadie asked.

"What kind of a question is that? Of course I didn't kiss her. I don't even like her."

Sadie hissed. "*Ach*, *bruder*, that is the biggest lie you ever told."

Chapter 8

"Mattie, you're washing the dishes like the house was on fire," Esther said, as she came into the kitchen.

Mattie took a deep breath and slowed her washing so Aunt Esther wouldn't get suspicious. "Why would anyone wash the dishes if the house was on fire?"

"I guess if you wanted to make sure the house was tidy for the fire department." Aunt Esther had a bright pink plastic straw behind her ear, a leftover from Winnie's dinner. Winnie liked to drink her milk from a straw.

It probably didn't matter how nonchalant Mattie tried to be. Aunt Esther had to suspect that Mattie was going out tonight to work on her campaign. But she wouldn't even ask to use the buggy. If she cut through two pastures and ran most of the way, she'd actually get to Cathy's almost as fast as if she took the buggy. Thanks to Bill Isom, she had to take the long way around in the buggy, and it just wasn't worth the trouble.

Esther started sweeping the floor, and Mattie took the broom from her. "I can do that. Go spend some time with Winnie before she goes to bed."

"You don't have to do that," Esther said. "I'm wonderful grateful, but you do plenty around here as it is. My house has never been so tidy."

"I'm just so *froh* you're letting me stay with you. You and *Onkel* Levi have been so kind."

Esther pulled the chairs from the table so Mattie could sweep under it. "You must be starting to like it here. A month ago you thought Colorado was a punishment."

Mattie curled one side of her mouth. "I did. And it was a punishment, or at least Dat meant it to be. But Colorado isn't so bad. My altitude headache is gone, and the toilet paper is crisp instead of damp. I do like that."

Esther's eyes widened. "I like that too, but I thought I was the only one who noticed."

Mattie laughed. "Freeman pointed that out to me, and that's when I started to appreciate the fresh, dry air. I miss the trees, but the mountains take my breath away every time I walk outside. I can't complain."

Esther leaned her hands on the back of one of the chairs. "I'm so happy to hear that. We want you to be happy here. We want you to make friends like Caleb and find fun things to do. Caleb knows all the fun places in the valley. And I know he'd be happy to take you anywhere you want to go."

Mattie liked Caleb well enough, but she didn't want to spend more time with him. Caleb was young and adorable, and Mattie preferred more interesting company, like Freeman. She felt her face get warm. Not Freeman in particular, but boys like Freeman, who could talk to a girl without breaking into a sweat or stumbling all over their words. Freeman was solid and mature, with a determination and a focus that only came with a few years of experience. Not only that, but at seventeen, Caleb didn't have the lean, muscular body that came from years of hard work. Mattie couldn't help but admire Freeman's broad shoulders and rock-hard arms and the way his eyebrows arched when she irritated him.

Ach, *vell*, his eyebrows had nothing to do with the strong arms, but they were still irresistibly attractive.

Mattie pressed her lips together and chased Freeman from her thoughts. He was attractive, but he was also rude and blunt, and what was on the inside was more important than his outward appearance. She shouldn't be so shallow.

But maybe it didn't hurt to let him show up in her daydreams.

Esther held the dustpan for Mattie, apparently not in a hurry to be anywhere else. Mattie pulled the mop from the closet, rinsed it under the faucet, and wrung it out. "You don't have to mop," Esther said.

"I know, but a little spot mopping makes the kitchen feel so clean, like the work is truly finished."

Esther again pulled the chairs out for Mattie. "*Denki* for being so nice to Caleb. You've already made a difference. I can tell."

"I'm *froh* I could help," Mattie said. Was now a *gute* time to tell Aunt Esther that she couldn't help with Caleb anymore? Surely Caleb had dozens of friends and family who could make him feel better about Lily What's-Her-Name. There was no reason Mattie needed to be involved. She didn't have time, and she didn't have the patience for it. She wanted to be helpful, but right now, being helpful meant getting on the town council so she could vote to get rid of the buggy ordinance. That would be a big help to Caleb—and the whole *gmayna*. She was thinking of the bigger picture here.

Someone knocked on the door, and Esther exploded into a smile. "Who could that be?" she said, though Mattie had a horrible feeling that Esther already knew who it was.

Mattie was rinsing her mop when Esther led Caleb into the kitchen. Mattie's heart sank. Caleb smiled tentatively and wiped the sweat from his forehead. It was hot out there, but someone only sweat that much when they were irrationally nervous. "*Hallo*, Mattie. Can you believe this crazy weather we're having?"

"I can't believe it," Mattie murmured.

"This morning, some of the clouds were as big as the mountains."

"It was a wonderful pretty day," she said, trying to figure out if she could escape without crawling out the bathroom window.

Caleb glanced at Esther. She gave him an encouraging smile. "We got to work in a house with air conditioning today. I really like air conditioning."

Mattie had to admire how hard he was trying, but she wasn't sure why he was trying so hard. He didn't want to date her, did he? Because even Caleb should be able to see that it was a ridiculous notion. Mattie wrung out the mop and held it like a staff between her and Caleb. "It's really *gute* to see you, Caleb," she said, deciding to pretend his visit had nothing to do with her.

"It's really *gute* to see you too, Mattie. Are you interested in a buggy ride? There's a special place not far from here where we can watch the sunset over the mountains."

Mattie forced a smile. The sunset wasn't for another two and a half hours. She didn't think she could sit with Caleb in his buggy and talk about the weather for two and a half hours, not to mention the fact that she needed to get to Cathy Larsen's house by six-thirty. "*Ach*, Caleb, I'm afraid I can't tonight."

Caleb again glanced at Esther, who nodded her encouragement. What was she up to? "I would be wonderful grateful if you would come. Nobody knows how to cheer me up like you do. There's a real nice spot to see the sunset, and it doesn't even matter if you've seen the sunset before."

Esther's smile was too wide. "You could go watch the sun set every night for the rest of the summer and it would be different every night. Wouldn't that be fun?"

Caleb nodded. "That would be so fun."

Mattie imagined sitting on a boulder watching the sunset with Caleb every night for the rest of her life. It was like one of those nightmares where she had to go to the bathroom but couldn't find a toilet. She couldn't do it. "That sounds fun, but I've got to finish the dishes and . . . do some weeding." She winced and chastised herself for not thinking of a better excuse. And she knew better than to try to use chores as a reason for not going. Aunt Esther was positively giddy at the thought of Mattie gazing at the sunset with Caleb. She must be very concerned about him. Aunt Esther would excuse Mattie from chores for the rest of her life if it might possibly cheer up Caleb.

Predictably, Aunt Esther snatched the mop from Mattie's hand. "You work too hard, Mattie. Go and have some fun with Caleb. The weeding can wait."

Caleb coughed as if he were choking on his own discomfort. "*Jah*. Let's go have some fun."

Mattie clenched her teeth. She was going to have to come right out and tell Aunt Esther that she couldn't watch the sunset with Caleb *ever,* because she had to go to Cathy's and work on her campaign. Aunt Esther had to understand that Mattie would be working on that campaign until November, when it would be too cold to watch the sunset until spring. Basically, she was going to have to make it clear that she wasn't available until April. Aunt Esther would not be happy, but with any luck, Caleb would find another girlfriend by then and quit coming over to annoy her.

She pressed her lips together. She shouldn't be so hard on Caleb. He was a nice boy, but she didn't have time for him right now, even if he was a heartbroken teenager who just needed a little cheering up. She could practically hear Mamm's voice in her head. *How can you be so insensitive, Mattie?* The shame nearly bowled her over. *Ach,* she should have more sympathy.

She cheered up when a *wunderbarr* idea hit her. Maybe she didn't have to choose between being cruel or having some compassion. "The sunset isn't for another two hours. Why don't you come back at eight and pick me up? I'll bring a treat." She didn't have time to make cookies or anything, but she did have some Tic Tacs. That would be good enough.

Caleb shuffled his feet. "I guess that would be okay."

Esther stomped all over that idea. "Of course it wouldn't. Caleb has ice cream in the buggy, and it will melt if you don't eat it soon."

Caleb nodded. "It's going to melt all over the vinyl."

The obvious answer was to bring the ice cream into the house and put it in the freezer until sunset. Or how about waiting until eight-thirty, walking out the front door, and watching the sunset from the comfort of Esther's front yard? But neither Esther nor Caleb seemed open to common sense. Esther just smiled and Caleb just perspired, and it seemed as if they were in on a joke that Mattie didn't understand.

Then the truth hit her like a softball to the nose, and she personally knew how that felt. Caleb was a diversion!

Mattie was so shocked, she had to sit down. She wouldn't be surprised if the whole story about Caleb's broken heart had been made up to get Mattie to feel sorry for him. Was he really as despondent as Esther claimed? Did he even know a girl named Lily? Aunt Esther didn't want Mattie running for office, but using her poor, innocent, irritating *bruder*-in-law to distract Mattie from working on her campaign seemed pretty sneaky, especially for someone who made beautiful quilts and was going to have a baby soon.

What to do now? She couldn't very well accuse her *aendi* of trying to derail her, and she couldn't very well demand that Aunt Esther stay out of her business. If backed into a corner, Aunt Esther might forbid her from campaigning at all.

If Aunt Esther could be sneaky, so could Mattie. She felt guilty for about two seconds and then decided to save it for after the election. Right now, she needed to concentrate on beating Bill Isom and getting that buggy ordinance repealed. As it was, Aunt Esther couldn't even walk out to the mailbox in her pregnant state. She'd be very happy when the buggy ordinance was gone and she didn't have to walk anywhere. Esther *had* given Mattie permission to run. Esther was just hoping Mattie would lose interest. Mattie smiled to herself. Caleb wasn't much of a distraction. Aunt Esther would have to do better than that if she wanted Mattie to give up her campaign.

Aunt Esther should have chosen someone like Freeman. For sure and certain Freeman could make a girl sit up and take notice. Of course his good looks didn't work on Mattie, but at least he wouldn't drip sweat all over her clean kitchen floor.

Mattie stood up and pretended to give in. "What kind of ice cream?"

Caleb beamed. "My favorite. Butter pecan."

Ach, *vell*, he would be eating that by himself. Whatever happened to *gute* old reliable chocolate? "Then let's get going. We don't want to be late for the sunset."

Caleb looked relieved. "*Ach*. Okay. It's going to be fun. The weather's been crazy, so the sunset should be extra pretty tonight."

Mattie went into the front hall and pulled her bonnet and

shawl from one of the hooks on the wall. Byler was hot during the day, but at night it cooled into the fifties. Perfect sleeping weather. It was just one more thing to like about Colorado. Freeman would be pleased. There were already half a dozen things on Mattie's list. "I'm ready," she said. "*Denki* for finishing the kitchen cleanup, Aunt Esther."

Esther waved away her thanks. "My pleasure. Go have fun."

Ach, Mattie would have a *wunderbarr* time. Caleb was going to be a little bit surprised and a whole lot *ferhoodled*.

They climbed into the buggy, and Mattie slid the tub of ice cream over so she could sit down. Caleb jiggled the reins and got the horse moving. "Turn left here, Caleb," she said when they came to the next road.

Caleb frowned. "Left? That's not the way. We're going to the park. It's where all *die youngie* go to watch the sunset."

Mattie cocked an eyebrow. The park was Caleb's special place? It was a *gute* thing she'd decided to railroad Caleb's plans or she'd be going insane with irritation right about now. "We're not going to watch the sunset."

"We're not?" Caleb's voice cracked.

Mattie motioned for him to turn, which he obediently did. "We're going to Cathy Larsen's house."

Caleb slowed the horse. "She doesn't have a *gute* spot for watching the sunset. There are three giant pine trees in her yard."

Mattie nodded as if she was fully aware of the limitations of Cathy's yard. "Freeman Sensenig is meeting us there."

"He wants to come with us to the park?"

Poor Caleb was getting more and more confused. "We're going to go to Cathy's and work on my campaign. I told you I was running, didn't I?"

He nodded slowly. "*Jah*. You told me."

"Much as I'd love to eat ice cream and watch the sunset, I need to make a flyer, design a yard sign, and find some people willing to give me money."

Caleb started sweating profusely. "Esther's not going to be happy about this."

"I know, but really, Caleb, does she have to know? We can eat ice cream at Cathy's and step outside later to watch the sunset."

"You can't see the sunset at Cathy's. She has too many trees."

"What if we walk into her neighbor's yard? He doesn't have trees."

Caleb swiped his hand across his mouth. "I suppose we could do that." Unfortunately, he seemed to think better of agreeing. His face twisted into a grimace. "Esther isn't going to like this."

Mattie laid her hand on Caleb's arm. He quit breathing. "What exactly did Esther ask you to do?"

He glanced at her as if he didn't want to get in trouble for what he was about to say. "She said you need a friend. She said if you had more friends, you wouldn't be so set on running for office." He pulled up on the reins and stopped the buggy. "Let's go to the park. They've got swings."

"*Ach*, *vell*, if they have swings . . ."

Caleb didn't notice the sarcasm in her voice, which was just as well. It would have hurt his feelings, and he was only trying to do what Aunt Esther had asked of him. He seemed to cheer up a bit. "*Jah*. Okay. I'll turn around."

"Wait. Let's talk about this." Mattie gave him her best smile, deciding that ordering Caleb to drive her to Cathy's house might work but would also hurt his feelings. She couldn't exactly consider herself a *gute* person if she bullied Esther's teenage *bruder*-in-law. "I do need friends, but what I really need are friends who will help me with my campaign. I know that nobody in the *gmayna* wants me to run for office."

"Well, I mean, we want you to win. We just don't think you should run."

"You see? You agree that someone needs to change the buggy ordinance, but if I don't win, it won't change. I want to help you, but I can't do it without your help."

Caleb seemed confused and encouraged at the same time. "You want me to help you help me?"

"You're obviously a very dependable and willing person or why would Esther have asked you to help me? She knows she can count on you. Can I count on you?"

Caleb furrowed his brow. "I still don't know if Esther will like it."

"She never has to know."

Caleb heaved a great sigh. "I suppose I can help you. But I don't even know what a flyer is, unless it's a goose."

Mattie laughed. "We can learn together. Freeman called Tami on the city council. He knows what to do, and he's going to help us."

"Just . . . just don't tell my *mamm*. She wouldn't like it if she knew I helped you run for office."

Mattie pretended to zip her lips. "Not a word." She didn't know whether to be glad that she had more help or worried that half the people working on her campaign didn't want anyone to know they were working on her campaign. And neither of them could vote.

They arrived at Cathy's house ten minutes late, but all things considered, it was an accomplishment they'd made it there at all. Caleb probably thought of himself more as a prisoner than a willing participant. Cathy answered the door, and the strong scent of menthol attacked Mattie's nose. "Sorry about the smell," Cathy said as she ushered them into her house. "Lon rubs Vicks VapoRub on everything, including his ingrown hairs. You kind of get used to it."

Mattie took off her bonnet. "Cathy, this is Caleb. He's Esther's brother-in-law."

Cathy nodded. "We know each other. Caleb sometimes comes over and helps us around the house. He's not a very *gute* weeder, but he put together one of those do-it-yourself shelves that are supposed to be easy but it takes three days just to read the instructions." She patted Caleb on the arm. "Are you here to help with the campaign?"

Caleb still didn't seem sure, even though Mattie had spent the majority of the trip trying to convince him that he was doing a *gute* and noble thing. "I guess."

Cathy shook her finger at him. "Don't guess, young man. You have to be committed. It's going to get rough, and if you're not all in, you'll crumble like a cookie in a blender."

Caleb's eyes grew wide. "What do you mean *rough?*"

"You can be sure Bill Isom will show no mercy."

Mattie almost laughed at the look on Caleb's face. Bill Isom's reputation was bigger and meaner than Bill was. "Do you think he'll get me in trouble with my *mamm?*" Caleb said. Apparently, Caleb's *mamm* was more frightening than anybody on the town council.

Cathy wasn't one to sugarcoat anything. "I don't doubt it. Bill will do whatever he can to win this election. But don't worry about your *mamm*. She's in my quilting group, and our bond is stronger than family." She patted Caleb on the shoulder. "I've got your back."

Mattie didn't know if that made Caleb feel better, but for sure and certain it made Mattie feel better. If things came to a head, Cathy could smooth things over with the entire family. Aunt Esther was also in Cathy's quilting group.

"I was starting to think you were dead." Freeman stood

in a doorway across the hall with his arms folded over his broad chest. He wore a wry smile that sent a zing of exhilaration directly to Mattie's heart.

"I'm not dead," she said breathlessly.

His smile got wider. "I'm *froh* to see it."

Mattie didn't know why her heart raced at his declaration. It was always glad news when somebody didn't die.

He looked past her, and his smile faded. "I see you brought a friend."

Mattie put her arm around Caleb as if she were his big *schwester*. "Caleb agreed to miss the swings at the park to help with the campaign."

Caleb's eyes darted from Mattie to Freeman and back. "Nobody knows I'm here."

"It's okay," Mattie said, giving his shoulder a squeeze. "Nobody knows Freeman is here either."

This news seemed to cheer Caleb up considerably. "You see, Mattie? It's not just me. Everybody is wonderful afraid of Bill Isom."

Mattie could almost hear Freeman's spine stiffen like cement. "I'm not afraid of Bill Isom."

"You're afraid of something," Cathy said. "Or else you wouldn't be sneaking around like a detective in some cheap spy novel."

"I'm not sneaking. It would simply be better if nobody found out that I'm helping."

"That's exactly how I feel," Caleb said. "I'm supposed to convince Mattie to quit, not help her." Caleb's eyes got big, and he clapped his hand over his mouth.

Mattie laughed. Caleb had finally come right out and said it. "It's okay, Caleb. I already know. But you're here now, and I really appreciate your help."

Cathy sighed. "Caleb doesn't want to get in trouble with his mom, and Freeman doesn't want to get in trouble with the church. And everybody's afraid of Bill Isom. Not the most promising start to a campaign. You're going to get creamed."

"I'm not afraid of Bill Isom," Freeman insisted.

Mattie tried not to get discouraged. Cathy was never a bright ray of sunshine. "I'm not quitting."

Cathy's wrinkles bunched on top of each other. "I didn't say you should quit. Abraham Lincoln started with less. He didn't even have a computer. Have you ever read *Hatchet*?"

The three Amish people shook their heads.

"Well, this kid gets stranded in the Canadian woods, and he has to survive. The first thing he does is take an inventory of what he has."

"What's an inventory?" Caleb asked.

"It's a list. We need to make a list of all our assets." Cathy frowned. "It's supposed to give us hope."

Mattie stifled a smile. Cathy's expression inspired nothing but despair. "Okay then, first on our list is that we have a purpose."

Cathy seemed impressed. "I was thinking of things like pencils and poster paper, but a purpose is probably the most important thing. We want to defeat Bill Isom and save the Amish people."

That was maybe overstating it a bit, but it was *gute* enough. Mattie smiled at Freeman, who was staring at her as if he couldn't look away. "Freeman knows someone at the copy center in Monte Vista who can help us with yard signs."

"And flyers," Freeman said. His smile nearly blinded her. Mattie never knew that the thought of flyers had the power to scatter her wits to the wind.

Caleb seemed to sense the excitement of the moment. "And I have feet."

"Yes, you do," Cathy said. "Someday you're going to grow into them."

"I mean, I can walk all over town and pass out those flyers. What good is a flyer if no one ever reads it?"

Mattie could have kissed Caleb on the mouth. "And we have Cathy's computer and telephone."

Cathy nodded. "I'm going to call all the neighbors and ask for money. I figure you'll need three hundred dollars to run the campaign."

Three hundred dollars! It seemed like a fortune.

Freeman looked at Mattie as if she were a piece of chocolate cake. "We forgot the most important thing. We have a candidate. She's brave and honest and smart. We're going to win."

Mattie truly thought she might faint, either because of what Freeman said or how he was looking at her. "I might not be the best candidate, but I'm the only one willing to do it. Cathy says Bill ran unopposed in the last election."

Caleb took off his hat and scratched his head. "What does 'unopposed' mean?"

"It means nobody ran against him," Cathy said. "Nobody wants to be on the town council. It's a thankless job, and they only pay you a thousand dollars a year."

Caleb's mouth dropped open. "They pay you?"

"It's not worth the money, unless you're power hungry like Bill." Cathy motioned them toward the door where Freeman was standing. "Let's go in the office."

"I'm not power hungry," Mattie said, following Cathy into a room barely big enough for a small desk and two chairs.

Cathy lowered herself into the rolling chair that sat next to the computer. "You're not power hungry. You're running because you want to change the ordinance. Bill is power hungry, and Fred likes being pals with Bill. Tami is trying her best to keep the town from descending into chaos." She pulled a piece of paper from the printer and a black marker from the desk drawer. "First thing we need to do is make a flyer. I wish I knew how to create one on the computer, but it will have to be handwritten. And I can't do it. My handwriting looks like a hen stepped in some ink and did a dance."

Freeman backed away from Cathy's marker as if it might bite him. "I can't do it. I have terrible handwriting."

Caleb took the marker from Cathy's fingers. "I can do it. Dat says I have steady hands." He drew his brows together. "But if we're going to pass this out, do you think Mamm will recognize my handwriting?"

"Not likely," Cathy said. "Your *mamm* isn't getting a flyer. She doesn't vote. We have to save money somehow."

Caleb looked relieved. He set the paper on the desk and took the cap off the marker. "What do you want me to say?"

Mattie gritted her teeth. Caleb was going to make a flyer right now, without a ruler or an outline of the words in pencil? She didn't see this going well. When one of the *fraaen* in the *gmayna* made a flyer for a benefit haystack supper in Leola, she always outlined the words in pencil first so she got them right.

Caleb looked at her expectantly, obviously supremely confident in his abilities. It was the first hint of confidence she'd seen from him ever. "What should it say, Mattie?"

Cathy tapped her index finger to her lip. "It should say something like 'Greetings, I'm Mattie Zook, and I'm running for town council. The buggy ordinance needs to be repealed, and Carson Road needs a street lamp.'"

Caleb wrote feverishly, with his tongue sticking out in concentration. "What comes after 'Mattie'?"

Freeman leaned against the wall. "Isn't this house on Carson Road?"

"Yes," Cathy said. "And we need a streetlight. The hooligans come out at night and ride their skateboards up and down our sidewalk."

Freeman's lips twitched. "Wouldn't a streetlight make them more likely to come?"

"I don't think so. They like to work in the dark." Cathy tapped her finger on Caleb's flyer. "You spelled 'council' wrong."

"How do you spell it?"

Unfortunately, they wouldn't be able to use Caleb's flyer. It looked like—well, it looked like a seventeen-year-old boy with big feet and wide ears had written it. He ran out of room for *Zook* on the first line and the two *O*'s and the *K* curled toward the top of the paper. Not only had he spelled *council* wrong, but *greetings, ordinance,* and *Mattie.*

Mattie turned her face from Caleb and grimaced at Freeman. Freeman grimaced back. "We're going to have to think of something else," he said. He pulled a slick blue pamphlet from his pocket and handed it to Mattie. He looked almost apologetic. "Sorry. I got this in my mailbox this morning."

On the front of the pamphlet was a photo of Bill Isom standing in the elementary school lunchroom where they held town council meetings, flashing a toothy smile at the camera. The caption read, "Bill Isom, Byler's best friend and your best friend too." Mattie groaned and unfolded the pamphlet. One section listed Bill's experience, which included a marathon, a hot dog eating contest, and twenty years as an accountant.

Cathy stood up and looked over Mattie's shoulder.

"Starting guard for the Monte Vista High School basketball team? What a lie. Bill was a benchwarmer."

The middle section was a photo of Bill and his wife on a beach, both wearing nothing but swimsuits. Mattie crinkled her nose. *Ach, du lieva.* Bill looked like he had a furry rug glued to his chest.

Freeman leaned in for a better look, chuckled, then wiped the smile from his face. Mattie didn't see anything funny about that picture. It was disgusting.

Cathy squinted at the picture. "I hope everybody gets this pamphlet. Bill's chest hair alone will win you the women's vote. I shave Lon's back twice a month. And his wife has definitely duct taped the back of her neck to reduce wrinkles." She took the pamphlet from Mattie's hand and drew it closer to her face. "'Byler is our beloved hometown,'" she read, "'but an outsider thinks she can come in and tell us how to run things. My opponent will bring her big-city values to our small town. Our peaceful neighborhoods and quiet way of life will be destroyed.'"

Mattie raised her eyebrows. "'Big-city values'? Has he ever been to Leola?"

Cathy grunted. "It's not the truth that matters in a campaign. The person who scares voters the most will win the election."

Mattie sank into Cathy's chair. "What can we do? Everyone will vote for his very impressive pamphlet."

Freeman shook his head. "Not with that chest hair."

Caleb turned bright red. "You shouldn't say 'chest hair' out loud." He leaned closer to Freeman and whispered, "Not in front of the girls."

Cathy snatched the marker from Caleb's hand. "I haven't been a girl for a very long time. And if you think 'chest hair' is embarrassing, you should try 'a bladder infection.'"

The laughter burst from Mattie's lips. "Okay, then. What can we do?" She gave Caleb a kind smile. "Caleb, I really appreciate your help, but after seeing Bill's pamphlet, I don't think we should use your flyer."

Caleb furrowed his brow. "Okay. I guess it does look a little messy. And I spelled *town* wrong."

Town was one of the few words he'd gotten right.

Cathy sighed and pulled her cell phone from her pants pocket. "I'm going to have to call in some favors." She pressed the little circle at the bottom of her phone and spoke slowly. "Call Dewey Markham."

The phone spoke back to her. "Calling Dewey Markham."

Cathy's lips formed into something like a smile. "I love voice recognition." She paused until someone answered on the other end. "Hello, Dewey? I have a computer emergency. I need you to come over right now." Another pause. "Nope. You don't have time to finish the next level. You shouldn't be playing computer games on a school night." Cathy listened for a few seconds. "Oh, all right then. I'm not too proud to admit when I'm wrong. I forgot it's summer break." Cathy glanced at Mattie and rolled her eyes. "Can't your mom drive you? Okay. See you soon." Cathy pressed the hang-up button on her phone. "That's my grandson. He lives in Monte Vista. He'll be over in ten minutes to help us make a flyer, or maybe he'll know how to make a pamphlet for us." She frowned. "Though I don't know if we can afford to print a pamphlet. I might need to find a corporate sponsor."

Mattie examined Bill's pamphlet again. "I don't think I need a pamphlet. It feels like too much. There are only twelve hundred registered voters in the whole town. I don't think it has to be fancy to get people to vote for me."

Cathy nodded. "You're right. If you just pass out a simple flyer, people will see you as a fiscal conservative."

"What does that mean?" Mattie said, hoping her ignorance didn't hurt her chances in the election.

"It means you don't like to spend money. We already pay too much in taxes. People want their money spent wisely or not at all."

Freeman pulled the other chair away from the wall and motioned for Mattie to sit. "While we're waiting for Dewey, we should talk about yard signs. What do you want them to say? And what color do you want them to be?"

Cathy sat in the rolling chair. "Red, white, and blue are patriotic. Voters like that."

Caleb lowered himself to the floor with his legs folded to his chest. "I like yellow. It's bright and catches people's attention."

"Green is a comforting color," Freeman said.

"But if it's green, people will want to know if you believe in global warming." Cathy pinned Mattie with a serious look. "Do you believe in global warming?"

Mattie grimaced. "I don't know."

"Nothing gets people riled up like global warming. It's best just to stay silent on the issue until after the election, then you can believe whatever you want. At January's council meeting, Glen Bateman threw a chair at Jim Palmer over an argument about the polar ice caps. Hopefully it won't come up in the debate."

Mattie's heart sank, and she chewed on one of her fingernails. "There's a debate?"

Cathy nodded. "Yes, but I wouldn't worry about it. If you don't know the answer to a question, just say something about Bill Isom's chest hair. Or you can change the subject and talk about the buggy ordinance. That's really the only thing you've got."

"Oh," Mattie said, deflating like a balloon. *Was* the buggy ordinance the only thing she had? It was going to be a very short flyer. And Bill Isom would certainly win. He had a whole pamphlet—with photos.

Freeman riveted his gaze to her face, and his eyes glowed with concern. "It's not the only thing."

Cathy stood up and walked into the hall. "Caleb, come and help me get three folding chairs so everybody will have a place to sit."

Caleb obediently stood and followed Cathy down the hall. There wasn't going to be room for five chairs, but Cathy would figure that out once she and Caleb came back.

Freeman knelt next to Mattie's chair and took her hand. Her heart hopped like a frog being chased by a raccoon. *Ach.* She was far too startled to pull away, even if she wanted to. His calloused hand felt pleasantly rough against her skin. "Mattie, I don't think you're foolish, but I just want you to know that there's no shame in quitting. Bill Isom has so much more experience than you. He's not going to go easy on you."

Normally, Mattie would tell Freeman to go jump in the lake, as she had before, but he'd thrown her off guard with the hand-holding. His touch was unnerving and exhilarating, but she also felt a little off-kilter at the thought of a debate with someone almost forty years older and much more educated than she. It sort of warmed her heart that Freeman was trying to protect her. She also found it sort of irritating. "I know. *Denki* for caring." She squeezed his hand because she wanted to reassure him and hide her annoyance at the same time. "I didn't know there was going to be a debate, so it surprised me a little. Bill Isom is a bully, and somebody needs to stand up to him."

"But why does it have to be you?"

"If not me, who?"

Freeman's lips curled upward. "Apparently, nobody."

"That's right. I'm doing what I think is right. You don't have to worry about me."

"I do anyway," he said.

Mattie's heart skipped a beat at the tenderness in his voice. If he was that worried, maybe he should quit the campaign. She didn't need the distraction of his flashing blue eyes and his troubled, handsome features. But she would never suggest that he go home. She needed his help, and for some strange reason, she enjoyed having him around. Why she put up with a rude, opinionated farmer was anybody's guess. "Do you know I actually had to testify before a judge in Pennsylvania?"

"Really?"

"It was when I filed that lawsuit. I was so nervous, I threw up before I walked into the courthouse. But the judge was wonderful nice, and she told me she was proud of me."

Freeman suddenly seemed to realize he was still holding her hand. He let go and stood up. "I'm proud of you too." He seemed a little breathless. "But I don't want Bill to make you regret running."

Mattie lifted her chin. "If anybody is going to regret running, it's Bill."

Freeman laughed. "I like your confidence. You're going to need it."

"I suppose I am." She pressed her lips together. Would it hurt to be a little grateful? "*Denki* for worrying about me, and *denki* for your help. I couldn't run for town council without you."

Freeman gave her a wry smile and shook his head. "So far I've tried to talk you out of running and refused to make the flyer. I've been no help at all."

"You're here. And there are only two other people in the whole world who have gotten this far."

Cathy and Caleb came back into the room. Caleb carried three folding chairs. Freeman took one chair from him, unfolded it, and set it next to the rolling chair. He set up another chair in the corner wedged to the side of Cathy's huge filing cabinet. "If we want room for our legs," Freeman said, "the last chair isn't going to fit."

"One of us will have to sit in the hall. But which one of us?" Cathy drew her brows together. "It feels like Sophie's choice."

Freeman set the last chair in the hall. "We can all stay in here as long as one of us stands. I don't mind standing."

Cathy seemed to like that answer. "To be self-sacrificing is to know happiness."

Mattie grinned at Freeman. Cathy was grumpy, but she definitely had a flare for the dramatic. Freeman smiled back, and just about knocked Mattie over with the brightness of his perfectly white, perfectly straight teeth. That boy had worn braces sometime in his life. Mattie couldn't look away.

The doorbell rang. "Aha," Cathy said. "Dewey has come. And please don't make fun of his name. His mother is a librarian."

Mattie didn't know what that meant, but she would never dare make fun of anyone's name, especially Dewey. He was going to help her make a flyer, and she was already extremely grateful. Cathy stepped out of the room to answer the door and came back with a slight, skinny boy who couldn't have been more than thirteen years old. His short white-yellow hair stuck up on the top of his head, the victim of an inconveniently placed cowlick. His hands were stuffed into the pockets of his jeans, and he looked as if he'd rather be anywhere but here.

Mattie felt for him. What kid wanted to be spending his free time making an election flyer with a bunch of Amish people? "*Hallo*, Dewey," she said. "Thank you so much for coming over. We are desperate."

Dewey shrugged. "It's okay."

Cathy hooked her arm around his shoulders, squished him close to her side, and gave him a loud smack on the cheek, never losing that irritated expression that she wore almost constantly on her face. "Dewey is a good boy, even though he's addicted to video games."

"I'm not addicted, Grandma. I'm going to be a professional gamer. They make bank."

Cathy smirked. "I don't want to crush all your hopes and dreams, but you're more likely to get hit by lightning."

Dewey didn't seem at all crushed. "If I get rich, I can support you in your old age, Grandma."

Cathy blew air from between her lips. "You're too late. I'm already in my old age."

"Then I could buy you a really nice casket."

"I don't need a casket. I'm donating my body to science."

Dewey pulled a face. "That's gross, Grandma."

"I'm just saying I won't need your money. Donate it to a worthy cause, like your own college fund." Cathy tapped the back of the rolling chair. "We can talk about funeral arrangements later. Right now, we need you to make us a flyer."

"We really appreciate it," Mattie said again.

Dewey smiled at Mattie. "It's okay. I don't mind. But I don't even know what a flyer is, unless it's a goose."

Caleb exploded into a smile. "That's what I said!"

The pit in Mattie's stomach gaped wider. "Um, I guess I could try writing something out. My handwriting isn't that bad." Not as bad as Caleb's anyway.

"You know what a flyer is," Cathy said. "Remember when you lost your dog. Your mom made a flyer to hang around town."

Dewey frowned. "Okay, I guess, but you don't have any pets, Grandma."

Oy, anyhow. How had the conversation gotten this far off track? "Maybe we should forget about a flyer," Mattie said. "Yard signs will be good enough."

Cathy pretty much ignored Mattie. "Dewey, Mattie is running for town council against Bill Isom."

Dewey puckered his lips as if he'd just eaten a whole lemon. "That guy who tried to run over Grandpa with his golf cart?"

"That's the one."

Mattie didn't dare ask.

Cathy motioned to Freeman. "Hand me the pamphlet."

Freeman pulled Bill's pamphlet out of his pocket and gave it to Cathy. She showed it to Dewey. "We need something like this. So people will vote for Mattie." She slid Caleb's attempt at a flyer across the desk so Dewey could see it. "This is what Caleb tried to do, and it's a disaster. Can you make something nicer for us on the computer?"

Dewey unfolded Bill's pamphlet. "Gross," he mumbled. "I can't make something this fancy, but I know how to do reports in Word."

Cathy nodded vigorously. "Yes, reports. That's all we need."

Dewey pressed one of the keys on the keyboard. "How do you turn it on?"

"How should I know?" Cathy said, pressing a few more keys to try to make something happen.

"It's your computer, Grandma."

"It was a Christmas gift. I've been meaning to figure it out, but I've been too busy quilting."

Dewey looked dumbfounded. "Somebody gave you this for Christmas? As a joke?"

"Of course not. Your mom and dad gave it to me before you were born."

"Grandma!" Dewey squeaked. "And you've never turned it on?"

Cathy and Dewey continued to discuss the computer, while Mattie, Caleb, and Freeman watched in varying degrees of dismay. Mattie didn't know whether to laugh or cry. She didn't usually resort to bawling, but if Caleb's flyer turned out to be their only option, she might just burst into tears. But it was also funny in a painful way that the success of her campaign depended on a thirteen-year-old who didn't know what a flyer was, two Amish boys who didn't dare be seen with her, and Cathy Larsen, whose best strategy was to accuse Bill Isom of having too much chest hair. Right now, the chest hair option was the only thing they had.

Mattie felt Freeman sidle close behind her. He leaned forward and whispered in her ear, "If you quit the campaign right now, I'll take you to my house for some pralines-and-cream ice cream."

She giggled softly. "If you're trying to get me to sell my birthright for a mess of pottage, don't bother. I'm not giving up. Besides, I don't like pralines-and-cream."

He dropped his jaw in mock outrage. "You don't like pralines-and-cream? What is wrong with you?"

"*Ach*, so many things."

"I don't think so." He looked at her like she was a bowl of pralines-and-cream ice cream, and a pleasantly warm sensation trickled down her spine.

She didn't even notice that the computer had been successfully turned on until Cathy and Dewey fell silent, and several beeps and buzzes coming from the old machine forced her to gather her wits. Cathy and Dewey leaned in and stared at the bright screen, and Dewey tapped several keys on the keyboard. "Grandma, Word isn't loaded on here. Neither is the Internet. About all you can do is play Spider Solitaire."

"Well, can you load Word on there for me?"

"I can't because your computer isn't connected to the Internet. I don't know that it can be connected. It's pretty old."

Cathy threw up her hands. "That's that then."

"Sorry, Grandma." Dewey stood up and pulled his phone from his pocket. "I'll call Mom to come get me."

Cathy pulled Dewey in for a stiff, quick hug. "You tried your best. That's all anyone can ask of you. Think about that the next time you play a video game."

Dewey grinned and rolled his eyes. His grandma's opinion on his video games was obviously a regular topic of conversation. "You won't mind so much when I buy you a Lexus."

"I won't hold my breath." She motioned for Dewey to sit. "Show me how to play Spider Solitaire before you go."

Mattie eyed Caleb's flyer. She didn't have great handwriting, but she could probably do better than that. If she used lined paper, the sentences wouldn't travel up and down across the page. She turned to Freeman. "Can you draw?"

He studied her face in puzzlement. "Not even stick figures."

"I think I can do the lettering, but it would be pretty to add flowers and vines around the edges."

He frowned and scrubbed his hand down the side of his face. "Sadie draws. Her bedroom walls are covered with horses and cats and butterflies. But . . ."

"If you asked her to help, she'd know you are working on my campaign."

"*Jah.*" He gave Mattie a half smile. "She can't keep a secret."

Dewey called his mom then finished showing Cathy how to play Spider Solitaire. Caleb had to move his chair for Dewey to get past.

Mattie's disappointment was deep. "It was nice of you to come over."

Dewey was already halfway out the door. "No problem." He hesitated, heaved a sigh, and stopped in his tracks. "My mom could make you a flyer. If you write down what you want, I can take it home, and she can type it up."

Cathy's wrinkles deepened around her mouth. "I should have thought of that."

"Oh," Mattie said. "That would be so nice."

Dewey pulled out his phone again. "I know you Amish don't like your picture taken, but Bill's got two pictures in his flyer. You're a lot prettier than Bill." A red flush traveled up his neck, and he cleared his throat.

"A picture is a good idea," Cathy said. "Folks nowadays don't read anything."

Dewey nodded. "My mom is always on Pinterest."

Cathy narrowed her eyes. "Everybody at that house is addicted."

"I haven't been baptized," Mattie said. "You can take my picture."

"Okay." Dewey held up his phone. "Smile."

"You . . . you want to take it right now?"

"Why not?" Dewey said.

Mattie turned to Freeman. "How do I look?"

His lips twitched into a grin. "Beautiful."

"Very funny. But is my *kapp* straight? Do I have any hair sticking out?"

He eyed her doubtfully then stroked his fingers across

her cheek as if brushing some hair from her face, but she hadn't felt anything out of place. Still, she froze at his touch, gluing her gaze to his, wondering what this strange feeling was that went all the way to her toes.

"You look just right." He moved away from her so he wouldn't be in the picture, and Dewey snapped a few shots while Mattie tried not to force her smile or look too severe.

Dewey squinted at his phone. "Do you want to see if you like them?"

Mattie took Dewey's phone, and Freeman leaned in to have a look. Mattie was almost irritated at how *gute* he smelled. She'd be able to think more clearly if Freeman wasn't in the room. "It's *gute* enough," she said. Blue was a *gute* color, and there was a friendly, vote-for-me kind of look on her face.

"We need to pass this out to everybody," Freeman said. "As soon as people see it, they'll vote for you just because you're so pretty."

Mattie laughed and smacked him in the shoulder. "Oh, stop it. I look fine, but I'm not pretty."

Freeman seemed surprised and a little annoyed. "You don't think you're pretty? What, are you blind?" He turned to Cathy. "Don't you think Mattie is pretty?"

"Very," Cathy said. "Let me see the picture."

Caleb cleared his throat. "Mattie is the prettiest girl in Byler, and she's not even from here."

Freeman grunted. "The prettiest girl in Colorado, if you ask me."

Mattie had always been unmoved by such flattery. "That's silly. 'Thou shalt not bear false witness.'"

Freeman pinned her with a serious glare. "You know I always tell the truth."

Mattie's mouth went dry, and she found it impossible to breathe, not so much because of what he had said, but because of how he was looking at her. *Ach*. No girl would have been able to keep her knees from going weak if she had gazed into those eyes. Now would be a *gute* time to sit down.

Cathy gave Dewey his phone back. "You look like a nice Amish girl. Freeman, see how much it costs to print flyers in color. This picture needs to be in color. I'm really going to need those corporate sponsors."

Dewey shoved his phone in his pocket once more. "I'll give these to my mom." He looked up at the ceiling and heaved another sigh, bigger this time. "You should probably have a Facebook page."

Freeman drew his brows together. "How does she get a Facebook page? Is it expensive?"

"It doesn't cost anything." Dewey frowned. "I could make you one, I guess."

"It will take time away from your video games. That's quite a sacrifice." Cathy reached out and patted Dewey on the cheek. "I've never been prouder of you."

Dewey shrugged. "I'm nice like that. It's why I'm going to buy you a Lexus, Grandma. Or a new computer."

"I don't need a Lexus. I'll settle for more time with my grandson."

Dewey grimaced. "That's so sweet, I want to throw up."

Cathy made a face. "Me too."

"If you want my mom to make a flyer, you need to write down some stuff I can give her."

Mattie snapped out of whatever daze she'd been in and pulled a piece of paper from Cathy's printer, which apparently hadn't been used either since she got the computer because dust motes floated off the paper and into the air when she picked it up. She sat at the desk where Dewey had been and picked up a pencil. "Okay, then. Everybody help me. What should the flyer say?"

Cathy pulled a chair next to her. "Write this down. 'Hello, Byler residents. My name is Mattie Zook. I'm running for town council. The buggy ordinance needs to be repealed, and Carson Road needs a street lamp.'"

"I think we should leave out the street lamp part," Freeman said. "We don't want people to think Mattie will do favors for her friends just because she's in office. That's what Bill does and it's wrong."

Cathy puckered her lips. "I suppose you're right, but once she gets on the council, I'm going to lean on her and Tami very hard."

Dewey pointed to her paper. "You need like a . . . I don't know what the word is. Like a motto. Something you can put on your posters."

"A slogan. That's a very good idea, Dewey. There's hope for you yet."

"Thanks, Grandma."

Caleb looked to be concentrating very hard. "How about 'Vote for Mattie'?"

"Too boring," Cathy said.

Dewey scratched his head. "You need to think of a good word that rhymes with Mattie."

Cathy tapped her lips with her index finger. "Chatty. Fatty. Catty. None of those are very complimentary words."

Freeman leaned over Mattie's shoulder, and she caught that *wunderbarr* smell again. Could he not be so distracting for half a second? "What about 'Mattie Zook for all of Byler,' with *all* in capital letters?"

"That's the one," Cathy said.

Mattie gasped. "I love it. *All* of Byler." She wrote it down on her paper along with a few other things she wanted people to know about the buggy ordinance. She left out the part about the streetlight but put in a sentence about being willing to listen to all citizen concerns. She glanced up at Freeman. "What do you think?"

His smile was like a mug of warm cocoa on a frosty day. "I think it's perfect."

Mattie folded the paper and handed it to Dewey. "Will you give this to your mom?"

"Okay," Dewey said. "She'll type it up."

"And if it's not too risky, I still want to ask Sadie to draw me some flowers."

Freeman thought about it. "I guess that would be okay, but we'll have to let Sarah in on the secret. Sadie would never be able to keep it from her."

"Is that okay?"

"My parents won't like it, but Lord willing, if Sadie can keep her mouth shut, Mamm and Dat will never find out."

Lord willing indeed.

Mattie took a deep breath and smiled. A burden shared was a burden lightened, and if Sadie and Sarah said yes, her number of campaign workers would double. She practically had a whole crowd of supporters.

Bill Isom had better be ready. She was definitely going to win.

Chapter 9

Freeman tromped up the stairs to his sisters' room and knocked on the door, with dread growing like toxic mold in his chest. How would his sisters react to his request? He wasn't altogether sure that one of them wouldn't march right down the stairs and tell Dat that he was working on Mattie's campaign. Sarah was levelheaded and sensible while Sadie was enthusiastic and unpredictable. Which one of them was more likely to tattle?

When there was no answer, he knocked again, louder. Sadie opened the door. "What do you want?" she said, with just a tinge of resentment in her voice.

She hadn't yet forgiven him for sending her away that day in the potato field. *Ach,* she was touchy. "I need you to come out to the barn."

She folded her arms as if ready to stand her ground for a week. "It's your turn to muck out. I did it yesterday."

"I already mucked out. I need to talk to you. And Sarah too."

Sadie narrowed her eyes. "About what?"

"For once could you do something without asking a million questions?"

"For once could you not boss me around?"

A growl came from the other side of the door, and Sarah

yanked it open. "Sadie, why do you always have to make it so hard? Freeman wants to talk to us. Is that so wrong? Maybe he's got ice cream in the barn he wants to share."

Sadie pinned Freeman with a piercing gaze. "Do you have ice cream in the barn?"

"*Nae.*"

She turned to Sarah. "See? No ice cream. He's going to make us do chores or something."

Freeman bit down on his tongue. If he didn't care about Mattie so much, he'd tell Sadie to go jump in the lake. "Okay then, you don't have to come. Sarah and I will leave you out of the secret."

He could feel Sadie wavering. "It's a trick."

Sarah sighed. "Sadie, what kind of a trick do you think it is? He can't make us do chores, and if we don't like what he has to say, we can come back up here and pretend it never happened."

Sadie tilted her head to one side. "Why don't you just tell us right here?"

He gave her a withering look. "That's part of the secret."

Sarah came out of the room and clomped down the stairs. "Well, I'm going, and don't think I'll tell you the secret later when you change your mind."

Sadie threw up her hands. "All right. I'm coming. Let me get my shoes on."

Freeman followed Sarah down the stairs, and it only took about half a minute for Sadie to catch up. Freeman smiled to himself. No matter how much she protested otherwise, Sadie didn't like to be left out of anything, especially not a secret. It was why she was so mad at Freeman to begin with.

They strolled into the barn, and Freeman led his sisters to the stall where Mattie was waiting for them. Sadie caught sight of Mattie and gasped. "*Ach, du lieva*. What is the secret? Are you two engaged?"

Mattie's cheeks turned a lovely shade of pink. Freeman's heart jumped up and down like a kid on a trampoline. The thought of being engaged to Mattie made him a little dizzy.

He certainly didn't have the time or the brain power to think about that now. "Calm down, Sadie. We are not engaged. Mattie has something she wants to ask you."

Sadie grabbed Mattie's hand eagerly. "Do you want me to be one of your attendants?"

"Sadie," Freeman snapped. "We're not getting married."

Sadie pulled her hand away and gave Freeman the stink eye. "You don't have to be so grumpy about it."

Freeman raised his hands and backed away. "Why are you mad at me? I didn't do anything."

Sadie glanced from Freeman to Mattie and back again. "*Nae*, you haven't done anything. Boys are so *dumm*."

Freeman huffed out a breath. "I give up."

Mattie had more patience than Freeman. "I've actually come to ask for your help."

Sadie made a face in Freeman's direction. "If you want us to get Freeman to ask you to marry him, you can forget it. He's hopeless."

Mattie giggled. "It's not that. But first, I'm hoping you'll keep this to yourselves. We don't want anybody to know."

Sadie's lips formed into an O. "You *are* engaged."

Sarah rolled her eyes. "Sadie, would you just be quiet and listen."

Freeman was about to order Sadie out of the barn, but Mattie just grinned. "I'm running for town council."

Sadie deflated like a balloon. "We already knew that."

"The big secret is that Freeman is helping me."

Sarah and Sadie eyed Freeman as if he'd grown antlers. "But you've been baptized," Sadie said in disbelief.

Freeman had expected this sort of reaction. "I have, but it's not against the Ordnung to help with a campaign, and Mattie needs me." Her words, not his.

"Dat wouldn't like it though," Sarah said.

Freeman sighed. "I know. That's why it's a secret. I'm not doing anything wrong, but it would upset Mamm and Dat if they knew, so I'm not telling them." He stood up straighter to make himself look more intimidating. "And you aren't going to tell them either."

Sadie puckered her lips and wrinkled her nose at him. "Fine, fine, big *bruder*. Don't get all huffy about it. I won't tell, but only because I like Mattie so much."

Freeman raised a cynical eyebrow. "You don't like me?"

Sadie shook her head. "You're too bossy. And sometimes you're rude. And you hog all the food at dinner. I have to take seconds *and* firsts or I don't get any."

Freeman chuckled. "Okay. Whatever you say. I don't care."

"I know you don't care," Sadie scolded. "It's like you don't even have a heart or something."

Mattie grabbed Sadie's wrist, probably to try to focus her attention. It was quite an impossible task. "The reason I told you about Freeman is because I am wondering if you would help me on my campaign too."

Astonishment popped on Sadie's face. "Me?"

"Both of you." Mattie looked at Sarah. "I need both of you to help me."

Sarah's eyebrows inched closer together. "*Ach, vell*, Mattie, I don't know. Dat wouldn't like it."

"I know," Mattie said. "And if you're not comfortable, I completely understand."

Sadie worried her bottom lip with her teeth. "We're in *rumschpringe*, Sarah. Even if Dat got mad, he wouldn't do anything about it. It's not like we're buying a car or smoking cigars inside the barn."

Freeman frowned. "Do you smoke cigars *outside* the barn?"

Sadie gave Freeman that look she always gave him when she thought he was being stupid. He saw it a lot. "Very funny." She turned to give her full attention to Mattie. "Just ignore my *bruder*. You know how rude he is."

Mattie's eyes flashed with mischief. "Oh, I know."

"Hey," Freeman said in mock indignation. "I'm standing right here."

Mattie pulled the folder from the shelf in the stall and handed it to Sadie. "Here is a copy of the flyer I'm going to hand out to the voters."

Sadie opened the folder and took out one of the four flyers inside. "*Ach,* look how pretty you are."

"*Denki*. The photo turned out fine." Freeman liked that Mattie wasn't one to make a fuss about her appearance.

Mattie's flyer wasn't nearly as fancy as Bill Isom's pamphlet, but it was neat and concise, with "Mattie Zook for ALL of Byler" printed across the top and a picture of Mattie right in the center of the page. Even though Mattie didn't care much about it, the picture of her was indeed very pretty. Dewey's mom had done a *gute* job on the flyer, and unlike Caleb, she hadn't misspelled any words.

Mattie pointed to the white space around the edge of the paper. "It wonders me if you would draw flowers and vines and such around the border. Freeman says you're a *gute* artist."

"She is," Sarah said. "She's painted butterflies and flowers all over our walls, even though Mamm thinks it's vain."

Sadie smiled tentatively. "I could, but it would take me days and days to draw flowers on each flyer."

Freeman hooked his hand over the stall door. "*Nae,*

Sadie, you just need to color one, and then we'll take it to the copy store and make five hundred copies."

Sadie got breathless. "Five hundred copies? All those people will get to see my drawings?"

Sarah was not one to let Sadie get carried away with herself. "*Ach*, Sadie, you shouldn't do it if you're tempted to be proud."

Sadie was deeply offended at such a suggestion. "I'm not proud. If my flowers make people happy and help Mattie get elected, why shouldn't I get excited about that?"

Mattie smiled. Freeman was coming to think of that smile as absolutely essential to his life. "Then you'll do it for me?"

Sadie beamed with delight. "Of course."

"*Ach*," Mattie said. "*Denki* so much. For sure and certain your flowers will help me get elected."

Sarah nodded. "Lord willing."

"Lord willing," Mattie and Sadie said in unison.

Mattie handed Sadie the folder. "I had Dewey's mom print out four flyers, just in case you make a mistake and want to start over. But remember, this is a secret. I don't want to make trouble between you and your parents."

Sadie waved her hand in the air. "I don't care about that. I'm in *rumschpringe*."

Sarah glanced at Freeman. "But Freeman isn't. We have to keep the secret for him."

Sadie eyed Freeman with suspicion. "Are you ashamed that you're helping Mattie with her campaign?"

Ach, Sadie jumped to conclusions like a frog jumped from lily pad to lily pad. Freeman frowned. Or maybe she was just annoyingly perceptive. "Not ashamed. Just cautious."

Sadie turned to Mattie. "He's scared."

"I'm not scared."

Sadie ignored his protests. "So, Mattie, tell me what colors you want me to use."

Mattie looked at Freeman. "What colors do you think?"

Sadie intentionally turned her back on Freeman. "*Ach*, he's a boy. He doesn't care."

Freeman never lost his temper, but Sadie was really starting to irritate him. "I do *so* care."

Mattie stunned him into silence when she hooked her elbow around his arm and pulled him into the circle of girls. "*Cum*," she said. "Help us decide what Sadie should draw."

Shocked by Mattie's gentle touch, Freeman kept his mouth shut for fear he'd stutter. He'd be able to speak when his heart returned to normal speed. He watched Mattie out of the corner of his eye. His heart would never return to normal speed as long as Mattie stood next to him looking like an angel in that yellow dress.

Sarah held up the flyer so the four of them could see it. "You could use blue to match her dress in the picture."

Sadie nodded. "Or yellow and red are cheery. What's your favorite flower, Mattie?"

"I like daisies, but white petals won't show up on the white paper."

"Oooh," Sadie said. "What about red and pink hearts?"

Freeman finally found his voice. "Too cutesy."

Sadie gave him that look again. "Hearts aren't cutesy. They make people think of love."

"You want the flyer to be pretty," Freeman said, "not look like some teenage girl wrote a love letter to her boyfriend."

Sarah nodded. "He's right. Hearts don't work on a campaign flyer."

"How do you know?" Sadie said. "None of us know what a campaign flyer should look like."

Freeman pulled Bill's pamphlet out of his pocket. He kept it there to remind himself why he was helping Mattie with her campaign. "Look. This is Bill's."

Sarah and Sadie looked through it, their eyes getting wider when they saw Bill in his swimming suit. "That's disgusting," Sadie said. "He should have used some hearts."

Mattie grinned. "I'm sure you can do better than that, Sadie."

Sadie giggled. "Our horse Lucky could do better than that. Don't worry, Mattie. I won't disappoint you."

"I know you won't."

Once again, Freeman was glad he'd kept that flyer. It motivated people the way nothing else could. Bill's own pride was his greatest weakness.

Mattie helped Aunt Esther fold the baby quilt into thirds before hanging it over a plastic hanger and hooking the hanger over the pole Uncle Levi had installed spanning the wall in the living room.

Aunt Esther stood back and admired the row of quilts hanging on display, a black marker tucked neatly behind her ear. "That looks very nice."

"*Jah*. So pretty and colorful."

Yesterday, Mattie had helped Aunt Esther make a poster to put out front by the mailbox. It read: QUILTS FOR SALE. OPEN FRIDAY AND SATURDAY, 10–6. CLOSED SUNDAY.

Almost all of the Amish businesses in town were run out of people's homes. The Millers sold vegetables and eggs at a stand in their front yard, the Yoders stitched fancy cowboy boots in their basement, and Mary Hostetler's *dat* had built an addition onto their house so Mary could have her own bakery. At every house where there was a business, shoppers were given a hand-drawn map of all the

Amish businesses in the area. That was all the advertising anyone ever did. There wasn't a lot of traffic because Byler wasn't a tourist town like Bird-in-Hand, Pennsylvania, or Sugarcreek, Ohio, but the Amish did well enough with the locals to make a little money. Byler hadn't had a quilt shop until today, and Esther was very enthusiastic about her new project. Mattie wasn't sure that the timing was right, since Esther's baby would come any day now, but Mattie wasn't about to discourage her. Mattie knew how frustrating it was when people tried to squash your dreams.

"Should I move the pink one to the end? It's brighter than the blue one."

"*Nae*," Mattie said. "They are all so beautiful. Don't move a thing or you'll be rearranging them forever."

Uncle Levi's *mammi,* Nanna Kiem, was a famous quilter, and about a third of the quilts hanging on the pole were from her. With an Englisch quilter's help, Nanna sold her quilts on the Internet and at a fancy quilt shop in Boulder. Aunt Esther also sold her quilts in fancy stores. Buyers who were willing to go off the beaten path were in for a real treat.

Esther smiled and ran her hand along the hanging quilts. "They are *wunderbarr*." She fingered a blue-and-white Nine Patch. "This one is Cathy's. Rita even gave me two to sell. There aren't more beautiful quilts in the whole state. People are going to love these."

Mattie glanced quickly at the clock and smoothed her fingers along the edge of a pink baby quilt with hearts sewn into the squares. "This is my favorite. It's just adorable."

"I like that one too. I made it from some scraps from Nanna Kiem."

"Maybe you will use it for your own baby."

Esther cradled her hands around her round abdomen. "Maybe. Or the blue one. I think it's a boy."

"*Ach,* how *wunderbarr*. Winnie will be so excited."

Esther laughed. "I don't know about that. She's been the center of attention for so long, she's bound to be jealous. A sibling will be *gute* for her. No one should grow up believing they're the most important person in the world."

Mattie clasped her hands together. "Do you need anything else, *Aendi* Esther?"

Esther's smile faltered. "Going somewhere?"

Mattie tried to deliver the bad news gently. "You know I am. Tonight is town council meeting." And it was Meet the Candidates night. Mattie had a five-minute speech prepared. She was both terrified and exhilarated.

Esther pressed her lips into a hard line. "I don't see why you need to go to every meeting. They can't be very exciting. Wouldn't you rather stay here and do a puzzle? Caleb will be very sad if you didn't stick around for the fun."

Mattie furrowed her brow. "Caleb is coming?" He knew better than to show up on Meet the Candidates night.

"He's bringing a new puzzle and some homemade root beer. For sure and certain you'll want to stay for homemade root beer."

"It sounds *appeditlich*, Aunt Esther. It really does, but Cathy is coming to pick me up. We've already made arrangements."

"But what will I tell Caleb? He'll be heartbroken."

Mattie seriously doubted that. Caleb was so busy trying not to get caught helping with the campaign that he didn't have time to be heartbroken. Had there even been a girl named Lily? If there was, Caleb hadn't said a word about her. And though Aunt Esther wouldn't like to hear it, Mattie's enlisting Caleb to help on her campaign was doing more to heal his maybe-broken heart than any puzzle ever would.

Mattie would have to right-out refuse to stay home

tonight. The election was less than two months away, and she was going to be gone more and more often. She felt a little bit bad about not being fully available to help when the baby came, but Mattie didn't have a job, so she could still spend a lot of time during the day and in the middle of the night helping Aunt Esther with the new baby.

So far, Mattie had managed to lull Aunt Esther into a sense of security. After Sadie finished the flyer, Freeman had made five hundred copies at the copy store in Monte Vista. Mattie, Cathy, and Dewey had passed them out to every non-Amish house in Byler. It had taken almost two weeks, because when most of the people who worked on your campaign didn't want to get caught, you didn't have a lot of help passing out flyers. They'd met a lot of nice people, and they'd only been chased by a dog once. Dewey had a way with animals and a pocketful of doggie treats, so none of them had been bitten. Mattie probably wouldn't win the election if she got rabies.

Mattie traced her finger around one of the hearts on the pink baby quilt. Freeman and Sadie had argued for a *gute* ten minutes about whether Sadie should draw hearts on the flyer, and it seemed Sadie had only argued because she liked getting under Freeman's skin. It was obvious that Freeman adored his *schwesteren*, even if they drove him crazy.

Mattie looked up from the quilt. Aunt Esther was watching her curiously. What did she see? What did she suspect? Self-consciously, Mattie smoothed the quilt back into its place on the pole and cleared her throat.

Ach, everything made her think of Freeman, even though there wasn't a heart to be seen on Mattie's flyer.

In spite of Mattie's objections, Freeman had spent his own money getting that flyer copied. Then they had spent a very pleasant evening folding the flyers into thirds so they'd look more official when Mattie passed them out. The best part about running for town council was being with Freeman. As they got yard signs ready to distribute, he told her all about the valley and the sand dunes and farmland. He entertained her with stories about his *schwesteren* and his parents and how he'd broken his arm three times. He expressed his concern again and again that Bill was going to hurt her feelings, and she found it sweet that he was worried about her. And he never once told her that she was foolish or snobby.

Aunt Esther smiled at her, a twinkle of understanding in her eyes. "Something's different about you."

Mattie glanced behind her. "Me? Has my appearance suddenly changed?"

Aunt Esther shook her head. "*Nae*. It's been coming on for weeks. That worry line between your eyes has disappeared, and you smile more, like you don't have the weight of the world on your shoulders."

Mattie felt her face get warm. Every time she thought about Freeman, she couldn't help but smile, and lately, she just couldn't bring herself to worry about much of anything. "The altitude headache is gone."

"That was gone months ago," Esther said. "This is Caleb's doing. For sure and certain you've cheered him up, but he's done the same for you. He's such a dear boy and so fun to be with."

Ach, vell, Aunt Esther could certainly believe that if it made her happy. And Caleb *was* a dear boy, an awkward teenager who was so eagerly chipper that sometimes Mattie wanted to smack him. Well, not really smack him. In spite of his very bad flyer, Caleb had been an amazing help with the campaign. Not only had he given Mattie rides and secretly hung flyers all over town, but he hadn't breathed a word to Levi or Esther. As far as Mattie knew, they were still blissfully ignorant of how much work was going on for the campaign.

A movement outside caught Mattie's attention. Caleb was walking up to the front door. *Ach.* He really was coming for a visit. He knew she had town council meeting tonight. What was he up to?

He knocked on the door, and Aunt Esther all but fainted with happiness. "He's here." She looked at Mattie, pleading with her eyes. "He's come all this way. Why don't you stay and do a puzzle with us? Surely you can miss one town council meeting."

Aunt Esther opened the door, and Caleb strolled into the entryway. "*Hallo*, Mattie. *Vie gehts?*" he said, the sweat beading on his upper lip.

She might as well be nice, even if her annoyance was about to boil over. "I'm fine. How are you?"

"Looking forward to spending time with you," he said.

Ach, she was going to gag on his sincerity. "That's wonderful nice, but . . ."

His gaze flicked in Esther's direction before landing squarely on Mattie. "It wonders me if you would like to go on a drive. The sunset is wonderful nice at the park."

Mattie's irritation dissipated like morning dew. Watching the sunset at the park was their secret code. "I would like that." She rushed past Aunt Esther, grabbed her bonnet and shawl off the hook, and took a deep breath. "Shall we go?"

Esther raised her finger. "Wait. You need something to snack on while you watch the sunset." She ran into the kitchen and with astonishing speed, returned with an entire picnic basket. "Here are some bread and cookies and a jar of apricot jam." She drew her brows together. "Do you want butter?"

"I think we'll be just fine without butter," Mattie said,

taking the basket from her and feeling only a slight twinge of guilt.

Esther smiled serenely. "I don't think anyone is fine without butter, but this should be *gute* enough."

Caleb hesitated at the door, but Mattie pulled him out of the house, down the porch steps, and into his buggy. Caleb drew a hanky from his pocket and mopped the sweat from his face. "This is bad, Mattie. I'm going to be sick."

Mattie's heart lurched. "What? What happened? Is someone hurt?"

"Every time I bear false witness to Esther, I feel like I'm going to throw up." Groaning as if he was just hit with a wave of nausea, he leaned forward and pinched the bridge of his nose.

Mattie pressed her fingers into the back of his neck and made her voice low and soothing. "It will be all right, Caleb."

"I'm going to throw up."

"Well, stick your head out the window so you don't ruin the vinyl."

He slid open the door and leaned the upper half of his body out of the buggy. Mattie patted his back while he took several deep breaths. After a few seconds, he sat up straight. "Now I think I'm going to faint."

"Put your head between your knees." Caleb sort of folded in half with his face toward the floor of the buggy and breathed even louder. "Not too hard or you'll hyperventilate."

He suddenly went silent, though she could see his chest moving up and down. At least he wasn't holding his breath. After a few more minutes, he took one deep, solid breath, sat up, and combed his fingers through his disheveled hair. "I'm sorry, Mattie, but I think we're both going to hell."

Mattie did her best to suppress a smile and her guilty

conscience. "*Ach*, Caleb. I'm so sorry. I didn't mean to put you in an awkward position with your *bruder* and *schwester*-in-law."

He paused as if he was thinking about that. "Well, I suppose Esther put me in the awkward position first, but every time I hang a flyer, it feels like I'm betraying her. She made us a picnic basket, and I don't deserve it because I'm a big, fat liar."

"You are not a big, fat liar. I'm sorry you feel like throwing up. You're just trying to be a *gute bruder*-in-law."

"*Jah,* I am."

"I don't feel bad about running for office, and I've tried to be truthful with Esther. But I do feel bad about dragging you into this. As far as I can tell, neither of us is going to hell, but if you want to quit, I understand."

He stared at her for a very long minute. "But then I wouldn't get to see you."

What did that mean? "Don't take it personally, but if you come over, I won't be hanging around to see how the puzzle turns out."

Caleb nodded and sat up straighter. "Daniel didn't lose his courage, even when they threw him in the lions' den. If you're brave enough to run for office, I'm not going to quit on you." He picked up the reins. "Let's get you to that council meeting."

Mattie couldn't argue with that.

The leaves on the few trees in Byler had just begun to turn red and yellow, and there was a hint of fall in the air. The mountains were dotted with golden aspens and bright orange scrub oak in what Freeman called "Froot Loops" season. The colors were different but just as vibrant as in Pennsylvania. It was why fall was Mattie's favorite time of year.

There were more cars than usual parked at the elementary school when Mattie and Caleb arrived. Three buggies stood next to the playground. Mattie eyed them curiously. She'd never seen a buggy at a town council meeting, not even that first time when Freeman had shown up to speak. Freeman had never come to a council meeting again. Mattie had gone to every one.

Caleb frowned and guided the horse next to the other buggies. "Do you think the elders are here?"

"I don't know."

His Adam's apple bobbed up and down. "I think I'll go to the park and watch the sunset. It's safer that way."

"Okay," Mattie said. "*Denki* for the ride."

Caleb's expression was saturated with guilt. "I'm sorry to abandon you, Mattie. I'm just not as brave as you are, and I never will be. I might as well admit it and get on with my life."

Mattie gave him a reassuring smile. "Don't worry, Caleb. I know you'll enjoy the sunset. Maybe some of *die youngie* will be there."

"I don't wonder but they will be. Everyone loves a sunset."

Mattie walked into the school, and her heart leaped at the sight of at least a dozen Amish young people milling in the front hall. Sadie Sensenig caught sight of Mattie and rushed to her side, pulling Sarah along with her. "Isn't this *wunderbarr*, Mattie? We told everybody we know to come to the meeting tonight. Cathy picked us up and brought us so we could hear you speak. You're going to speak, aren't you? Cathy said you were going to speak."

Mattie nodded, somewhat dazed at the sea of *kapps* and straw hats surrounding her. She spoke during the public comment period at every council meeting. It was a way to show Bill Isom she was serious and to make people aware of who she was. They always let Bill's wife speak right after Mattie. Bill's wife said nice things about Bill and all he was doing for the town, and she always gushed about how nice it was to drive on the roads without having to dodge buggies and manure.

Tonight Mattie would be up in front, speaking for several minutes and answering questions from the audience. "I am going to speak," she said. A wave of gratitude washed over her. "*Denki* for coming. It is wonderful nice to see so many friendly faces." She searched the group for the one person she most wanted to see but knew she wouldn't find. Freeman just couldn't risk coming. It made her feel just a little bit lonely.

Sadie pulled Mattie in for a quick hug. "We all think you're so brave. I told Sarah that we all need to be as brave as you are, didn't I, Sarah?"

Sarah rolled her eyes. "She did. Everybody."

Mattie frowned. "But I thought you were going to keep it a secret."

Sadie grunted. "*Ach,* we're keeping Freeman a secret, even though I told him he needs to be as brave as you are. I told him that, didn't I, Sarah?"

"She did. Freeman gave her the stink eye."

A twinge of pain in her heart caught Mattie by surprise. "Oh, please don't be mad at Freeman. He's helped me so much, even though he knows he could get in trouble with the *gmayna*."

Sadie didn't seem concerned. "*Ach*, Mattie, I couldn't ask for a better *bruder*. But sometimes his love smothers me."

"That's silly, Sadie," Sarah said.

"It is not. He's so bossy, I just want to throw dirt at his head sometimes. I know he wants to do what is exactly right, but that doesn't mean I have to go along with it just because he's my *bruder*. It's like he can't even let me live my life."

Freeman was always very concerned about doing the right thing. How it must have pained him to go behind his *dat*'s back—just like fooling Esther bothered Caleb. But if campaigning was so hard for Freeman, why had he volunteered to help her?

The answer was obvious. Freeman had a *gute*, kind heart. For sure and certain nobody in the district wanted to see Mattie get hurt, but Freeman was the only one who had been willing to try to protect her. The thought momentarily stole her breath.

"You should have seen Freeman's face when I told him we were coming tonight," Sadie said. "He got all quiet and grumpy."

Sarah wrapped her fingers around Mattie's wrist. "But he did tell us to watch out for you."

Sadie giggled. "As if we wouldn't. But guess what else, Mattie? We are all going to vote for you."

Mattie's mouth fell open. "You're going to . . . what do you mean?"

"Those of us who are eighteen and older registered to vote. We're in *rumschpringe*. They can't stop us."

"But won't your *dat* be upset?"

Sarah grabbed Mattie's hand. "It's okay. We've already told him. He didn't like it, but I told him if he let me vote—"

"And he can't say no, because we're in *rumschpringe*," Sadie added.

Sarah shot Sadie a reproachful look. "I told him if he let me vote, I wouldn't get a cell phone."

"You shouldn't have promised that," Sadie said. "I'm going to get a cell phone next week. Simeon says there's a *gute* plan at Walmart."

Sarah sighed. "I know, but it made Dat feel better. And he'll only let you use it in the barn."

Most of *die youngie* got cell phones during *rumschpringe*. Some parents were adamantly against cell phones and wouldn't allow them in the house. Other parents wanted their children to have cell phones because parents liked borrowing them for their own use.

Mattie gave Sarah a hug. "That's a wonderful big sacrifice. Are you sure about this? Because I understand if you'd rather have a cell phone."

"I'm voting and getting a cell phone," Sadie said. "I'm in *rumschpringe*, and Dat and Freeman can be as mad as they want."

Sarah grunted. "That's why Dat paces the floor at night worrying about you and not me."

"Why would he worry about me?" Sadie said. "I'm just living my truth."

Mattie frowned. "I don't even know what that means."

Sarah cocked her eyebrow. "Sadie has been talking to her *Englisch* friends."

Sadie practically bounced with enthusiasm. "Who are all going to vote for you, for sure and certain."

Mattie couldn't help but be touched by her friends' support. "I don't know what to say but *denki*."

"This is for all of us," Sarah said. "The buggy ordinance is just plain mean."

They walked into the lunchroom. Every seat at the lunch tables was taken, and people had started setting up folding chairs along the back wall. Mattie was astounded. She'd never seen more than twelve people at a town council meeting, and there were more than sixty here before the meeting had even started. Her heart thudded against her chest like a galloping horse. This was going to be scarier than she thought.

Instead of the usual table and chairs, two microphones stood next to each other on the stage with two chairs behind them. Mattie climbed the stairs to the stage and stared at the chairs. Which one was she supposed to sit in? Was there a rule? Would she embarrass herself if she sat in the wrong one?

Tami Moore was suddenly at Mattie's side. "Mattie, so nice to see you."

Mattie resisted the urge to give Tami a hug. "Where should I sit?"

Tami smiled. "It doesn't matter. Just pick one. Be sure to speak nice and loud." She lowered her voice. "And don't let Bill bully you."

"I won't," Mattie said, with more conviction than she felt. She was a twenty-two-year-old Amish girl, raised to be quiet and modest. Her family and the *gmayna* were embarrassed by her behavior. Even Freeman, who had been so kind, would not publicly support her. It was easy to doubt herself.

"You're bright and brave, Mattie. Stand your ground. You have more friends than you know." Tami's gaze traveled around the room. "Look at how many Amish people showed up tonight, probably without their parents' approval."

"That's for sure and certain. It wonders me if their parents wouldn't rather they took up smoking."

"If it's any encouragement, I would rather my kids vote than smoke." Tami left the stage and sat off to the side on one of the uncomfortable lunch table seats. Mattie chose the chair to the right. Being a little closer to Tami made her feel that much more confident.

Cathy limped into the lunchroom with six more Amish young people in tow. Mattie hadn't realized there were that many *youngie* in all of Byler. Caleb would be watching that sunset all by himself tonight. Freeman, of course, wasn't among the new group of Amish, but Mattie had already resigned herself to the fact that he wouldn't be coming. She had never let it bother her before, but now a hollow space opened up in the middle of her chest. Try as she might, she couldn't ignore it. Freeman was not here, and he was the only person who truly understood why she was running and how hard it was to go against her entire community.

Cathy waved to her and hobbled up the steps to the stage. "I've been all over town recruiting Amish boys and girls," she said, breathing heavily from her trip up the three stairs.

"Thank you, Cathy."

Cathy took an inhaler from her purse and sprayed it into her mouth. "Marva Hirschi donated ten dollars to your campaign yesterday. I tried to get fifteen dollars out of her, but she's a tightwad." Cathy turned and tapped the microphone. "It's not working." She pointed to a janitor who was sweeping the stage. "This mic isn't working."

The janitor dutifully shuffled over to the microphone and examined it. "I don't think it's turned on yet. They're probably waiting for the meeting to start."

"All right then," Cathy said, dismissing him with a wave of her hand. "I should know better than to ask someone who isn't a tech expert." She eyed Mattie, licked her thumb, and swiped it across Mattie's chin. "You have a smudge right there. It's gone now."

Mattie did her best not to cringe. Cathy was just trying to help her. "Okay. Thanks."

"If I were you, I'd bring up his hair plugs and that swimsuit picture first thing. Nothing gets votes like a scandal." With that cheery piece of advice, Cathy descended the stairs and sat in the back amongst the Amish young people who were attending the meeting instead of watching the sunset with Caleb Kiem. At least they weren't out smoking. Their parents could be happy about that.

Bill climbed the steps to the stage as if he owned the entire lunchroom. He wore a royal blue suit with a bright yellow tie. He was likely trying to look intimidating, but all Mattie could think about was that photo of him in a swimsuit. It would probably take years to get that image out of her head.

"Well, Mattie, I guess you got the memo," he said, smiling at her like a snake. Mattie had never seen a snake smile, but she imagined the expression would look just like Bill's.

She tried not to let him make her doubt herself, but she hated that she didn't understand his meaning. "The memo?" If you were unsure, you always answered a question with a question. Freeman had told her that when he helped her with her speech.

He fingered the lapel of his suit. "We're both wearing blue. Who do you think looks better in it?"

Mattie clenched her teeth. Why had she chosen the blue dress to wear tonight? *Ach*, *vell*, she knew exactly why. Freeman had told her the color brought out the blue in her eyes. The dress made her think of Freeman. Unfortunately, every dress she wore made her think of Freeman because he complimented her, no matter what she wore. But she also found it strange that Bill cared at all. She gave him a weak smile. "We Amish avoid anything that would tempt us to be proud. For sure and certain it looks better on you."

Bill liked that answer. He preened like a prize pig at the county fair. "I'm glad you Amish are so humble. Humble people don't get elected to office."

"I guess we'll see."

"After tonight, it will be very clear who the winner is." His smile stretched wider. "But I don't want to give away all the surprises at once." He examined the two chairs on the stage. "I need to sit where you're sitting, Mattie. The light is brighter, and people can see me better. Since you don't care about being seen, you don't mind, do you?"

Mattie's smile was still pasted to her face, even though she seethed on the inside. This had less to do with the lighting and more to do with the fact that Bill wanted to boss her around. She took a deep breath. *Whosoever is angry with his brother* and all that. Tami had encouraged Mattie to stand up to Bill, but was a chair worth getting heated up about?

She didn't know, but she suspected if she backed down on the small things, Bill would push her harder to back down on the big things. She pressed her lips together and remembered why she was running for town council. Aunt Esther and Uncle Levi were counting on her, even if they didn't want her help. "I'm sorry, Bill," she said, immediately regretting her choice of words. It was a mistake to apologize to Bill for anything, unless she truly was in the wrong. "What I meant to say is, I'm not sorry." She pointed to the other chair. "That is a perfectly good chair. I'm sure you'll like it."

Bill had obviously expected her to cheerfully give in—who made a fuss over who sat where? He stiffened like a starched collar and momentarily lost his charming and insincere smile. "I guess you Amish folks aren't so humble after all."

"I guess we aren't," Mattie said. She pretended not to care, but Bill's words hurt more than she thought they might. Of course she should have expected he would say something mean, but he probably didn't realize how often Mattie had been admonished for her pride by her family, the *gmayna*, and Freeman. And maybe it hurt so much because deep down, she knew she *was* proud. It was pure pride for an Amish girl to think she knew better than the church. One minister had even accused her of thinking she was smarter than Gotte. "*Gelassenheit,* Mattie," he had said. "Running for election is not yielding to Gotte. You cannot add one inch to your height by thinking about it. Gotte's will is always right, and you are acting as if you don't think He's doing a *gute* job."

Why now, of all times, did that conversation have to play over in her head? She thought she had made peace with the fact that the whole *gmayna* was against her and that Gotte probably was too. Couldn't she just win the election, change the ordinance, and get baptized later? She frowned. That sounded a lot like deathbed repentance.

It didn't help that Freeman didn't want her to run. Freeman was fast becoming a very important part of her life, and his absence made it clear what he thought of the whole election and her part in it.

Mattie watched as Sadie grabbed two folding chairs and carried them right up to the front. Sadie motioned for Cathy to sit by her, and Cathy left *die youngie* in the back and joined Sadie. Sadie beamed at Mattie as if she were the smartest, most interesting girl in the world. Mattie forgot all about deathbed repentance and focused on Sadie Sensenig, who had come to hear Mattie speak even though her *dat* opposed it. She would see this through for Sadie and every other Amish person who needed her to fight for them. She didn't care if she went unappreciated. She was doing the right thing. Surely Gotte wouldn't fault her for that.

The mayor stepped onto the stage, grabbed one of the microphones, and called the meeting to order. Once everyone had found a seat and quieted down, the mayor glanced back at Mattie. "Are you ready?" he asked.

Mattie nodded, her heart clamoring to get out of her chest.

"It is my pleasure to introduce our candidates for town

council. Each candidate will have five minutes to speak, and then we will open the floor for questions. Please remember that this is not a debate. We just want to get to know the candidates and where they stand on important issues."

Mattie swallowed hard. The most important issue was the buggy ordinance, but Cathy had filled her in on some of the other issues like the plat approval process, impact fees, and water rights. She didn't know very much, but Lord willing, she knew enough that she wouldn't embarrass herself.

The mayor read from an index card she'd given him earlier. "Mattie Zook is from Leola, Pennsylvania, and is running for town council because she wants to represent all of Byler." He turned and handed Mattie the microphone and stepped off the stage.

Mattie stood up and *die youngie* in the room exploded into applause. Even most of the Englischers clapped for her, some enthusiastically, others politely. Sadie and Cathy were the most boisterous of all. Cathy yelled so loudly, Mattie feared she might strain her vocal cords. Sadie whooped and stomped her feet and clapped. As if that wasn't enough, she put her fingers between her lips and blew an ear-splitting whistle that had a few people glancing at her in surprised alarm. The reception was a bit overwhelming. What if she made a fool of herself? What if Freeman was right? Mattie's tongue felt like a piece of dry toast, and every word she wanted to say flew out of her head. *Ach,* how she wished she'd had the *gute* sense to write down her speech.

A movement from the door caught her eye. Freeman, looking like he'd just come from the potato fields, edged into the lunchroom and found a leaning spot against the back wall. He folded his arms, grinned in her direction, and might have winked. The lunchroom was dim and he was far away, so she couldn't be sure it was a wink, but she chose to take it as a sign that he approved of her, even if he wanted her to quit. The sleeves of his royal blue work shirt were rolled up past his elbows, revealing hardened biceps and forearms, and his trousers were smudged with dust and mud. But he was here, and it looked like he'd gotten the memo. His shirt was the exact color of hers.

Ach, she was wonderful glad she'd decided to wear blue.

Mattie drew in a deep breath to calm her racing heart, but it didn't do any good. Freeman's arrival had completely stunned and thrilled her, and she couldn't contain the feeling that she was floating three feet off the ground. He was taking a great risk by being here. Had he come for her?

Keeping her gaze glued to his, she slid the microphone into its stand and smiled. "Hello. I am Mattie Zook. I am running for town council because I think the council should represent and care about all the people who live in Byler, not just the ones who elect them."

The room once again erupted into applause. Sadie beamed widely but didn't whistle again. She must have decided it was too much.

Most of Mattie's speech was about the buggy ordinance and how unfair it was, especially since the Amish paid local and state taxes that helped maintain the roads. She mentioned that the Amish were peaceful people and that she felt compelled to be their voice because they would never fight for themselves. When she finished, there was another round of clapping more enthusiastic than the first time. Freeman didn't clap, but he winked—this time she was certain—and made Mattie feel quite giddy.

Mattie turned and sat down. She hadn't embarrassed herself, and she'd said what she wanted to say. That was all she could have hoped for.

Bill Isom stood and pulled the microphone from its stand. He walked back and forth across the stage while he talked, as if giving a performance instead of a speech. "Hello," he cooed into the microphone. "I'm Bill Isom."

Bill's wife sat in the front row a few seats to the right of Sadie. She stood and clapped and shouted, and about a dozen other people followed her lead. The other Englischers in the audience clapped politely. Mattie caught Sadie's eye and nodded her encouragement. *Die youngie* would look petty and sulky if they didn't clap for Bill. Sadie understood immediately and clapped her hands while nudging the Amish boy next to her to do the same. Soon everyone in the room was clapping. Bill's reception wasn't as enthusiastic as Mattie's, but at least he wouldn't have another reason to resent the Amish. Freeman stood as stiff as a post, but he hadn't clapped for Mattie either, so Mattie didn't care. Mattie smiled to herself. As long as he didn't wink at Bill, he could do what he wanted.

Bill paced back and forth, droning on and on about the buggy ordinance and why it was necessary, using big, important-sounding words that Mattie couldn't begin to decipher. "I know how to make the hard decisions, even if they're not popular or convenient. I will always do what is best for the town."

His wife and the others who were obvious Bill supporters clapped and jumped up and down and made a tremendous amount of noise. Mattie didn't encourage any applause. Bill was wrong, and there was no cause to cheer for his pride.

Bill pointed to a young man sitting at the middle lunch table. The young man turned on a projector, and Bill pulled a string that hung a few feet over his head. The string was attached to a screen, and Bill pulled the bottom of it almost to the floor. "Margaret, please get the lights."

Margaret, who seemed to be at Bill's beck and call whether she liked it or not, turned out the lights. It was completely dark except for the white square of light projected on the screen.

"I want to show you what happens when we let buggies on our streets and roads." Bill nodded to the young man below, who typed something into his computer. A picture of a splintered, broken buggy appeared on the screen. "This is a picture of a buggy accident in Sugarcreek, Ohio, where they have buggies all over the place. This buggy ordinance is for everyone's safety, including the Amish." Another photo, this one of a decimated buggy sitting next to some train tracks. Bill held up two fingers. "Two fatalities."

Mattie didn't know which emotion was more powerful, horror or fury. How dare Bill use other people's tragedies to get what he wanted! She held on to the edge of her chair with both hands to keep from jumping up and pulling the screen off the ceiling.

"It's not the buggy's fault," someone yelled from the back. "People need to slow down and share the road."

"Yeah," someone else shouted.

"Share the road!" one of the Amish boys yelled.

Soon the lunchroom was a jumble of noise and confusion. *Die youngie* took up chanting, "Share the road," while Bill's supporters just cheered and clapped louder. The mayor tiptoed onto the stage. "Now please, everyone, please be polite. And, Ronald, turn off that blamed slideshow. We've seen enough."

The young man frowned but did as he was told. Margaret turned on the lights, and the noise finally died down. Bill stopped pacing, clasped the microphone with two hands, and looked directly at the audience. "I wanted to fully explain my position on the buggy ordinance. People are dying out there. I'm trying to save lives. I truly care about each and every one of our citizens." He pulled the bottom of the screen, and it rolled itself up again with a wonderful loud bang. "When I get reelected, I hope that people will stop arguing about this." He turned and looked directly at Mattie. "I'm confident that the Amish will return to their peaceful and submissive lives and stop interrupting our town council meetings."

Bill was arrogant. There was no getting around that.

And Mattie was furious. There was no getting around that either.

Bill motioned to his wife. She fluttered like a butterfly onto the stage and handed Bill a piece of paper. He raised the paper in the air. "Right before this meeting, I received word that Miss Mattie Zook failed to submit her campaign financial disclosure statement by the deadline."

Mattie's heart jumped into her throat. Had she done something wrong?

Bill's voice boomed through the lunchroom. He dramatically loosened his tie as if the tightness was too hard to bear. Had there been a podium, Mattie was convinced he would have pounded on it. "As per campaign rules, Miss Zook is disqualified from running, and her name will be removed from the ballot."

A collective gasp rose from the audience. Sadie's mouth fell open with an expression of shock. Freeman looked as if he was made of stone, his spine rigid and straight, his frown permanently etched into his face.

Mattie forgot how to breathe. Was this really happening? One mistake and she was out of the race? She couldn't believe it, but it made all the sense in the world. She hadn't known what she was doing. She hadn't known the basic rules for running a campaign. Her own ignorance had ruined her chances of making things better for her Amish friends. Was it too late to bring up that swimsuit picture?

The mayor conferred with Margaret, the woman who took minutes at every council meeting, then he jumped up on stage and grabbed the microphone from Bill. "I think it's best we adjourn this meeting until we can sort out this mess. We won't waste more of your time. Thanks, folks."

There was a considerable amount of talking and murmuring as the Englischers began to file out. The Amish stayed seated, as if shock had welded them to their chairs.

Bill snatched the microphone back from the mayor. "Don't forget to mark your ballots for me in November. Bill Isom, for *all* of Byler."

Mattie's composure nearly snapped. If she hadn't been trying to be an exemplary Amish girl, she would have jumped out of her chair and tackled Bill to the floor. Instead, she sat silently, wondering how long it would take before steam started coming out of her ears.

Cathy didn't have the same reservations. She stood up and cupped her hands around her mouth. "Boo, boo," she shouted. "Get off the stage, you Communist."

Mattie tripped quickly down the steps and put her arm around Cathy. "It's okay," she whispered, even though she could barely speak, and nothing was okay.

Cathy's distress always came out as anger. She glared daggers in Bill's direction. "He stole your slogan. That Communist stole your slogan."

Mattie swallowed past the lump in her throat. "I guess I won't be needing it anymore."

Sadie and Sarah were suddenly right next to her, along with all *die youngie* who had come to hear her speak. Sadie's eyes pooled with tears. "I don't understand, Mattie. What did you do wrong?"

"I didn't turn in a form I was supposed to. I guess it's the rules."

Cathy growled. "Isn't that just like Bill Isom? He has to make a production of everything. Well, if he thinks I'm voting for him, he has another thing coming. I'm writing in Beyoncé on my ballot." She stomped her foot then grimaced and pressed the heel of her hand to her hip. "Never stomp your foot if you've got a titanium hip."

Sarah gave Mattie a hug. "I'm so sorry, Mattie. It doesn't seem fair. You've gone to all this work."

"My flyer flowers were so pretty," Sadie sobbed. She sniffed and glanced at Sarah. "At least you'll get your cell phone now."

Sarah huffed out a breath. "How can you think of a cell phone at a time like this?"

Sadie's sobbing resumed in earnest. "You're right. I'm a terrible friend. I'm sorry, Mattie."

"You did real *gute* on your speech," Davey Hostetler said.

Susie Miller nodded. "I got teary when you said how the Amish people just want to live our lives and we would never hurt a fly."

"We still love you, Mattie," Sarah said. "And we're glad you came to Colorado, even if you're out of the election."

Sadie dabbed at her nose with a handkerchief. "We were all glad you came, even before we knew you were running."

Mattie had never been more grateful for loyal friends. Most of the *gmayna* had been against her campaign, but *die youngie* still stood behind her. It didn't lessen the pain, but their support made the blow easier to bear. She looked around the lunchroom for Freeman and couldn't see him anywhere. He must have slipped out the back before anybody noticed him. Mattie tried to ignore her profound disappointment. He wanted to be discreet, but just this once, when she needed his comfort so badly, couldn't he have waited around?

She squared her shoulders. She had Cathy and Sadie and Sarah and everybody else. She'd be ungrateful indeed if she couldn't take comfort in the friends who were here.

Sadie sighed. "What do we do now?"

Mattie glanced at the clock on the back wall. "Let's go catch the sunset."

Mattie sat on the picnic table next to Caleb and tried to pretend she was interested in the last orange glow of light in the west. The only person who seemed sincerely excited about the sunset was Caleb, and he watched with awe as the sky turned from muted orange to brown to deep blue. Mattie couldn't muster a tenth of his enthusiasm, but she tried to be interested, for his sake. He, after all, had nearly thrown up in his buggy, and she was eager to make amends.

The post-Meet the Candidates night had turned into a gathering. All *die youngie* who had come to the meeting were at the park, listening to something that passed for music on Davey's boom box and talking about how unfair the buggy ordinance was.

All Mattie could think about was how foolish she had been. Her head had been in the clouds when she should have been filling out financial forms and learning the rules for running a campaign in Byler. Now she was deeply embarrassed and had a hundred useless yard signs. It was all so humiliating.

At the meeting, she'd been expecting an attack on her character or her opinions or even her outfit, but she hadn't expected that Bill would wipe out her entire campaign on a rules violation. He was smart, but the mistake had been her own. She needed to apologize to Cathy, Dewey,

Dewey's mom, Sadie, and everyone else who had spent hours working on her campaign. Her apology to Freeman was going to be the hardest of all, because she so hated that she had been wrong and he had been right.

She had been foolish and proudly stubborn. She had lost to Bill Isom before a vote was ever cast. Then he'd stolen her slogan. How dare he? It made her furious, which is exactly how she wanted to feel, because as soon as she stopped being mad, she'd burst into tears.

She wanted to go home, shut herself in her room, and pound her pillow to a pulp, but Caleb was eager to watch the stars come out, and he was her ride. So she sat there, her gaze directed at the sky, feeling more lonely than she'd ever felt in her life. Dat would tell her it served her right for going against the *gmayna*. Aunt Esther would secretly take credit for the demise of Mattie's campaign. Caleb wouldn't have to feel guilty for sneaking around anymore. Freeman would go back to his life, glad that he didn't have to work on a campaign he hadn't wanted to work on in the first place.

Some of *die youngie* were kicking a soccer ball around, though it would soon be too dark to see the game. All of them had risked their families' displeasure to support her. She felt bad she wouldn't be able to change the buggy ordinance for them.

Caleb pointed to the sky. "Do you see the Big Dipper, Mattie?"

"*Jah*," she said unenthusiastically.

"If you follow those two stars in a line, you'll come to the North Star. And there's Orion's Belt."

Mattie nodded. Hopefully he wouldn't feel the need to point out every constellation in the sky. There were too many, Mattie didn't care, and she would rather be home with her pillow.

Someone slid next to her on the picnic table, and she turned to see Freeman smiling sadly at her. Her heart did a double flip before settling into an uneven rhythm. There wasn't much room between Mattie and the edge of the table, so he had to sit close to her or risk tumbling to the ground. His warmth immediately enveloped her, even though only their arms were touching. "*Hallo*, Mattie."

"*Hallo*."

"*Vie gehts*, Freeman?" Caleb said, more animated than Mattie had ever seen him. Of course he was happy. He was looking at the stars, and he was free from the terrible secret of Mattie's campaign. "Do you see the Big Dipper? If you follow the two bright stars on the edge of the dipper, you can see the Little Dipper to the right and Polaris at the very end of the handle."

"You know your dippers," Freeman said, obviously as interested in the stars as Mattie was. He scooted an inch closer to her. "I'm so sorry."

The compassion in his voice rendered her temporarily mute. She *would not* cry, no matter how Freeman's sympathy touched her. Bill Isom didn't deserve her tears. She propped her chin in her hand. "What? Aren't you going to say 'I told you so' or mention how foolish I am or give me a lecture on the importance of paying attention to small details?"

He shook his head, a grin playing at his lips. "I won't 'tell you so,' you're not foolish, and how were you to know about the finance rule? I should have asked Tami more questions."

Mattie nudged him with her shoulder. "Don't you dare blame yourself. This is my fault and only mine. I should have read everything more carefully. We went to all that work for nothing."

He studied her face. "I'm really sorry." He pushed his hat higher on his forehead. "I can't believe Bill Isom got elected the first time. He doesn't deserve to be elected again. It just makes me so angry."

"Me too! I'm mad, and there's nothing I can do about it."

"It feels like a dirty trick."

"*Ach*, did you see that shooting star?" Caleb pointed to a spot just above the mountain.

Sarah sidled closer to the picnic table. "I want to see." She sat next to Caleb and gazed up at the sky.

"You have to stare and stare and not take your eyes from the sky for one second," Caleb said.

Freeman chuckled quietly. "She's going to get a stiff neck for sure and certain," he whispered.

Mattie smiled. Did Sarah know any constellations? Because she was about to get a lesson. "*Denki* for coming to my speech, even though I wasted my breath."

"You did so *gute*. I don't wonder but most of the Englischers there changed their minds after hearing you explain it so clearly. Anyone with a sense of fairness knows what a bad rule it is." He paused and drew his brows together. "I should have been there to support you after the meeting, but like a coward, I sneaked back to my buggy because I didn't want anybody to see me."

"I'm sure you didn't sneak, and I understand your feelings. You don't want to get in trouble with the *gmayna*. Caleb feels the same way about Aunt Esther."

"But I should have been more of a friend to you."

"*Ach*, *vell*, you're here now. That's all that matters." He had no idea how much it mattered. Her heart might never return to normal rhythm. She sighed. "It wonders me if Aunt Esther will send me back to Leola."

His gaze grew more intense, as if he was trying to read her thoughts. "Do you . . . do you think she will?"

She shrugged. "I don't know. There's no reason for me to stay."

"That's not true," he said, with what seemed like a great deal of emotion. "You didn't have a reason when you came. You decided to run for town council after you got here."

"I came because my *dat* wanted to keep me out of trouble, but I think he realizes I find trouble no matter where I go."

"You should at least stay a full year. You haven't really seen Byler until it's covered with snow."

Mattie smiled in mock surprise. "You get snow here? It's hard to believe it snows when it doesn't even rain."

He laughed. "Okay, I'm guessing the snow is more spectacular in Pennsylvania, but they have snowshoeing at the golf course in Monte Vista."

"It sounds thrilling. I just might have to stay to see that."

"Now you're just mocking me."

She pumped her eyebrows up and down. "You will never know for sure." She loved Freeman's smile, especially on a bad day like today. "I suppose I do have a very *gute* reason to stay. Esther's baby is coming anytime, and I know she would appreciate my staying. Even my *dat* wouldn't mind if I stayed here to help her. There's no one else on her side of the family in Colorado except her sister Ivy, and Esther can only take Ivy in small doses."

Mattie nearly jumped out of her skin when Freeman wrapped his hands around hers and squeezed them tightly. "I want you to stay."

"You . . . you do?"

"*Jah.*" He seemed to realize that he was holding her hands right there in front of everybody. He let go, cleared his throat, and scooted a few inches away from her, though he couldn't go far without falling off the table.

"You want me to stay? Even after all the trouble I've caused? Even though you think I'm a snob?"

"You're not a snob."

"Even though I'm likely to find another office to run for?"

He grimaced. "Let's hope not."

"You don't want me to run for office?"

He shook his head. "I didn't want you to run the first time."

"But you said you're mad about the election."

"Of course I'm mad, but I'm also relieved it's over. I worried about you all the time. My teeth have been permanently clenched for months. It's why I had to come to the meeting tonight. I had to see that you would be okay, and if Bill had said anything to hurt your feelings, I was planning to shout him off the stage." He leaned back on his hands. "I'm sorry that this is how it ended, but I'm not sorry it's over. Now you can be a normal Amish girl who quilts and cooks and gardens, and I can stop worrying."

Mattie's earlier anger returned with a red-hot vengeance. Of course Freeman didn't appreciate all she had tried to do for the *gmayna*—neither did any Amish person over the age of twenty. "Well, I wouldn't want to make your life harder by trying to make your life easier."

He was smart enough to be wary. He pressed his lips together and eyed her doubtfully. "I have no idea what you mean."

"I fought that buggy ordinance for you and every other ungrateful Amish man in town."

"Mattie, I'm not ungrateful."

"*Nae*, you're not ungrateful. You're relieved. Everybody is so relieved. I'm not going to stay where I'm not appreciated. And I'm finished trying to help people who don't want my help." She stood up, grabbed Caleb's sleeve, and pulled him with her. "*Cum*, Caleb. I need to go home and start on that quilt I've been meaning to sew."

Wide-eyed and unsure, Caleb did as he was told, looking back over his shoulder at Sarah as if begging for her help.

Mattie turned to Freeman, who looked just as dumbfounded as Caleb. "See you later, Freeman. I hope you have fun walking all over town, because that's what you're going to be doing from now on."

Chapter 10

"*Ach*, Esther, he is the most beautiful *buplie* in the whole world. I love his hair." Mattie bent down and gave little Levi Junior a kiss on the top of his head. His dark, sticky-uppy hair tickled her nose.

Esther eased herself into a chair at the table and played with Levi Junior's feet while Mattie held him and watched Caleb try to do the puzzle by himself. Esther cooed and clicked her tongue at her baby, even though Junior was fast asleep in Mattie's arms. "He has more hair than Winnie had at one year old. I hope it turns out curly like Levi's. I love Levi's hair."

Three weeks ago, Esther had given birth to an eight-pound baby boy the day after the disastrous Meet the Candidates meeting. Mattie had woken up that morning planning to mope all day when Uncle Levi had rushed out of the bedroom and told her that Esther was in labor and could she please watch Winnie while Levi took Esther to the hospital. There was no moping after that. Levi Junior had been born at eight that evening, and Esther had come home the next morning. Since the Amish didn't have health insurance, they paid all their medical bills with cash. Long hospital stays were out of the question.

"I don't think that goes there," Esther said, pointing to

the puzzle where Caleb had been trying for the last minute to fit a blue piece into a green tree.

Caleb didn't seem troubled in the least that he was failing miserably with the puzzle. He glanced at Esther. "*Ach*, I'm not real *gute* at puzzles, but I for sure like doing them here with all of you and seeing the *buplie*. He looks *gute* in your arms, Mattie." Caleb smiled at Mattie as if she were the nicest girl in the whole world.

Caleb was a sweet boy. He really was. He was always willing to help with the dishes or *die kinner* or any odd jobs Esther needed him to do around the house. But Mattie couldn't figure out why he kept coming over. The campaign had been dead for three weeks, and there was a new baby in the house. Aunt Esther didn't need Caleb to distract Mattie anymore. He had fulfilled his duty to his *schwester*-in-law, and Esther might even believe Mattie's failure was Caleb's doing. He would probably be her favorite relative forevermore. He had nothing left to prove. So why was he sitting at Esther's table doing a puzzle he couldn't even do? Why wasn't he out having real fun with boys and girls his own age? There was no way a seventeen-year-old boy was that interested in Esther's new *buplie*.

"Did you notice there was a tiny bit of snow in the mountains this morning?" he said.

"It looks like powdered sugar on top of a cake." Esther had a baby thermometer tucked behind her ear and a burp rag slung over her shoulder.

Mattie sighed inwardly while she stroked Junior's head and did her best not to think about that brown puzzle piece Caleb was trying to fit into the sky. She hadn't seen hide nor hair of Freeman for three weeks. She didn't know whether to be irritated, angry, or deeply hurt. Was he pouting because she'd gotten mad at him at the park? Had he decided that Mattie was just one big headache? Was he glad to be through with her? Had he set his sights on a nice, normal Amish girl and forgotten that he ever knew a girl named Mattie? It's not like they had been courting or anything, but they had been friends, and it hurt that he hadn't said so much as "boo" to her in three weeks.

She tried to be irritated, but working up her righteous indignation was hard when she was the one to blame. She'd been angry, and he had just been trying to make her feel better. It was a clumsy attempt, but Freeman often said the wrong thing with a *gute* heart. She shouldn't have gotten mad at him for being honest. She shouldn't have gotten mad at him at all.

While still holding Junior, she found the dog's nose and popped it into place in the puzzle then glanced up to see Esther and Caleb staring at her. "Is something wrong?" she asked, even though that was a silly question because everything was wrong, and she didn't know how to fix it.

"That's the third time you've sighed in the last three minutes," Esther said.

"*Ach.* I'm sorry. I didn't realize." She would have to concentrate harder on not thinking about Freeman or the election or the loneliest three weeks of her life. There was no reason for feeling so alone. Esther had a new baby. There was plenty to do around the house, and when Mattie needed a smile, she could always hold the *buplie*.

Aunt Esther gave her a weak smile. "I'll take the *buplie*. You and Caleb should go for a buggy ride."

"There's nowhere to go." Mattie cringed. She sounded so sulky.

"*Ach*, Mattie. I'm sorry about the election. I know you're disappointed."

Once again, Mattie did her best to tamp down her irritation. Aunt Esther wasn't sorry about the election. It had turned out exactly the way she'd wanted it to. But she'd snapped at one too many people about the election, and she wasn't going to alienate Aunt Esther because of it. "*Denki*. I'm very sad, but I suppose it was Gotte's will."

"Of course it was," Aunt Esther said. "It always is."

Someone knocked on the door, and Esther went down the hall to answer it. She came back into the room looking none too pleased. "Mattie, it's for you."

Mattie frowned. They'd had several visitors in to see the *buplie*, but none to see Mattie. Nobody came to visit her except Caleb, and he was already here. Maybe it was Freeman coming to apologize or coming to get an apology.

Esther held out her arms. "Here, let me take Junior. It's almost his bedtime."

Mattie handed Junior to his *mater* and hurried to the front door.

Freeman, Cathy, and Tami Moore stood on the front porch. Freeman leaned against the brick with his arms folded, a neutral expression on his face. Mattie's heart did cartwheels at the sight of him. He looked two shades tanner, one inch taller, and ten pounds stronger. Cathy didn't seem exactly eager—she never seemed eager about anything—but she did have that determined look in her eye that always made Mattie a little nervous and a little intrigued. Tami smiled as if she just couldn't wait to tell Mattie something. What were they doing here together? It wasn't likely that they'd come to hear Freeman's apology. Freeman would have come alone for that, and he didn't look as if he especially wanted to apologize about anything.

"Hi," Mattie said. "Did you come to see the baby?"

Cathy had already been over twice to see the baby. Maybe Cathy thought Junior was so cute that she wanted Tami and Freeman to see him. Cathy looked past Mattie. "How is that baby? Is he asleep? Can we see him?"

"Um, sure. Aunt Esther was just about to put him to bed."

Aunt Esther came out of the kitchen with Junior in her arms. She tried to hide a frown, though Mattie could see it in her eyes.

"Oh, look how darling," Tami said. "My sister is going to have a baby soon. I just love babies."

Without asking permission, Cathy stepped into the house, took the baby from Esther, and cuddled him like a seasoned mother. "I like babies well enough, but teenagers are my favorite."

Aunt Esther was very fond of Cathy, but she didn't seem happy about seeing the three people who were most closely associated with Mattie's campaign for town council. She probably suspected their visit had something to do with the election. But despite her misgivings, she was a naturally hospitable person and certainly wouldn't let anyone stand out on the porch when she could welcome them into her home. "Come in," she said, after a short hesitation. "Why don't you sit in here?"

Esther steered the three of them to sit in the living room, which was a feat because not only did Esther have all the quilts for sale taking up one end of the room, but there was an unfinished quilt on frames that commanded the rest of the space. Together, Esther and Mattie pulled the quilt frames away from the sofa so Cathy and Tami would at least have room for their knees. Freeman opted to stand near the window on the opposite side of the quilt. He curled his lips when he caught Mattie's eye and made her pulse race wildly.

Tami's eyes lit up. "Oh, look at the quilts! I've been meaning to get over here and take a look. I want to give my sister a quilt for her new baby."

Aunt Esther suddenly seemed much more cheerful about having these three in her house. "Is she having a girl or a boy?"

"A girl. Do you have anything for a girl?"

"Oh, yes! I've got seven baby girl quilts. Let me show you."

Esther showed Tami all the baby quilts. She took the ones Tami was especially interested in off the hangers, and Mattie helped her spread them out so Tami could see them better. Tami had a hard time choosing one but finally landed on a lime-green and pink quilt with a plump pink pig appliquéd in the corner. It was one of Mattie's favorites.

"She's going to love that one," Mattie said.

Tami pulled cash from her wallet. "I'm definitely going to be the favorite aunt after this. I'm going to tell everyone I know that they need to get over here and look at your quilts. They're beautiful."

Esther, who seemed to be feeling quite cheerful at the moment, stuffed the money into her apron pocket. "Thank you, Tami. I'd really appreciate that." Her smile faded but didn't completely disappear. "I suppose I should put Junior to bed and let you four have a chat."

She said *chat* as if it were the most unhappy thing in the world. *Ach*, *vell*, there was nothing Mattie could do about Aunt Esther's feelings except give up trying to change the world. But it wasn't in Mattie's nature to be compliant, not even to make those she loved happy.

Esther took the baby from Cathy and bounced him out of the room.

Tami sat down next to Cathy and smoothed her new quilt with her hand. "I love quilts. And babies. What a fun house." She looked up and grinned at Mattie. "I suppose we should get to what we came for. We have some really good news. You can still run for town council."

Mattie drew her brows together. "I don't understand. I've been disqualified."

Cathy looked as if she'd eaten something unpleasant for

dinner, but it was one of her most pleasant expressions, so Mattie wasn't too worried. "Your name has been taken off the ballot. But you can still run as a write-on candidate."

Tami shook her head. "That's *write-in* candidate, Cathy."

"Isn't that what I said?"

Mattie glanced at Freeman, who seemed content to look at her but not entirely happy about what Tami had just said. "What's a write-in candidate?"

"Your name isn't on the ballot, but people can still write your name down if they want to vote for you."

Mattie's dashed hopes found a spark of life. "You mean, I can still win?"

"*Jah*," Freeman said.

Was it strange that at that moment she wanted to squeeze around the quilt frames and plant a kiss right on Freeman's lips? Instead, she gave him a teasing smile. "Are you officially helping with this campaign, or should I pretend I don't know you?"

He rolled his eyes. "I'm pretending I don't know you."

"You're not doing a very good job of it," Cathy said. "You're looking at her like she's a chocolate doughnut with sprinkles on top."

Mattie forgot how to breathe. That was truly how Freeman was looking at her.

Freeman blew a puff of air from between his lips. "I'm here, aren't I? I'm planning to help."

Mattie couldn't have been more thrilled. Her campaign was back on, and Freeman was going to help. "I don't know what to say."

Tami laughed. "Say yes."

"Of course I'll say yes."

Tami laughed. "I'm so glad. I wish I could do more to help you with your campaign, but since I'm on the town council, I feel that I should be somewhat neutral. But just know that I am pulling for you in my heart, and there's no harm in answering your questions and maybe steering you in the path of some donors."

Mattie clasped her hands together. "Thank you so much, Tami. Where would I be without your help? There's so much I don't know yet."

Tami opened her wallet and pulled out a hundred-dollar bill. "Gena Treiter asked me to give this to you."

Mattie looked at the money in awe. She couldn't remember ever seeing a hundred-dollar bill before. "This is too much. I can't accept it."

Tami held up her hand when Mattie tried to give it back. "Gena said it was a good potato crop this year, and she refuses to give a dime to her son. She says he just sits in the basement and plays video games." Tami smiled. "I told Gena that I'm pretty sure you don't play video games, and if you do, I can't imagine you're very good at them."

"I wouldn't know how to turn the game on."

Tami reached in her purse again and pulled out more cash. She placed the bills one by one into Mattie's hand. "This twenty is from Sally Whittaker. Forty from Mr. and Mrs. Granger. This is from my husband, who feels no obligation to be neutral."

The thought of such generosity rendered Mattie temporarily mute. Tami had just given her three hundred dollars. She felt like a millionaire.

Cathy eyed Mattie's handful of money. "That should pay for a full color pamphlet and more yard signs."

"Be sure to keep a very careful accounting of what money you are given and what you spend. If you win, you have to submit a financial disclosure form within thirty days after the election, even as a write-in candidate." Tami pulled a piece of paper from her pocket. "Here are the names of everybody who gave me money to give to you and how much they donated. Don't lose it."

Mattie nodded. "I won't make that mistake again."

Tami stuffed her wallet into her purse and stood up with the baby blanket tightly in her fists. "I've got to get home, or the kids won't get their baths. I gave Freeman a list of people you can call to ask for money."

"I don't know what we'd do with it," Mattie said. Three hundred dollars would buy plenty of yard signs.

Tami curled one side of her mouth. "You'd be surprised."

With what seemed like a lot of effort, Cathy stood up. "I need to go too. Lon likes to watch *Survivor* reruns with me. But let's get together next week and plan out our strategy." Her gaze flicked between Mattie and Freeman. "My house on Tuesday?"

"Okay," Freeman said.

Mattie nodded her agreement.

Freeman followed Tami and Cathy out the door. Mattie wasn't happy to see him go. She really wanted to apologize to him and let him apologize to her. *Ach, vell*, it would have to wait for another day.

The giant maple that wasn't even on Aunt Esther's property dumped a lake of leaves on their grass every day. Tami and Cathy waved goodbye, and the leaves crackled under their feet as they crossed the lawn to their cars.

Freeman glanced up at the tree. "Where can I find a rake?"

"*Ach*, you don't need to rake. I'll do it in the morning."

Freeman gave her a wry smile. "It looks like you've got plenty to do around here without having to rake leaves. Besides, I'm trying to make peace with Esther. She's never going to forgive me when she finds out you're back in the race."

"Believe me, she won't connect you with my campaign."

"I came over tonight with Cathy and Tami. She's going to know I had something to do with it."

Mattie couldn't argue with that. She should probably mop Esther's floor and clean her toilets every day, but if she thought that would butter Esther up, she would have tried it already. She pointed to the side of the house. "There's a rake in the shed."

Freeman disappeared around the corner of the house and soon returned with the new rake that Uncle Levi had bought for leaf season.

Mattie closed the front door behind her, not sparing more than a passing thought for Caleb working on the puzzle inside, and watched Freeman rake Uncle Levi's leaves. He was so irresistible . . . so capable . . . so Freeman. She just wanted to be near him. "I haven't seen you for three weeks," she said.

He already had a pile three feet high. "I've been harvesting potatoes."

"Harvesting potatoes?"

"*Jah*. If you leave them in the ground too long, they rot."

"I didn't know that," Mattie said.

He picked up a stick. "I also helped with the Potato Festival. I was in charge of the fish pond."

Mattie scrunched her lips together. "Sounds like you were pretty busy."

He didn't look up. "I was."

"Too busy to come over and see the *buplie*?"

"I wanted to wait until the crowds died down."

"Too busy to let your friend Mattie know you were still alive?" she said.

He seemed to rake with more vigor. "Wonderful busy."

Mattie switched her weight from foot to foot. "Wonderful busy?" she repeated.

He stopped raking and frowned at her. "If you must know, I was mad at you."

Ach, vell. At least he was honest. "I suppose I deserve that. I wasn't very nice."

"Nice? You just about tore my head off. I've met rattlers nicer than you."

"Do you ever try to soften your criticism, even just a little?"

He propped his hand on the top of the rake. "You will always hear my honest opinion, Mattie, even if you don't like it. My integrity is more important to me than your feelings."

"Keeping your opinions to yourself isn't dishonesty. It's tact."

He shrugged. "I'm fully aware that I have no tact. Sadie reminds me daily. But you didn't exactly curb your tongue either."

Mattie sighed. "You're right. I'm sorry I got mad at you, and I'm sorry you like rattlesnakes better than you like me."

His lips twitched upward. "I never said that. Rattlesnakes are dangerous and unpredictable. You're original and surprising."

She couldn't seem to catch her breath. "Do you like surprises?"

"Not really."

"*Ach.* I see."

He laughed. "I mean, I don't like surprise parties or surprise visitors, but I like you."

Now she completely forgot how to breathe. He *liked* her?

Freeman stuffed his hand in his pocket. "I like trying to guess what you'll do next. You refuse to be a modest, normal Amish girl."

"That's no surprise to my *dat*."

"I like the way you are," Freeman said. "You're recklessly brave when you believe you're right, and you truly want to help people. Most of us never have that kind of courage. You're one surprise after another."

Mattie felt pleasantly dizzy after all those compliments. "I'm sorry about what I said at the park. I didn't mean to hurt your feelings."

He frowned as if he'd bitten into a lemon. "You didn't hurt my feelings. You can't hurt my feelings. I don't get my feelings hurt. Sadie would say I have no feelings. I was mad at you, but I'm past it now. I thought if I just let it be, you'd come around to my way of thinking and realize I was right."

"Not likely."

"*Ach*, I know. I was mad that you got mad at me for being honest. I truly was relieved that the campaign was over. I didn't want Bill to hurt your feelings over and over again."

Mattie grinned. "Bill didn't hurt my feelings. Bill can't hurt my feelings. I don't get my feelings hurt. I've got a very thick skin."

He smiled then shook his head. "I saw you that night, Mattie. You were devastated. And Bill hadn't even done his worst."

She pressed her lips together. "I guess it does no *gute* to argue about what might have happened or how I might have felt."

"*Jah*. All I know is how I felt. I was relieved. And mad at you for being mad that I was relieved."

She shrugged. "Such a tangle of emotions."

"The potato harvest gave me time to think. I realized that even though *I* was happy about the end to the campaign, *you* would think you had failed all the Amish people in

Byler, even though it wasn't your fault and it wasn't your fight."

"It was too my fault."

Freeman held up his hand to stop more protests. "It doesn't matter, and I don't want to argue."

Ach. Freeman could be so aggravating. "Just because you don't want to argue doesn't mean you're right."

He ignored her very logical argument. "I knew you wouldn't be happy until you'd shoved Bill's face into the dirt."

Her mouth fell open. "I would never do that."

"It's just an expression," he said, arching his eyebrows as if to say she'd brought him to the edge of his patience. She shut her mouth, determined not to interrupt for at least twenty seconds. "You want justice and fairness, and Bill needs to be stopped. You feel that it's your duty to stop him, even though there are hundreds of other people in town who could do it."

"*Won't* do it."

He gave her the stink eye. She pressed her lips together and concentrated on not wanting to kiss him. "After weeks of harvesting potatoes, I had an idea. I remembered seeing an unusual election sign in someone's yard two years ago. It said '**WRITE IN KERMIT THE FROG FOR PRESIDENT.**'"

"A frog?"

"I asked Tami about it. She said people could vote for you even though your name isn't on the ballot. So I used her phone, found the registered voter rolls, and started calling everybody I knew, asking them to vote for you."

"Everybody you've helped over the years."

He lowered his head, deflecting the praise. "We're neighbors. We help each other. Englisch and Amish alike."

"I know, but you seem to be an especially helpful neighbor. Cathy isn't the only one who loves you."

"There is only a handful of people Cathy loves, and I'm not one of them. I'd say she tolerates me."

Mattie laughed. "Me too. Except I think she only puts up with me."

Freeman dragged the rake over the grass then tapped it on the ground to clear out the leaves stuck in the tines. "I disagree. Since you decided to run for office, you're her second favorite person next to Dewey."

Mattie sat on the porch step and wrapped her arms around her knees. "So, are you still my campaign manager?"

"I thought Cathy was your campaign manager."

"*Nae.* She told me she's my chief of staff. I don't even know what that is."

Freeman propped the rake against the house and sat next to her. "I'll be your campaign manager. I'm not that mad at you anymore." His eyes flashed with a tease.

"Don't try to deny it. I hurt your feelings, and you're still pouting about it."

He narrowed his eyes in mock indignation. "Sadie pouts. I don't pout."

She laughed at the expression on his face. "*Ach*, I'm sorry to offend you." She leaned closer to catch a whiff of his pleasant smell—autumn leaves and crisp air. "Remember when I told you that I didn't need your help?"

"Believe me, I remember."

She nudged him with her elbow. "Okay, okay, you don't have to rub it in my face. I can admit I was wrong. I need your help badly. You know I can't do it without you."

"That's a wonderful nice thing to say, but for sure and certain you could do it without me. With all the support you have, I don't see how you could lose."

"Don't say that too loudly. Gotte doesn't like it when we make our own plans."

Chapter 11

He couldn't keep his eyes off her.

Even though she was so busy campaigning that she barely noticed him. Even though she found him irritating and rude and testy.

Freeman couldn't help being testy. He worried about Mattie every hour of every day, and she would be deeply offended if she knew how he fretted. Bill Isom was clever, and he wouldn't rest until he'd done everything in his power to win this election. When Freeman thought about the looming election his stomach tied itself into one big knot. When he thought about how Mattie wasn't even on the ballot, he considered taking up smoking. When he thought about Mattie's devastation if she were to lose, he was sick to his stomach.

Their campaign bonfire and hot dog roast had turned into quite an event. The bonfire had been Dewey's idea. He said everybody loved a hot dog roast, and it would be a *gute* chance for Mattie to meet more voters. With some of the money they'd raised, they made up a flyer inviting the whole town, and Sadie, Sarah, and their friends had passed it out.

Mattie stood near the fire, visiting with Marion Whittaker, who had lived in the San Luis Valley his entire life.

Marion roasted a hot dog while he and Mattie talked about rezoning and water rights. Freeman drew his brows together. *Ach, vell,* they weren't so much talking as Marion was giving Mattie a lecture. Freeman didn't like it. He didn't care how worked up farmers got about their water, nobody should take out their frustration on Mattie. None of the problems in Byler were her fault, and people should be nothing but grateful that she had the courage to run against Bill Isom. There wasn't much she could do about water rights anyway. That was for the state and the canal companies to figure out.

Finally, Freeman couldn't stand it anymore. He grabbed a hot dog and a stick and pretended to want to roast it. He walked right up to Marion and interrupted his tirade about why the canal company shouldn't pipe the ditches. He stuck out his hand. "Marion, nice to see you. How did the potatoes go this year?"

Marion seemed a little put out that he'd been interrupted, but he also had a hard time resisting talk of farming. "I got a bigger crop than ever. Sally says it's because I started going to church every week. I think it's because I used new seed potatoes. But I don't mind if Sally wants to give credit to God. Going to church gets me out of a scolding."

"I hope you don't mind, but I need to talk to Mattie," Freeman said, which wasn't a lie because he always needed to talk to Mattie. He needed to be with her kind of like he needed to eat.

Mattie gave Freeman a look of pure gratitude.

Marion handed his stick to Freeman. "I've got to get home anyway. Sally warned me not to talk your ear off."

"Don't you want to eat first?" Mattie said.

"No. Sally made me promise not to eat anything. She's got me on a strict diet for my heart. I can only eat stuff that doesn't taste good. I'm not even allowed to eat my own potatoes."

"I'm sure it's a comfort to know she's watching out for you," Mattie said.

He nodded. "Her first husband died after three years of marriage, but she didn't like him much. I'm glad she wants to keep me around."

Freeman couldn't let Marion go without one last request. "Thanks for coming. Can we count on your vote?"

The wrinkles around Marion's eyes bunched together. "I still don't understand how an Amish girl can run for election. All the Amish I know are pacifists. I don't think you know enough to be on the town council, but I don't know as I like Bill Isom any better. He thinks a little too much of himself, and I don't trust a man who dyes his hair. Let nature take its course, I always say." Marion fingered the whiskers on his chin. "The way I figure it, you are the lesser of two evils."

Mattie curled one side of her mouth. "I appreciate your confidence."

He nudged his hat up and scratched his head. "I'll try to remember your name long enough to write it on the ballot."

They were quickly finding that making sure Mattie's name was written correctly on the ballot was going to be their biggest problem. If her name were on the ballot, people could have just remembered to vote for the girl running against Bill Isom. But her name had to be spelled correctly by the people writing her in, or it wouldn't count as a vote for her. Freeman handed Marion a little card with Mattie's name printed on it. "Here you go. Take this with you on Election Day. It will help you remember."

Marion stuffed the card into his pocket. Lord willing, it wouldn't end up in the washing machine before the election.

"Okay, well, good luck to you. Be sure to look up that water study I told you about. The state is making a mess of it."

"Thank you for helping me understand." Marion walked away, and Mattie waited until he was out of earshot. "*Denki*. He got so worked up, I thought he was going to have a heart attack."

Freeman nodded. "I don't like that he got so mad at you. Just because you're running for office doesn't mean he has permission to be rude."

"Some people think they are allowed to say anything just because you're willing to listen."

"They shouldn't treat you that way."

Mattie laid her hand on his elbow, a gesture that sent a zing of electricity all the way up his arm. "I'm okay. Really. Please don't worry. They can't hurt my feelings."

"Of course they can."

"*Ach*, *vell*, they haven't hurt my feelings yet. I'll be okay. But *denki* for being concerned."

He was more than concerned, but he didn't know what to do about it. She didn't want him to worry, and if he told her how worried he was, she'd think he was trying to get her to quit the campaign. That hadn't gone over well the last time. Besides, this whole mess was his fault. If he hadn't asked Tami about a write-in campaign, Mattie wouldn't have been the wiser. But when it came right down to it, he would rather see Mattie happy, even if that meant he'd be worried sick for three more weeks.

The best he could do was try to shield her from irritated voters like Marion Whittaker and do his best to protect her from Bill Isom's petty lies. Bill had already spread the rumor that Mattie was being investigated by the Campaign Finance Violations Committee, even though Byler had no such committee and there was nothing to investigate. It would be funny if it weren't so deceitful. How would he ever protect Mattie from all of that without her knowing that he was protecting her? She'd get grumpy if she found out.

"Are you going to eat that hot dog?" Mattie said.

Marion burned it to a crisp. He tossed the hot dog and the stick into the fire.

Mattie grinned and stuffed her hands into her coat pockets. The bonfire was seven feet high, but it was a cold night. "It wonders me if there aren't fifty or sixty people here."

"How many have you been able to talk to?"

Mattie counted to herself. "*Ach*, probably twenty. It would have been more, but Marion had a lot to say."

"I talked to another twenty. The rest are Amish who've already been baptized. They came for the food."

She sighed. "*Ach*, *vell*, I don't mind feeding them, even if they're not going to vote for me."

Freeman pursed his lips. "I mind, but it wouldn't seem charitable to refuse to let them have a hot dog. The Amish can't resist a free meal."

She laughed. "We have plenty of hot dogs. Cathy bought ten dozen. They can't vote for me, but maybe they will put in a *gute* word with their neighbors."

"You mean campaign for you? I think my *fater* would rather shave his beard than have anything to do with an election."

Mattie's eyes danced. She didn't seem the least bit upset that her Amish neighbors weren't going to be much help. "*Ach*, *vell*, maybe they'll at least earn us some sympathy from the Englisch. I don't mind if people vote for me out of pity." She lost her smile and studied his face. "How are things between you and your *dat*? Does he know you're helping with my campaign?"

"He knows."

"And how does he feel about it?"

Freeman wasn't sure how to answer that. He refused to burden Mattie with his troubles. His problems were between him and the *gmayna*. "He's not happy about it, but the potato harvest was *gute*, and I painted the barn last week and oiled every hinge in the house, along with my regular chores. He can't complain that I'm not pulling my weight."

"I don't want you to work yourself to death on my account, and that's not just because you're my campaign manager. You need your sleep, and more importantly, I don't want to come between you and your *dat*." She pressed her lips together and looked genuinely worried. "If you need to quit, I'll understand."

He didn't want to quit, even though the deacon warned him there would be consequences to continuing with the election. The campaign was his only connection to Mattie, and he couldn't bear the thought of not seeing her regularly. "I'm not quitting."

Her expression relaxed. "Are you sure? I told you I needed you, but Caleb would probably love to be my campaign manager."

Freeman grunted in mock indignation. "Caleb? He doesn't even brush his teeth every day. It would be like asking a toddler to compete in the spelling bee."

"Caleb doesn't brush his teeth every day?"

"I made the choice to work on your campaign. And now that you're a write-in candidate, we're going to have to work harder than ever."

Mattie's piercing gaze stole his breath. "You didn't have to ask Tami about that. I never would have known I could be a write-in candidate."

"I wanted you to be happy."

"You did?"

"I do." The firelight reflected in her eyes, and he thought

that she'd never looked so beautiful. The desire to kiss her seized him by the throat and nearly choked him. He took a half step away from her and tried to think about anything but Mattie's lips. A distraction came in the form of the deacon, who set a chair on the opposite side of the fire, sat down, and started roasting a marshmallow. He was probably here to spy on Freeman. "I . . . I think I convinced at least three Englischers to vote for you."

Mattie took a deep breath and smiled. "So far tonight, I've gotten six yeses."

"And Marion Whittaker says you are the lesser of two evils. That's got to make you feel *gute*."

Laughter burst from between her lips. "So *gute*."

Ach, he still wanted to kiss her, but the sight of the deacon definitely made the feeling less urgent. "We just need to talk to a few people every day. Bill Isom has offended just about everyone in town for one reason or another, so they'll vote for you if they know you're still running."

Sadie, looking quite unhappy, ran up to Mattie with an Englisch girl in tow. "Mattie, look what Kirsten found on YouTube."

Kirsten, Sadie's Englisch friend, pulled her phone from her pocket. Freeman moved behind Mattie and looked over her shoulder at Kirsten's screen. "My boyfriend told me that Bill Isom's son posted a video," Kirsten said. She tapped on the screen, and a video started playing. There was no talking, only eerie, dark music and words that scrolled over the picture of a campaign sign. "Is Mattie Zook stealing Bill Isom's campaign signs?" it read.

Mattie growled. Freeman stiffened like a board.

"One Byler resident reported an Amish girl lurking suspiciously around his yard in the middle of the night. The next morning, his VOTE FOR BILL ISOM sign was gone. Then two Amish boys were seen taking Bill Isom signs from several yards on Sunday. And we thought they believed in keeping the Sabbath day holy!"

Sadie was breathlessly offended. "Can you believe it, Mattie? He's accusing you of stealing."

Kirsten squinted at her screen. "It already has seventeen views."

Freeman clenched his teeth so hard, he thought they might crack. This kind of behavior from Bill was what Freeman had feared all along. Poor Mattie. From behind, he curled his fingers around her shoulders. "I'm so sorry, Mattie. That man has no shame."

He had momentarily forgotten that Mattie didn't get her feelings hurt. She got angry. "*Ach, du lieva.* What are we going to do about this?"

Kirsten put her phone in her back pocket. "Do you want to toilet-paper his house? I'll go with you."

Sadie was on the verge of tears. "This is terrible. People are going to think you're a stealer."

Mattie narrowed her eyes and huffed out a breath. "When you say it has seventeen views, does that mean seventeen people have seen it?"

Kirsten scrunched her lips together. "Well, I've watched it four times, and my boyfriend watched it twice, so maybe it's only eleven other people."

"That's not so bad." Mattie frowned, nibbled on her fingernail, and looked at Freeman. "Bill has probably watched it a couple of times. So, fewer than ten people have seen it. Do you think it changed their minds about who they are going to vote for?"

"Ha!" Kirsten said. "It probably made them want to vote for you."

Mattie burst into a smile. "That's right. I'm not happy about being accused of stealing, but this will help us more than it will hurt us. Anyone who sees it will know I'm still running, and it makes Bill seem a little desperate."

"Oh, he is," Kirsten said. "My boyfriend works at the market. Bill was in there the other day, and he ripped your flyer off the message board and tore it up. He's pretty mad."

Mattie nodded in satisfaction. "Then we're going to be okay. The more desperate Bill gets, the more people will see who he really is. Kirsten, if I gave you four or five flyers, would you give them to your boyfriend so he can hang up a new one every time Bill pulls one down?"

Sadie gave Mattie a quick hug. "You're so smart. I just know you're going to win."

"I'm going to write something rude in the comments," Kirsten said. "That'll show him."

Mattie held up her hand. "Don't do that. Say something like, 'Be sure to write in Mattie Zook for town council. She's not on the ballot, but she's still running.' Nothing rude."

Sadie nodded enthusiastically. "We don't want to stoop to Bill's level."

Kirsten pulled out her phone again, tapped some keys, and smiled. Then she and Sadie marched off arm in arm, probably to show the video to all *die youngie*.

Freeman folded his arms and eyed Mattie with admiration. "I don't know what to say."

She cocked an eyebrow. "About what?"

"You keep surprising me. I thought for sure and certain you'd get your feelings hurt. You barely even got mad."

She waved her hand in the air. "*Ach*, Bill Isom is aggravating, but he's not going to pull me into his dirty tricks. I've got to show people that I'm the better candidate—that I deserve their votes."

Freeman grinned. "*Ach, vell*, according to Marion Whittaker, you *are* the lesser of two evils."

"High praise indeed. I've finally figured out why we're commanded not to be angry. It's a waste of time, and it distracts me from what I need to do to win this election."

"This is *gute* news," Freeman said, unable to resist teasing her. "Does this mean you'll never get angry again?"

She laughed. "I don't think either of us can hope for that, but my goal is to never give anyone cause to call me a rattlesnake again."

"I didn't call you a rattlesnake," he protested.

"*Jah*, you did."

"I said I've met rattlesnakes that were nicer than you."

Mattie always laughed like she meant it clear down to her toes. "*Ach*, excuse me for trying to make it sound better than it actually was."

Cathy, who had been handing out hot dogs, hobbled from the other side of the food table still wearing her large plastic food handler's gloves. "I like you Amish people, I really do. But the ones who've been baptized are just here for the food. They're taking advantage of my good heart."

Mattie smiled at Cathy. "It's okay. I don't mind. There's plenty for everyone, and it never hurts to spread good cheer as far as it will go. If a hot dog will help my Amish neighbors see me more kindly, I'd say that's a good trade."

Cathy shrugged her shoulders. "You're more magnanimous than I am, but I suppose that's why you're running for office and I'm sitting at home listening to the police scanner for entertainment." Cathy pulled off one of her gloves with a loud snap. "Everybody who wants a hot dog has got one. It's time for your speech."

Mattie frowned. "I wasn't planning on a speech."

"You've got a captive audience of sixty-two people with full stomachs. You might as well make the most of it." Without waiting for Mattie's agreement, Cathy put two fingers between her lips and whistled. It was so loud, it no doubt would summon every dog in the county. "Everybody, we are here tonight in support of Mattie Zook, who has this crazy notion to run as a write-in candidate for town council. As we all know, you're more likely to be hit by lightning than to win as a write-in candidate, so she really needs your help."

Ach, vell, nothing like a dose of hopelessness to get the voters fired up.

Was Cathy single-handedly trying to sink Mattie's chances, or had she just made it more likely that Mattie would win? Cathy made Mattie's campaign sound like a lost cause, but maybe that was her strategy. Everybody loved an underdog, and people would be more likely to vote if they thought Mattie was desperate for their help. That, or they'd sit out the election because, what was the point? Freeman certainly didn't know if it was a *gute* plan. Cathy probably didn't either.

Mattie moved to the side of the fire where most of the Englischers were sitting. She wanted the good will of the Amish folks, but she wanted votes even more. "Thank you all for coming tonight. Can we show our appreciation to Cathy Larsen for her great work with the hot dogs?"

The crowd clapped, and Cathy made a slight bow.

Mattie talked for a few minutes about the buggy ordinance and about integrity on the town council. Freeman tried to pay attention, but he was distracted by the graceful curve of her neck and the glow of the firelight on her face. Mattie truly was an angel on earth. And suddenly he knew with his whole heart: He wanted to marry her more than he had ever wanted anything in his entire life. The realization pounded on his chest and nearly knocked him backward.

Then it slapped him upside the head.

What did he have to offer her? A dry, barren place where

he scratched a living off the land? A place she thought of as a punishment rather than a home? He had a strong back and two able hands, but he wasn't sensitive or romantic or particularly tender. What girl in her right mind wanted a husband like that? He was fiercely loyal to his family, but he often walked around with a chip on his shoulder. He always told the truth, but it often stung. You didn't woo a girl by comparing her to a rattlesnake.

Cathy's little speech had alluded to despair. Now he felt it all the way to his bones. He would never deserve Mattie, never be able to convince her to love him. The pain knocked the wind right out of him.

A smattering of laughter and more clapping. Mattie finished her speech, and three Englischers approached her, no doubt with more questions and concerns about town issues. Freeman took a deep, painful breath and marched to the food table where he picked up an uncooked hot dog and took a big bite. It was as bad as he'd anticipated.

"That's how I like my hot dogs," Cathy said. "But I had to give them up because of all the nitrates and nitrites. Now I eat vegan hot dogs. They're not too bad if you smother them in bacon."

He sheepishly studied his half-eaten hot dog. "I haven't eaten anything since lunch. I guess I got hungry."

"No," Cathy said. "You got frustrated."

"Frustrated about what?"

"Frustrated that you care more about the candidate than you care about the election."

Freeman's mouth felt as dry as a valley breeze. "How could you possibly know what I'm frustrated about?"

Cathy inclined her head in Mattie's direction. "I've got eyes, haven't I?"

If he hadn't been frustrated before, he certainly was now. "You told me you have cataracts. You can't see *that* well."

She waved away his logical argument. "I see well enough." She patted him on the arm. "And you're frustrated."

Freeman chucked his hot dog into the weeds and gave up trying to argue. "This is your fault. You pressured me into helping her with the campaign."

"Don't blame me. You made your own choices."

It wasn't a choice to fall in love with Mattie. That's why they called it "falling." It had just happened, and he was miserable. "Any suggestions of what to do now?"

Cathy patted him on the cheek. He drew back in annoyance. "Be patient."

"I am patient."

"Everybody thinks they're patient until their patience is tested." Cathy eyed him like she had his whole story figured out. "Be patient and don't get frustrated. There's nothing more unattractive than a frustrated Amish boy."

"Really? Nothing? What about Bill Isom in a swimsuit?"

Cathy narrowed her eyes. "You have a point."

Mattie came toward them, and Freeman's heart did a somersault. He didn't want to react that way to Mattie, but there it was. It was incredibly . . .

Ach! Cathy was right. He was frustrated. Frustration was probably oozing from his pores. He pasted a casual, how-do-you-think-the-campaign-is-going smile on his face and shoved his frustration to the back of his mind. Maybe Mattie wouldn't notice it.

She didn't look happy. Freeman wanted to kick himself. He should have ignored his earlier frustration and stayed by her after the speech. Had one of those well-meaning Englischers irritated her?

"That was a good speech," Cathy said. "But you have yet

to mention Bill Isom's chest hair in one of your rallies. It's a sure winner."

Mattie glanced at Cathy and gave her a brief smile, but her focus was squarely on Freeman. "Sarah says the deacon came to visit you yesterday."

Freeman's heart plummeted to the ground. She wasn't supposed to find out about that. "It doesn't matter."

"Why didn't you tell me?"

He tried to shrug off her concern. "There isn't much to tell."

"What about your integrity being more important than my feelings? Was that just talk?"

"This has nothing to do with your feelings," Freeman said.

Cathy shook her head. "He's trying to learn patience."

Mattie placed a hand on Cathy's arm. "Could I talk to Freeman alone for a minute?"

Cathy pointed an arthritic finger at Freeman. "Remember, there's nothing more unattractive than . . . well, you know." She walked to the hot dog table and pulled a hot dog from its package. After she skewered it on a roasting stick, she took it to the fire and held it close to the coals. Apparently, she had stopped caring about nitrates and nitrites. There really was nothing better than a hot dog roasted over an open fire. Some temptations were too hard to resist.

Mattie folded her arms across her chest. "What did the deacon say?"

"I told you. It doesn't matter."

She glared at him. "Don't be a martyr. Tell me what he said."

"A martyr? That's a little extreme, don't you think?"

"If I'm responsible for getting you shunned, and you don't

tell me, then you're being a martyr. May I remind you that your integrity is more important than my feelings."

"Stop saying that. You don't have to throw my words back at me. You're the one who said I should be more tactful."

A fire flared to life behind Mattie's eyes. "Stop avoiding my question. Are you going to tell me what the deacon said, or do I have to go over there and ask him myself?" She pointed to the deacon who was laughing with his wife and helping his young son roast another marshmallow. He seemed to be having a grand time.

Under no circumstances was Mattie allowed to interrupt the deacon's *wunderbarr* evening. Freeman pressed his fingers to his forehead. "What do you think he said?"

She gasped. "They're going to excommunicate you, aren't they? *Ach*, I'm so sorry, Freeman. I pushed you too hard, and they found out. I'm so sorry." She paced back and forth in a small area of space.

He took her hand and led her to a couple of camp chairs far from the fire. He didn't know who they belonged to, but he was going to borrow them for a few minutes. They both sat. "Mattie, they are concerned, but it's unlikely I'll have the *bann* put on me. It's a last resort, and the vote to excommunicate has to be unanimous. It's not like I've left the church. Most members in the district don't think my helping with your campaign is as bad as all that."

She fell silent and studied his face. "But . . . you're in trouble. They're going to punish you."

Ach. He wished he knew how to be tactful and honest at the same time. "There is talk of barring me from Communion. The deacon doesn't think I can honestly say the *Dorbeit* if I'm still helping you with your campaign." The *Dorbeit* was a statement that each member made in the ear of the minister at the conclusion of the Ordnung's *gmay* two weeks before Communion. Each member was supposed to declare that he was in unity with the Ordnung.

Mattie was genuinely upset. "Then you can't help with the campaign anymore. I'm an unbaptized outsider. Nobody cares what I do, but I have separated you from your community."

She looked on the verge of tears. He had been so worried about Bill hurting her feelings that he hadn't considered that he would be the one to upset her. Taking her hand, he scooted his chair closer. "Mattie, I chose to help you. I'm not going to vote, and I'm not running for office. I firmly believe I am still in good standing with Gotte and the Ordnung. If the elders do not agree, then I will accept their decision. I can wait and take spring Communion." She still looked worried. "You couldn't kick me out if you wanted to. We're doing this for the Byler Amish, and I'm willing to sacrifice for them." And Mattie. He was willing to sacrifice for her too, but he couldn't tell her that without sounding desperate or frustrated or pitiful. Cathy had counseled him to be patient. He'd do his best.

"I've been so ungrateful." She sat up straighter and took a deep breath. "I'm sorry I'm so mad at you all the time."

He chuckled. "Are you really mad at me *all* the time?"

Her lips twitched in amusement. "I guess maybe half the time. You make it so hard not to be mad at you."

He nodded in stiff, mock sincerity. "I'll try my best to do better."

"There really isn't anything you can do." She giggled. "You say something reasonable, and I don't want to agree with you, so I get mad."

"Maybe I should try saying only ridiculously stupid things."

She nodded. "That would be *gute*. I'd fire you as my

campaign manager, but at least I wouldn't be mad at you all the time."

He acted surprised. "You're mad at me all the time?"

She cuffed him on the shoulder.

They heard the faint and distant sound of a siren, probably on the highway. Freeman didn't think much of it until the blaring siren got louder, and he saw two pairs of flashing lights in the distance. Mattie stood up and looked toward the road. "Did you remember to get permission for the bonfire?"

"Weeks ago," Freeman said.

A police car and a giant fire truck pulled up next to the field. Thankfully they turned off their sirens, but their lights still flashed as if they were trying to attract the attention of all the people at the bonfire, airplanes flying overhead, and the entire state of Colorado. Two officers got out of their car. Freeman recognized one of them as the woman who had pulled over his *dat*'s buggy months ago. She looked even more embarrassed now than she had then.

Freeman frowned. Had Bill called the police on their bonfire?

Freeman and Mattie were the closest ones to the road, so the police made a beeline for them. Everyone fell silent, and the only sound Freeman heard behind him was the crackling of the bonfire and a dog barking in the distance.

"I'm sorry," the policewoman said. The apology was written all over her face. "We've had some neighbor complaints of fire danger, noise ordinance violation, and drug use in the area. I'm going to have to ask you all to leave so we can put out this fire."

The firefighters stood beside their truck donning fire gear as if they were getting ready to douse the entire pasture.

Freeman tried to step in front of Mattie, but she nudged him aside and stood her ground. "We got permission for this bonfire weeks ago from the county fire department. And the noise ordinance doesn't go into effect until nine P.M. We checked."

"Still, we have to investigate all complaints, ma'am."

"Did Bill Isom make these complaints?" Mattie asked.

"I'm not allowed to say, ma'am. We just need everyone to leave so we can put out the fire."

Freeman turned his head so that the people behind him would hear. "It isn't right that Bill Isom can shut us down just by complaining."

Mattie pulled on his jacket sleeve. "Don't, Freeman. Remember, we're not going to stoop to his level."

"Now would be a *gute* time to forget." She pled with her eyes, and he growled in resignation. It was hard to take the high road. He turned his back on the police. "This very nice officer says we have to go. Thank you all for coming, and remember to write in Mattie Zook for town council."

Cathy waved her hot dog in the air. "If anyone wants to take home some hot dogs, help yourself. But don't go crazy."

Freeman turned back to the police. "Would you like us to roast you some hot dogs before they put out the fire? They're wonderful *gute*."

"I'll take one," said the other officer. He looked young and hungry.

"Kyle," the policewoman said. "We shouldn't eat on duty."

"We eat on duty all the time. Come on. It won't hurt anything to have a hot dog."

The woman looked as if there was nothing she wanted more than a hot dog. "Okay, but we'll have to pay you for them."

Officer Kyle shook his head. "If they were free for everyone, then we don't have to pay. It's in the rules."

Cathy gave the policewoman the hot dog she'd been roasting and slid a cold one on her roaster stick. "One more coming up."

Amish and Englisch alike gathered their chairs and blankets and left. Nobody dared take more hot dogs, so Caleb and another Amish boy packed up all the food and carried it to Cathy's van. She'd be eating hot dogs for weeks.

Freeman was annoyed, but Mattie, he could tell, was livid. He leaned over to whisper in her ear, "As irritating as this is, it's also an unexpected blessing."

She cocked an eyebrow and pursed her lips into a sour expression. "You think so?"

"We won't have to figure out how to get everyone to leave."

Her lips twitched as if she were trying not to smile. "Do you remember when I told you I'd never get angry again?"

"As I remember, you said that neither of us could hope for that."

She nodded. "That's correct, because right now, I'm feeling like a rattlesnake, and Bill Isom is looking more and more like a mouse."

Freeman didn't know whether he should stay out of the way or warn Bill that the prettiest diamondback in the world was coming for him.

The look on Mattie's face told him it would be better to stay out of the way. Nobody wanted to tangle with a rattler.

Chapter 12

Mattie's heart sank as she, Caleb, and Cathy drove up to the elementary school. It wasn't the sight of the catering truck that upset her or the cars and buggies that filled the parking lot and lined the street in front of the school, but Freeman standing near the school's front doors, blowing on his hands and looking highly irritated. "You really can't make him stay away," Cathy said, pulling into the only handicap spot left. "You shouldn't have tried in the first place."

Mattie pressed her lips together. She wouldn't second-guess her decision to kick Freeman out of her campaign. He was in trouble with the *gmayna*, and it was all her fault.

"He's been baptized," Caleb said. "Mattie did what she had to do."

Caleb understood, because he still hyperventilated every time Mattie asked him to do something for her campaign. But she didn't have the same reservations about Caleb's helping because he hadn't been baptized. Caleb had plenty of reservations of his own. He was a *gute* boy, very dependable, and a great, if reluctant, helper. He lifted heavy boxes and sometimes hung flyers, but he still got twitchy whenever he drove Mattie to a rally or even to Cathy's house for a campaign meeting. The new baby hadn't distracted Aunt Esther for long, and she had redoubled her efforts to sidetrack Mattie from the campaign. She invited Caleb over almost every night to do a puzzle or play Scrabble. Caleb was terrible at puzzles and even worse at Scrabble. It was always a *gute* night when they could "go for a drive" and skip the "fun" activities altogether.

Since the sun set earlier and earlier, Mattie and Caleb would usually bundle up and go to the park to watch the sunset first. Caleb felt much better about telling Aunt Esther that they were going to watch the sunset when they actually watched it. Then Caleb would drive Mattie wherever else she needed to be. It was wonderful nice of him to use his buggy for Mattie's unapproved activities.

Cathy handed Mattie two foot warmers. "It's going to be a cold night. Put these in your shoes. We don't want your feet to freeze. Although if you lost a couple of toes to frostbite, it would make you a more interesting person."

Cathy must have truly thought Mattie was boring if she believed two fewer toes was all it would take to make her interesting. Mattie tore the foot warmers out of their package, unlaced her shoes, and stuffed them near her toes. "Do you think anybody will come?"

Cathy pulled a bright pink beanie over her ears. "If everybody is as tired of this campaign as I am, there will probably be about five people."

Mattie and Cathy were definitely in agreement about the campaign. Mattie was thoroughly sick of the whole thing. It was a *gute* guess Caleb shared their opinion. Somebody—and she wouldn't ever publicly accuse Bill—kept stealing her campaign signs, and every time Caleb or Sadie hung a flyer in the market or the barbershop or even on a telephone pole, it was gone within hours. More videos had popped up on YouTube accusing Mattie of everything from stealing signs to secretly working for the railroad to get tracks laid through every pasture and field in Byler. Bill had no shame, no respect, and no integrity. The only *gute* news was that Byler was a small town and people seemed to be paying attention. Mattie had visited nearly every house in Byler, and though many weren't convinced that she would make a *gute* town councilwoman, they were pretty sure that anyone would be better than Bill Isom.

Cathy pointed out the window at Freeman. "I'm usually on the girl's side, but you need to apologize."

Mattie frowned. "I'm just protecting him."

Cathy grunted. "Like he wanted to protect you? That didn't go over so well."

Mattie gazed out the window. Freeman paced back and forth, probably trying to keep warm. He should be home heating his hands by the woodstove. She didn't need him here. She didn't want him to be here. *Ach*, he made her so angry. "Do you have more of those foot warmers, Cathy?"

Cathy reached into her giant purse and pulled out a handful of foot warmers. "I have a year's supply."

"Okay. Would you both mind staying here while I get rid of Freeman?"

Caleb frowned. "Don't you want me to come with you?"

"Not necessary." Mattie grabbed four foot warmers and got out of the van. She marched across the lawn, straight toward Freeman. He didn't look happy to see her. "You shouldn't be here," she said, because "I feel guilty and ashamed" wasn't quite the greeting she was looking for.

He narrowed his eyes. "You could have told me you were planning to be here tonight. I had to find out from Sadie."

"I didn't want you to come."

"*Jah.* I sort of figured that out. You had a secret rally on Saturday and left me out."

"It wasn't a secret. Thirty people came."

His eyes were mere slits on his face. "It was a secret to me."

She felt horrible for leaving him out of that rally, but it was for his own good. She'd ruined Communion for him, and his reputation in the *gmayna* was in jeopardy. The price he had paid for her campaign was too high already. She held out the foot warmers to him. "Here. Put two in your boots and two in your coat pockets."

"I don't want them," he snapped, keeping his hands tightly buried in his pockets.

He was the most aggravating person she had ever met, and that included the attorney for her neighbor in Leola. "Why not? It's freezing out here."

"You can't butter me up with your kindness. I'm too mad at you."

She rolled her eyes. "I'm not trying to butter you up. I don't want your frozen body on my conscience. It's already guilty enough."

He studied her face. "Mattie, helping you with your campaign is my choice. I am willing to live with the consequences."

She turned her face from him to avoid the intensity of his gaze. "I don't like the consequences."

"You don't get to decide that for me. It's my choice, just like it was your choice to run for office."

"You tried to talk me out of it."

He nodded. "But I accepted your decision."

"You never accepted my decision. You called me foolish."

He huffed out a breath. "I helped you with your campaign. How much more acceptance do you want?" He bowed his head and lowered his voice. "I'm sorry to yell. But you make me so mad."

"You make me so mad. We're even."

"Look, Mattie, I'll admit I wanted to protect you from

the consequences of your choice. I tried to talk you out of running, but I was wrong to do that."

Mattie raised her eyebrows in pretend surprise. "Will you say that a little louder?"

He cracked a smile. "I was wrong to try to get you to do something you didn't want to do."

She nodded in satisfaction. "I accept your apology."

"That wasn't an apology."

She gave up trying to reason with him, and she gave up trying to hide a smile. "You can't be mad at me for trying to protect you when you have been trying to protect me since you became my campaign manager. That's why you showed up tonight."

He tilted his head as if trying to see her from a different angle. "And you left me out for the same reason. But I've been trying to tell you, I don't need you to protect me."

"And I don't need you to protect me."

He squared his shoulders. "So let me help."

She sighed. They were right back where they'd started from. "I can't ask you to go against the *gmayna*."

He finally pulled his hands from his pockets and curled his fingers around her upper arms. "You're not asking. I'm choosing, and I don't think I'm going against the Ordnung. My conscience is clear."

"I feel guilty all the same." She expelled a breath she felt like she'd been holding for a year. "Cathy isn't quite as *gute* with people as you are, and Caleb still gets nauseous every time I get in his buggy. I'm embarrassed at how much I need your help."

Freeman laughed as if he'd never been so happy. He leaned in and planted a swift kiss on her cheek. "Then come on. We've got a debate to get to. And it's freezing out here."

The kiss left Mattie feeling dizzy—like she'd been beaned in the forehead with a rock—and giddy—like she'd just played with a whole litter of puppies. Her wits scattered like feathers on the wind. "Um . . . wait," she said, as he pulled her toward the front doors. "We can't go in."

"We can't?"

"*Ach, vell*, I guess we can go in, but I can't go in as a candidate. Since my name isn't on the ballot, I'm not allowed to participate in the debate."

Freeman cocked an eyebrow. "So Bill is going to debate himself?"

Mattie curled one side of her mouth. "I guess so."

He glanced in the direction of the parking lot. "*Ach*, there are a lot of people here."

"Don't feel too bad about it. Bill advertised that he was hosting a Texas barbecue in the lunchroom before the debate. I guarantee that most of the people came for the free meal."

Freeman's eyes danced. "At least the Amish."

Mattie laughed at the expression on his face. "We've always been a smart bunch."

"So if you can't debate, why are you here?"

"*Ach, vell*, that was Caleb's idea. When people come out of the school, we're going to hand them a flyer. I'm here to answer questions and make sure people know I'm running."

"Is there anyone in Byler who doesn't know you're running?"

She handed him the foot warmers and smiled. "I can't think of a single person. Everyone who wanted to come to a rally has already come to a rally. Everyone who wanted a hot dog has already eaten a hot dog, but Cathy says I need to keep myself fresh in their minds. She says we can't be complacent. I had to look that word up."

He tore open a foot warmer. "No wonder you brought these."

"I don't know how long we'll be here. Dinner started at six, and the debate starts at seven. I thought we should be here before the debate starts in case some people wanted to leave after dinner."

"*Gute* idea. Where are the flyers?"

Mattie motioned for him to follow her. "They're in Cathy's van. I wanted to scold you before I got the flyers out."

He laughed. "I'm glad I was on your to-do list."

They went to Cathy's van, and Freeman pulled out the box of flyers and hefted it onto his shoulder. Caleb climbed out and grabbed the homemade posters, courtesy of Dewey and Dewey's little sister. Both of them said **WRITE IN MATTIE ZOOK FOR TOWN COUNCIL**, and Dewey's little sister had painted a cat beneath the words on both. Or at least Mattie thought it was a cat. It could have been a puppy or a mouse or possibly an otter.

Cathy finally stepped out of the van, looking quite colorful in her sparkly pink parka, her pink beanie, and her lavender snow boots.

"I don't know how long I'm going to last out here," she said, zipping up her coat. "My arthritis acts up when it's cold."

Freeman winked at Mattie. "Why don't you just stay in the van, Cathy? The two of us can hand out flyers."

Cathy shut the van door. "I may have arthritis, but I won't let it be said that I don't pull my weight."

Mattie opened the door again. "Cathy, you always pull your weight, but it's cold, and Freeman and I don't have arthritis. You don't want to lose any fingers or toes to frostbite."

"Although that would make me a more interesting

person." Cathy considered her options for a few seconds. A frigid breeze kicked up and tickled the faux fur lining of her hood. That was all it took. "Okay. I'll wait here, but if you have a rush, just wave to me, and I'll come help."

"For sure and certain," Mattie said. "We'll be fine. Caleb can help us."

Caleb seemed extraordinarily pleased and uncommonly nervous. He liked to be helpful, but he didn't want to be seen being helpful.

Freeman set the box of flyers on the sidewalk near the front doors. They barely had time to pull a stack out of the box when the doors opened and more than a dozen Amish youth came out of the school. Freeman's *schwesteren* Sadie and Sarah were among them.

Freeman widened his eyes. "What were you doing in there?"

Sarah practically glowed red. "*Ach.* I don't know. We didn't think you'd be here."

Freeman glared at his *schwesteren*. "You mean you didn't think you'd get caught eating dinner with the enemy?"

Sarah looked at Sadie. "I told you we shouldn't have come."

Sadie was completely unashamed. She propped her hands on her hips and scowled. "We are supposed to love our enemies and do *gute* to those that despitefully use us."

"By eating their food?"

Sadie was like a bird with ruffled feathers. "'Judge not that you be not judged.'"

"Don't quote Scripture to me to justify your sins," Freeman said.

Sadie pulled a face. "Don't be so self-righteous. We didn't do anything wrong, and it was wonderful *gute* barbecue."

Caleb's ears perked up. "Is there any left?"

Sadie nodded. "If you hurry. They're just cleaning up before the debate."

Freeman held out his arm and blocked Caleb's escape. "Don't even think about it."

Mattie giggled. "You might as well go, Caleb. It would be a shame to let the leftovers go to waste."

Caleb's eyes darted in Freeman's direction. "I could hand out some flyers while I'm in there."

"*Gute* idea." Mattie took a stack of flyers out of the box. "Be sure to give one to Bill."

Caleb's face turned white. "I can't do that. He might yell at me."

Mattie giggled. "It was a joke."

Freeman wasn't done with either of his *schwesteren*. "I expected more loyalty from you."

Sadie stuck her nose in the air. "It was a free meal that Bill paid for. You should be thanking us. That's money he can't spend on campaign signs."

"I'm sorry, Mattie," Sarah said. "I didn't mean to offend you."

"You didn't offend me. Sadie's right. Why pass up a free meal?"

There wasn't much Freeman could say when his own candidate approved.

Sadie popped a breath mint into her mouth and handed one to Sarah. "We're ready to help pass out flyers. There's lots of people in there, but they'll be coming out as soon as they're done eating. Nobody wants to get stuck hearing Bill talk to himself."

Mattie squeezed Sadie's hand. "I hope so." She handed Sarah and Sadie each a stack of flyers. They were half-page flyers with **WRITE IN MATTIE ZOOK** across the top. Sadie had drawn a cute picture of a horse and buggy in the bottom right-hand corner. It wasn't colored like the first flyer, because they didn't have the money for color copies, but it was a nice flyer that drew people's attention to the words at the bottom: **MATTIE ZOOK FOR *ALL* OF BYLER**. Sadie had drawn a heart around *ALL* and written "Buggy Love" and a heart down the margin.

Sadie smiled at the flyer. "This looks real nice."

"Don't be proud, Sadie," Sarah scolded. She always felt the need to put Sadie in her place.

The Amish young people milled around the front of the school, always eager to support Mattie, always so kind. Mattie felt their strength and their goodness, and she was grateful they had spent so much of their free time helping her out. More Amish families exited the building, and most avoided even looking in Mattie's direction. They didn't need to be embarrassed. Mattie didn't care that they'd eaten Bill's food. Bill had probably been irritated by their attendance. It seemed like just what Bill deserved—a bunch of Amish people getting under his skin.

They didn't have to wait long for the Englischers to start trickling out of the school. The catering truck pulled out of the parking lot, and the trickle became a wave. Mattie couldn't help but feel a tiny bit smug. The Amish weren't the only ones who'd come just for a free meal. Mattie and Freeman handed out dozens of flyers to mostly friendly people. Caleb soon joined them. Sadie and Sarah stood on either side of the front doors and held up the cat/otter posters.

Two women, wrapped in fluffy sweaters, asked Mattie if she was concerned about Amish people getting hurt in buggy accidents. While Mattie talked, a small group huddled around her and listened. Freeman stopped handing out flyers and parked himself behind and a little to the right of Mattie. It was his way of watching over her without being overbearing. She probably should have been irritated, but his concern felt more like a warm blanket and a mug of hot cocoa.

That Ronald guy, the one who had shown pictures of Amish buggy accidents at the Meet the Candidates meeting, stuck his head out of the front doors, eyed the poster Sarah was holding, and scowled. Mattie didn't know why, but the look on his face momentarily stopped her heart. He soon disappeared back into the school, and Mattie inched a little closer to Freeman to borrow some of his courage.

Mattie didn't know how many people were inside listening to Bill, but after about fifteen minutes, there were no buggies and only a few cars in the parking lot and along the streets. Nine Amish young people were in the crowd, as well as about twelve Englischers. There couldn't have been many more than that inside. Two teenage boys Mattie hadn't noticed before stood behind the group of people Mattie was talking to. They weren't wearing coats, which was strange as well as foolish. But they each wore a T-shirt that said "Vote for Maddie," written in black ink. The writing wasn't very neat and they'd misspelled her name, but Mattie was touched by the thought that those boys had been willing to ruin two perfectly *gute* T-shirts to support her campaign. But they really should put on their coats.

An Englisch boy about sixteen years old and a girl who looked to be about Mattie's age strolled out of the school and stopped to listen to Mattie describe her plan for safer, buggy-inclusive roads. She made her voice louder so the growing group could hear her.

"We don't want any Bill Isom supporters here!"

Mattie sucked in her breath. One of the boys wearing a "Maddie" T-shirt glared at the pair who had just come out of the school. Mattie pointed to the one who had yelled. "We welcome everyone here," she said.

"Not Bill supporters," the boy growled. He grabbed the lower edge of his T-shirt and pulled it tight so people could more easily read what it said. "We're for Mattie."

His companion pointed to the boy and girl on the other side of the crowd. "Get out of here. We want Mattie. We want Mattie."

Many in the crowd grew uneasy. Folks started whispering to each other and casting uncomfortable glances behind them. Freeman stepped up next to Mattie. Mattie thought she might be sick. Contention was not the way to win an election. "If you can't be polite," she shouted, "please go home, and please don't vote for me."

Three or four of the Englischers also told the boys to leave, but they just kept chanting, "Mattie, Mattie, Mattie."

Freeman slid a protective arm around her shoulders. "We should go," he whispered in her ear.

Mattie shook her head and nudged him away from her. She pointed to the bigger boy and made her tone stern. "You boys need to leave now. This is not the way I am running my campaign."

The boy and girl who had just come out of the school yelled back at the two chanting boys, and pretty soon, the four of them were screaming at each other. Mattie heard several words that she knew weren't nice, even if she didn't know the meaning of them.

Freeman grabbed her arm. "We need to leave, Mattie. Now."

Mattie wasn't sure what happened next except that above the yelling and chanting, something that sounded like a gun exploded above her head. A woman screamed, and the impromptu rally descended into pandemonium. Mattie's ears rang, her heart raced, and the air around her filled with the sharp smell of smoke. In a lightning-swift movement, Freeman grabbed Mattie from behind and pulled her against his chest. The Englisch girl turned to run, and crashed into Sarah, knocking Sarah down and ripping her poster. The teenage boy grabbed the girl's hand, and they bolted into the school while everyone else ran in dozens of different directions.

"Sarah," Freeman yelled. He let go of Mattie and ran to his *schwester*.

An *Englisch* man tripped on a sprinkler head in the grass, and Mattie rushed to help him from the ground. He thanked her then hurried to the parking lot, where most of the crowd was now headed. Mattie turned toward the school in time to see one of the boys in a "Maddie" T-shirt light a string of firecrackers and toss it in Sadie's direction. Sadie, being the feisty, fearless girl she was, used her poster like a baseball bat and swatted the firecrackers away from her body. They landed on the sidewalk where they exploded with a deafening noise.

Mattie wasn't going to let them get away with trying to hurt her friends. One of the boys had his back turned to her. Even though he had a *gute* fifty pounds on her, she charged at him, determined to tackle him to the ground before he lit another firecracker. But to her surprise, he suddenly turned and ran right at her. Before she had time to get out of the way, he plowed her over, knocking her flat on her back. With her face turned toward the sky, she saw the other boy run by. "Vote for Mattie. Vote for Mattie," he chanted as he ran away.

"Mattie!" Sadie screamed.

"Mattie!" Freeman yelled. Mattie wasn't sure which one of them sounded more hysterical. Freeman was suddenly kneeling beside her, fear etched on every line of his face. "Mattie, Mattie, are you okay?"

Panic overtook her as she realized she couldn't draw a breath. "I can't . . . I can't . . ." she gasped.

Freeman placed a gentle hand on her shoulder and made his voice soft and low. "It's okay, *heartzley*. It's okay. You got the wind knocked out of you. Try to relax. Slowly let the air fill your lungs. Don't force it." Concern filled his eyes, but he pasted a pleasant, I'm-so-calm-I'm-going-to-fall-asleep look on his face.

Mattie tried to follow directions, mostly the part about relaxing. In a few seconds, she was able to take a shallow breath and then a deeper one.

"That's right. In and out," he coaxed.

She started to breathe easier, but Freeman panted as if the weight of a buggy sat on his chest.

"You too," she whispered.

He leaned closer. "Me too, what?"

"Just take some deep breaths."

Irritation flashed in his eyes. "Focus on your own breathing and leave mine alone."

Mattie laughed, then coughed, then grimaced in pain. She held out her hand. "Help me up."

"Just lay quiet for a minute."

"Help me sit up, Freeman. It makes it easier to breathe."

He furrowed his brow. "Are you sure?"

Sadie knelt next to Freeman and grabbed Mattie's hand. "For goodness' sake, *bruder*, help her sit up." She pulled Mattie to a sitting position. "Are you okay? He was twice as big as you."

"I'm just happy to be able to breathe again." In truth, every part of her body ached, but she didn't want to worry anybody.

It seemed Freeman was just barely hanging on to his composure. He reached out and cupped her cheek in his hand. "You're okay," he whispered. "Everything is going to be okay."

Sadie blinked four times, and one big, fat tear rolled down her cheek. "Boys are so *dumm*," she said.

Mattie nodded. "Boys are so *dumm*."

Freeman pulled his hand from Mattie's face and scrunched his lips together. "*Denki* for the kind words."

Sadie smacked him on the arm. "Not you. Those stupid boys wearing those stupid T-shirts."

With Caleb awkwardly holding on to her elbow, Sarah hobbled over to Mattie. "Oh, no, Sarah," Mattie said, pointing to Sarah's ankle. "You're bleeding."

Sarah lifted her dress. Both knees were scraped, and blood trickled down her right leg. "I'm okay, but for sure and certain my knees hurt."

"*Ach*, I'm so sorry."

To Mattie's surprise, Sarah bloomed into a smile. "Did you see the way Sadie batted away those firecrackers? Like she was hitting a home run."

Sadie giggled, half in shock, half in amusement. "I didn't even think. I just saw them coming and remembered what Freeman said about keeping my eye on the ball."

Worry lined Freeman's face. "No one gives me enough credit, but I'm a *gute* coach." He stood up, pulled Sadie with him, and drew her in for a stiff hug. "I've never been more proud of you."

Sadie clutched Freeman, buried her face in his neck, and whimpered softly. After a few seconds, the dam broke, and she sobbed like a baby. Freeman patted her on the back and whispered sweet-sounding words into her ear. After a few minutes of Sadie's crying, Freeman nudged her away from him and handed her a handkerchief. "Let's go home," he said. "I think we could all use a warm bath and some Band-Aids."

Mattie could use a painkiller. Her ankle, her wrist, and her neck were throbbing.

"One minute I'm sitting in the car listening to Barry Manilow and the next minute it's Armageddon." Mattie turned to see Cathy limping across the grass. "You told me you wouldn't need me. Famous last words. I could have used my pepper spray."

She stopped six feet away from them and put her hands on her hips as if she were surveying the damage from a house fire. "Would you like to explain what happened here?"

"These two boys started yelling, and then they started throwing firecrackers." Sadie bit her bottom lip. "They were Mattie supporters."

Cathy grunted. "They were wearing 'Vote for Maddie' T-shirts, but they weren't Mattie supporters. I got them on my camera." She pulled her phone from her parka pocket, came closer, and showed everyone the photo she'd taken. It was the two boys in their "Maddie" shirts, plain as day. "They came running my way, so I turned on my headlights and took a picture." She pointed to the boy on the right. "That is Bill Isom's nephew."

Mattie's jaw dropped. "His nephew? But why was he wearing a Maddie T-shirt?"

Cathy shook her head in disgust. "It's a trick called a 'false flag.' You do something bad and blame it on your enemy."

Mattie tried to bend her knee and grimaced in pain. "So that people will blame me and vote for Bill?"

"That's about the size of it," Cathy said.

A fire leapt into Freeman's eyes. "That's despicable."

Mattie was beyond angry, but she was also beyond cold. Sitting on the frozen ground didn't help. Cathy might get her wish of an eight-toed Mattie.

Sarah frowned. "Mattie, you're shivering."

Freeman grabbed her hand and anchored his other hand under her arm. "Come on. Let's get you out of this cold."

Mattie tried to stand and just about passed out when pain shot up her leg. "*Ach*, stop, stop! Let me down."

Caleb's gaze traveled to her foot, and his eyes nearly popped out of his head. "Look at her . . ." He turned a light shade of green, clapped his hands over his mouth, and ran around the corner of the school, presumably to throw up in private.

Mattie eyed her ankle, and her stomach roiled like waves on a stormy lake. Her foot jutted out from her leg at an unnatural angle, and now that she really paid attention to it, the pain was almost unbearable.

Freeman gasped. "Mattie, I think you've broken your ankle."

There was no "think" about it. Her foot flopped to one side, and she found it impossible to move anything below her knee. She'd obviously rolled it when T-shirt Boy had bowled her over, but she'd been too busy trying to breathe to notice. The tilt of her foot, the excruciating pain, and the bitter cold made her dizzy. "I don't think I can walk," she panted.

Freeman looked as if he were feeling the pain right along with her. "*Ach*, Mattie. I'm so sorry. I don't want to hurt you, but do you think you could stand it if I picked you up and carried you to the van?"

"Just leave me here to die."

She had never seen Freeman so upset and yet so outwardly calm. He tightened his arm around her, even as his eyes deepened with concern. "As tempting as that sounds, I can't have your frozen body on my conscience." He was trying to distract her, but his arm around her shoulders was distraction enough.

"Okay, but just go slowly or I might pass out." She held her breath as he slid one arm under her knees. This was going to hurt something wonderful.

Before he could lift her off the ground, the front doors burst open, and Bill came running out of the school, along with three other men and the two young people who'd engaged in the shouting match with the T-shirt Boys. Bill held his phone as if he were ready to snap some pictures.

Mattie shook her head slightly at Freeman. Freeman pulled his arm from under her knees and crouched on his haunches. They didn't look completely natural, but it certainly didn't look like they'd been in the middle of a riot only minutes earlier.

Bill came to a halt at the edge of the sidewalk and lowered his camera. "We heard gunshots," he said. Righteous indignation was written all over his face, but he was also clearly disappointed about something. Disappointed that he wouldn't be getting photos of a riot? Disappointed that there were no angry bystanders shouting at Mattie and the other Amish people? He narrowed his eyes. "What's going on here?"

Sadie and Sarah were too afraid of Bill to speak up. Cathy was busy recording the whole exchange on her camera. Freeman was livid and didn't look as if he would do anything but give Bill a nasty scowl. Mattie would have to be the one to talk. "We're just enjoying a lovely fall evening, Bill. How was the debate?"

Bill pointed to the Englisch girl who had shouted some very naughty things at the T-shirt Boys. "Becca says some of your voters attacked her."

Mattie shrugged. That small movement zinged through her broken ankle. "There was certainly a lot of noise, but it was two of your supporters shouting at two of your relatives." She tried to look sufficiently shocked. "And then your nephew started throwing firecrackers, and Becca tackled Sarah, and she scraped her knee."

"I didn't tackle anybody," Becca said, as if she resented the whole world.

Bill puffed out his chest. "Your voters are thugs. They tried to disrupt the debate and hurt Becca and Mike." Bill glanced at the people he brought out with him. "This will be in all the papers by tomorrow, and your campaign will be finished. But we all knew it was finished weeks ago."

Cathy stared at the screen on her camera. "And by *all* the papers, do you mean the *Byler Town Newsletter* that comes out once a month?"

Bill pointed a threatening finger at Cathy. "Oh, no. The Byler riot will make all the Denver and Colorado Springs papers too. You can be sure of that."

Cathy didn't seem to be listening. She tapped her phone screen. "I'm sending you a photo you can use in the paper so people can see who really started the Byler riot."

Bill's phone vibrated. He scowled when he saw what was on the screen. "Nobody will believe I had anything to do with this."

Cathy cocked an eyebrow. "Your nephew is literally wearing a 'Vote for Maddie' T-shirt, and he's got a handful of firecrackers. And he can't spell."

"That doesn't prove anything," Bill said. His pride truly had no bounds. "Nobody knows that's my nephew. He lives in Alamosa." He eyed Mattie, still sitting on the ground, still shivering so hard, she thought her teeth might crack. "Keep your voters in line because I'm prepared to call the police if there's any more trouble."

Mattie wanted to stand up and give Bill the greatest, most fiery lecture of her life, but standing was impossible and it hurt to move her lips. She stayed silent in hopes that Bill would take his minions and go back into the school so Mattie could escape with some of her dignity. She could just see the headline if Bill learned about her broken ankle:

CANDIDATE INJURED BY HER OWN VOTERS.

Thank Derr Herr, Bill hadn't brought his coat out with him. He'd obviously been in too much of a hurry to record something incriminating. His nose was already bright red, and his short-sleeved white shirt didn't offer much protection. He turned on his heel and marched back inside, his friends and accomplices following.

Once Bill had disappeared, Freeman wasted no time. He quickly but gently lifted Mattie into his arms. She groaned as her foot left the ground. Freeman grimaced. "Sorry, Mattie."

She wrapped her arms around his neck and rested her head on his shoulder. She'd never been in this much pain. It stole her breath and made her light-headed. Closing her eyes, she focused on Freeman's nice smell, his soft coat, and his rock-hard arms. Being this close to him was the only *gute* thing about breaking her ankle, except for maybe the fact that everything had become clear to her in the last five minutes.

Getting into the van was another ordeal. Sarah held her hands so Mattie could prop her foot on them, which minimized some of the jarring but left her gasping for air by the time she was in the seat.

Caleb came running from the side of the school just as Cathy put the van into reverse. He jumped into the back next to Sadie and buckled his seat belt. "I'm wonderful sorry about that. I've always had a touchy stomach."

Cathy pulled out of the parking lot and turned in the direction of Monte Vista.

"Wait," Caleb said. "Where are we going?"

Cathy turned around and looked at Caleb, taking her eyes off the road and giving Mattie a heart attack. "Where do you think, Caleb? Even though I'm not fond of doctors, we need to take Mattie to the hospital."

Caleb's mouth fell open. "But . . . how long will it take?"

"Emergency rooms are notoriously slow. We're looking at three or four hours. They should bring in a consultant from Chick-fil-a. Those folks know how to get people in and out."

Caleb groaned. "*Ach, du lieva.* Esther isn't going to believe we watched the sunset for four hours."

Mattie pointed to her foot. "I think a cast might make her a little suspicious."

Caleb ran his fingers through his hair. "She's going to kill me. Esther is going to kill me, and I'm too young to die."

Chapter 13

Freeman pulled in front of Esther and Levi's house, set the brake, and slid out of the buggy. The fact that it had taken him half an hour to get here on the back roads only added insult to injury. He clutched a bouquet of blush-pink roses in his fist, hoping that Mattie liked flowers. What girl didn't like flowers? Amish men rarely gave flowers to their sweethearts, but Englischers did it all the time, and Freeman figured it couldn't hurt.

He was looking forward to seeing Mattie, but he wasn't looking forward to having this conversation.

He slumped his shoulders and tromped up the porch steps, seriously doubting that roses would soften the heart-to-heart he needed to have with Mattie. Because as much as she didn't want to hear it, it was time for her to quit the campaign. Too many people had been hurt, including her.

Freeman hadn't been physically hurt, but it just about tore him apart to see Sarah and Sadie in danger. And when that boy had knocked Mattie over, Freeman's heart had stopped beating altogether. He hadn't been able to keep the people he loved from getting hurt, and the feeling of helplessness was a tight knot in his gut.

The hospital had been almost as bad. When the doctor examined her ankle, Freeman had felt Mattie's pain as if it were his own, and by the time the doctor had put on the cast, Freeman was more determined than ever to talk her into quitting. If she was too stubborn to withdraw because of a broken ankle, surely she could be persuaded to do it for Freeman—who couldn't bear the thought of seeing her get hurt again—or Sarah, who'd needed four stitches in her knee.

Freeman wasn't surprised when Caleb answered the door. When Caleb wasn't working with his *dat* remodeling houses, he was almost always at Esther's house with Mattie. He had definitely taken seriously Esther's request to distract Mattie from the campaign, or at least Caleb wanted Esther to think he'd been distracting Mattie instead of helping her. After last night, Caleb was probably in the doghouse with Esther, and he was likely now doing his best to make amends. Lord willing, after today, Caleb wouldn't need to distract Mattie because the campaign would be over.

"*Hallo*, Caleb. I've come to see Mattie."

Caleb eyed the flowers in Freeman's hand. "*Ach, vell*, okay, I guess." He leaned his head out the door and whispered, "But just a warning. Esther won't be very nice. She's already smashed a banana with her fist, and she has a knitting needle tucked behind her ear. I think she wants to stab something."

Freeman widened his eyes for Caleb's benefit, but he wasn't worried. Esther would be glad he'd come once she found out what he wanted to say. "I'll be careful."

Caleb motioned him into the house. Mattie lay on the living room sofa, her arms folded across her chest, her casted leg propped on a pillow, and her eyes clamped tightly shut. She didn't open her eyes when he walked into the room, but unless she'd gone deaf, for sure and certain, she'd heard him come in. A pair of crutches leaned against the wall behind the sofa.

"*Vie gehts*, Mattie? How is the ankle?"

No answer.

A blue-and-mustard-yellow quilt was stretched on Esther's quilt frames, and there was barely enough room to maneuver around it. The quilt frames wobbled even though Freeman did his best not to bump them on his way to the sofa. Thank Derr Herr, there was a chair on one side of the quilt where it looked as if Esther had been sitting to take some stitches. Freeman pulled it out and sat down.

To Freeman's annoyance, Caleb settled in. He leaned against the wall and stuffed his hands in his pockets, and then Esther appeared from the direction of the kitchen, carrying a chair. She placed it in the entryway and sat down where she had a view of the whole living room. Didn't she have a toddler and a new baby to look after?

"Welcome to our home," Esther said, which was a strange greeting. Maybe she meant it as a warning that she wouldn't hesitate to throw Freeman out on his ear if he said anything Esther didn't agree with.

Freeman clenched his jaw in frustration. He had wanted to talk to Mattie alone. Then again, there was wisdom in having allies. Esther was most definitely on his side, and Caleb's conscience was slowly eating away the lining of his stomach. And maybe Mattie would temper her anger with her *aendi* sitting not ten feet away.

"If you've come to give me a lecture, you can save your breath," Mattie said, her eyes still closed.

Mattie was by far the most exasperating girl Freeman had ever met, and that included Sadie. He did his best to tamp down his simmering annoyance. He'd only just gotten here, and he'd rather not engage in a shouting match before he had a chance to give her the flowers, which were supposed to be a peace offering. He loved Mattie, for goodness' sake. Why did she annoy him so?

He pressed his lips together and tried to think happy thoughts. Not one happy thought came to mind. "How is your ankle feeling?"

"It hurts," she said curtly.

Esther wasn't ready to unbend, but she obviously felt sorry that Freeman was trying to carry on a conversation with a post. "Linda brought over some essential oils. I think they've helped the pain."

"I'm *froh* to hear it." Freeman tried again with Mattie. "Can you get around okay on the crutches?"

"*Jah*. They're fine."

He swallowed his frustration and made his voice low and soothing so she would know how bad he felt for her. "I'm sorry you broke your ankle."

Mattie remained rigidly mute.

"How is Sarah?" Esther asked. "Caleb said she had to get stitches."

"*Ach*, not too *gute*. Both her knees are bruised, and she's going to have a scar. And her hands were scraped up pretty bad."

Mattie didn't open her eyes, but the lines around her mouth deepened. "Why don't you just say, 'I told you so' and get it over with?"

Freeman frowned, mere inches from losing what little patience he had left. "It wonders me if you could sit up and look at me when I talk to you."

"My ears are working just fine."

He bit his tongue. "I brought you some flowers."

Mattie peeked out of one eye. "That was very nice of you."

She wouldn't think he was so nice if she could read his thoughts. "Could we talk? Face-to-face?" He picked a rose from the bouquet, reached out with the stem, and brushed the petals against her cheek.

Mattie flinched, opened her eyes, and batted the rose away from her face. "Stop that. I thought it was a spider."

He pumped his eyebrows up and down. "I have a jar of spiders in my pocket, and if you don't sit up, I won't hesitate to use them."

"You do not."

"What if you're wrong?"

Mattie growled, gingerly slid her cast off the sofa, and sat up. This was progress. She folded her arms and turned her face away from him. "I feel terrible, just terrible that Sarah got hurt."

"I do too," he said.

She expelled the air from her lungs. "I don't want anyone else to get hurt so I'm quitting the campaign."

Esther beamed and sighed as if she'd been holding her breath a long time. Freeman couldn't keep a grin from taking over his face. Things were better than he could have dared imagined. Mattie was obviously irritated, but she had made the right decision without his advice or his admonishment. He didn't have to lecture her, she didn't have to get defensive, and they didn't have to argue.

Mattie raised her palm to stop Freeman from saying anything. "Don't gloat or I'll throw up all over your boots."

Freeman wiped the smile off his face so fast, it was as if someone had pinched him. "Why would I gloat?"

"You tried to warn me something like this would happen. You were right. That ought to make you wonderful happy."

"It doesn't make me happy."

She cocked an eyebrow. "Maybe not. But for sure and certain you're relieved."

Esther tried to be helpful. "We're all relieved, Mattie. It's better to stop before anyone else gets hurt."

Freeman nodded. "Enough damage has been done already. You broke your ankle. Sarah had to get stitches."

Mattie's expression darkened like the sky in a looming storm. "You don't have to remind me. I was there."

He was making Mattie feel worse when he only wanted to help her feel better, to assure her she'd made the right decision. "You're very wise to withdraw from the campaign. I'm proud of you for being so sensible."

She stared at him, and her eyes were like two icy blue marbles. "That's quite a compliment coming from you."

"Uh, *jah*," he stuttered, unsure what she meant.

"You said I was foolish. I'm thrilled to finally meet with your approval."

He laughed uncomfortably. "You've always met with my approval."

"I'm sure I have," she said, as if she thought he was lying, as if she didn't care anyway.

She hadn't reacted to his praise the way he thought she would. He cleared his throat and tried again. "That's not really what I meant to say. You don't need my approval. You are intelligent and independent, smart enough to make the right decision on your own."

He wasn't quite comfortable with the way she looked at him—as if she were a cat stalking a mouse, backing him into a corner where there was no escape. What was he doing wrong? "Smart enough to make the decision you wanted me to make all along."

"That's beside the point, Mattie," Esther said, again jumping in to save him from something he didn't rightly understand. "You feel bad about quitting the race, but you feel worse that Sarah got hurt and that there was nearly a riot. None of this is Freeman's fault, even though you're eager for someone to be mad at."

Freeman furrowed his brow. Mattie was mad at him? Of

course she was, not because he deserved it, but because it was easier to be mad at him than to accept she'd been wrong in the first place. "It's no weakness to admit you made a mistake."

Esther gritted her teeth and shot a warning glance in Freeman's direction. "Not that you made a mistake, Mattie. How could you have known what Bill was capable of?"

Mattie frowned. "Freeman knew."

A tiny voice came from the room across the hall. Esther patted her hands on her knees and smiled at Freeman. "*Ach, vell*, there is Winnie from her nap, which means Junior will be up soon too." She took her chair back to the kitchen, slipped into Winnie's room and brought Winnie out.

Winnie rubbed the sleep from her eyes and reached for Caleb. "Hold me, Laleb," she said.

Esther bounced Winnie on her hip. "Not now. Caleb is talking to Mattie. He can hold you later." Esther disappeared into the kitchen with Winnie.

Freeman was on his own because Caleb was no help at all. Freeman held out the bouquet to Mattie, who took it grudgingly. She laid the flowers across her lap. Freeman propped his elbows on his knees. "In the end, it doesn't matter who was right or who was wrong. It's not a contest, and there's not a winner or loser. You've chosen to do the right thing. That's what matters. You'd be selfish indeed if you didn't withdraw from the election and let things get back to normal."

Mattie's eyes flashed with an intense emotion. She was angry, for sure and certain, but it was plain he'd also hurt her feelings. "You think I'm selfish?"

How quickly could he backpedal? "What I mean is, you've made an unselfish decision by getting out of the race."

She looked at him as if he were Bill Isom's campaign manager. "But you thought I was selfish before?"

A little voice in his head told him to just stop talking, but he had to convince her that they had both been right. That he had been right earlier than she had been shouldn't have made a difference. "I didn't think you were selfish before. You just didn't know what you were getting into. Now that people have been hurt, you'd be selfish if you kept going with the race. Quitting is the unselfish decision—the most unselfish thing I've seen you do. I admire your courage to do the unselfish thing." If he kept filling the space with words, maybe she'd find one or two that she agreed with. "I'm sorry. I know how much this campaign meant to you."

"Do you?"

"Of course. We all want to see the ordinance changed. It just wasn't Gotte's will."

Of all the things he'd said, this one seemed to upset Mattie more than the others. "*Nae*. It wasn't Gotte's will."

He nodded. "I'm not saying it's easy to submit, but humility makes us more fit for the kingdom of Gotte."

Caleb chimed in. "Maybe Gotte gave you a broken ankle to teach you a lesson."

At that moment, Freeman wanted to toss Caleb out of the house, but this wasn't his house, and Esther probably wouldn't have liked it. "That's the dumbest thing I've ever heard," Freeman said.

Caleb eyed Mattie. "I'm sorry. That's what some people are saying."

Mattie didn't seem all that upset with Caleb. She was too busy staring daggers at Freeman. "I'm selfish, proud, and foolish. How can you stand to be in the same room with me?"

"You are willfully misunderstanding me, Mattie. We all must learn humility, myself included."

She set the flowers next to her on the sofa, as if she didn't like them all that much. "I can't see as how you need to work on much of anything. You're nearly perfect, and I willfully misunderstand people."

Now he should most assuredly stop talking because if he didn't, he was going to say something he regretted, like "Stop being so childish." He scrubbed his hand down the side of his face, took the deepest breath he had ever taken, and counted to ten. Why did Mattie make him so angry? And why, when he was this angry, did he still want to gather her in his arms and kiss her until they were both breathless? It was aggravating and puzzling and exhilarating all at the same time.

Willing his blood to stop boiling and his pulse to slow down, he reached out and took her hand. She flinched but didn't pull away, and he savored the feel of her skin against his. "I'm sorry, Mattie. I'm saying it all wrong. I know you wanted to help us, but there is nothing else you can do. Somehow we will work around the buggy ordinance. It is hardly the worst hardship we Amish have had to face. The most important thing for the community is to put this behind us and get back to the peaceful lives we had before this whole mess started."

She reacted as if he had slapped her. Her face twisted in pain, her eyes filled with tears, and she pulled her hand away. "You can say it, Freeman. You all were much better off before I came to Colorado." She buried her face in her hands and began to sob.

Freeman was paralyzed with shock. He had never seen Mattie cry before, and the sight shook him to the core. He quickly shifted from his chair to the sofa and slid his arm around Mattie. To Freeman's irritation, Caleb abandoned the wall he was holding up and sat on the other side of Mattie. Caleb also put his arm around her, which ended up not being so much around Mattie as being on top of

Freeman's arm. Didn't this kid know when to stay out of grown-up problems?

Despite his annoyance, Freeman's first concern was for Mattie. He did his best to ignore Caleb's arm on top of his. "It's okay, Mattie. It's okay."

She paused her sniffling while her puzzled gaze traveled from Freeman to Caleb and back again. *Jah.* Caleb was acting strange. Or maybe she thought both of them were acting strange. "I am trying to live with *Gelassenheit* in my heart, but I truly thought Gotte wanted me to run for office."

Freeman patted her on the back, all the more awkward because Caleb's arm was holding his down. "You were doing what you thought was right."

"I don't know if Gotte wanted you to run," Caleb said, "but I know Esther didn't."

Freeman handed her a tissue. "I'm sorry I hurt your feelings. Please don't be sad."

She looked at him as if he were crazy. "You can't hurt my feelings, and I'm not sad. I'm mad. I cry when I get mad."

His lips curled upward. "Then I would have expected to see you cry every time you and I talk to each other. You're always mad at me."

Her mouth twitched. "That's true, but this is not one of those times that I can just put you in your place."

She was feeling better already, but he just had to set her straight. "You have never put me in my place."

She cracked a smile. "You can believe that if it helps you sleep at night." She blew her nose and dabbed at her face with the tissue. "This is a more intense kind of anger, like I've fallen off a cliff and my broken body is lying in a ravine."

Caleb frowned. "That would make me angry."

She sighed. "I'm angry because Bill's tricks hurt people. I'm angry because I didn't do anything wrong, but I still feel guilty. I'm angry because Bill won, and he won by being devious and dishonest. I'm angry because the *gute* people don't always prevail. I'm angry because the *gmayna* was fine before I came, and you'll be fine after I leave, like I don't even matter."

"Of course you matter," Freeman said. Did he dare say more, like the fact that she had come to matter very much in his life—to the point of him not being able to think about anything else?

"Everybody wishes I had never come to town."

Caleb finally removed his arm from Mattie's shoulders. "That's not true, Mattie. I'm wonderful glad you came to town."

"Well, that makes one of you."

Freeman shouldn't have to say it. Mattie knew how he felt, didn't she? "I'm *froh* you came to Colorado too."

Without warning, Caleb snatched Mattie's hand as if they were playing a game of Spoons and her hand was the last spoon. "I'm wonderful *froh* you came to town," he repeated, "because, well, Mattie, I've fallen in love with you."

Mattie's mouth fell open.

Freeman would have swallowed his gum if he'd been chewing any. Love? What did a seventeen-year-old boy know about love? Not as much as Freeman did, that was for sure and certain. Freeman was the one who loved Mattie. The only one, and if Caleb thought he was going to intrude on what Freeman and Mattie shared, he was sorely mistaken. Freeman snatched Mattie's other hand. "Mattie, he can't be in love with you because I'm in love with you."

The color drained from Mattie's face, and she moved her lips to say something, but Caleb cut her off. "You don't know how I feel, Freeman." He puffed out his chest like a rooster. "I love Mattie, and you can't talk me out of it."

"Uh," Mattie said.

Freeman's heart hammered against his rib cage. "What do you know? I love Mattie, and it's more than just your teenage puppy love."

"You sure don't show it. All you do is scowl at her and tell her she's foolish and proud . . . and . . . and selfish."

Mattie jerked her hands away. "I'm not . . ."

"I don't think she's foolish or selfish," Freeman growled.

"Maybe," Caleb said, narrowing his eyes as if he were suspicious of Freeman's integrity. "I have never called her foolish. I love her so much that I would crawl on my hands and knees all the way to Denver to prove my love."

Freeman had never seen Caleb quite so sure of himself, as if he'd aged ten years in a few minutes. Love did strange things to people, like make them say ridiculous things. "I would crawl to Pennsylvania to prove my love."

Caleb wasn't impressed. "I helped with her campaign when you were hiding in your potato fields."

"I carried her to the van while you were busy throwing up."

Mattie clasped her hands, pressed her lips together, and stared at Freeman as if she didn't know who he was. Right now, he didn't recognize himself either. He'd been pulled into an absurd bragging contest with a lovesick teenager.

Caleb clasped both his hands around Mattie's. "You have to believe me. No one has ever loved a girl the way I love you."

Mattie pushed off the sofa and stood up on one leg. "Oh, stop it!"

"Mattie, I love you," Caleb begged.

Mattie held up a finger and hissed. That was enough to shut Caleb up.

Freeman didn't want to appear pathetic, like Caleb, but he felt an overwhelming need to make Mattie see the truth. "I'm sorry, Mattie. I'm not sure what's gotten into me, but I love you. I have known it for a long time. I should have told you sooner."

Mattie pressed her fingers to her forehead. "You are the most aggravating . . ." She reached for her crutches. Caleb grabbed them before Freeman could, obviously trying hard to prove the depth of his love. Mattie propped her crutches under her arms. "I have a broken ankle, a bruised rib, and I just dropped out of the election. Could you have picked a more inconvenient time?"

Caleb pled with his eyes. "There's no convenient time for love."

Mattie gave Caleb, then Freeman, the stink eye. "Save your breath. I don't want to hear it." She blew a puff of air from between her lips. "I've got enough problems without having to sort this one out. Go home. I'm sick of you both."

"But, Mattie."

"Go."

Caleb and Freeman stood up at the same time. Freeman ground his teeth together until they squeaked. Caleb had sat on Mattie's roses, flattening them like pink, leafy pancakes. That boy was like an abscessed tooth.

Caleb gave Mattie one desperate look and walked out of the house like a dog with his tail between his legs. A single pink petal stuck to his bottom.

Freeman followed, wondering just where the conversation had gone wrong and why Mattie had been so irritated. He'd just professed his love. She hadn't outright rejected him, but she could have at least been more polite.

Maybe he shouldn't have brought the flowers. They'd pushed her over the edge.

Chapter 14

Freeman finished mucking out the barn and leaned against the wall with his hand propped on top of the stall fork. It was the first time in his life that he had no idea what to do next—not with the farm, not with his life, not with Mattie Zook. Even after the potato harvest, he usually had a list of daily chores as long as his arm. But today, he didn't have the heart to walk the fences or check the cover crops or even sharpen his tools. The only thing he wanted to do was stare in the direction of Mattie's house and think about how much he loved her.

And she couldn't stand the sight of him.

He really should make a plan to win her heart, but he had no idea what to do to make her fall in love with him. Bringing her roses had been a big mistake. Trying to make her feel better about dropping out of the race seemed to make things worse. Telling her he loved her had only made her mad. It hadn't helped that Caleb had professed his love not one minute earlier. Had Mattie not believed him? Did she blame him for . . . any number of things?

Freeman had felt a connection between them when he carried Mattie to Cathy's van after she'd been injured. If that hadn't prompted her to at least notice him, he wasn't sure what would have. She had been upset about having to quit the race, but if she felt anything for him, couldn't she have given him a little encouragement? He'd spilled out his deepest feelings, and she'd ordered him out of the house.

He'd been walking around in the stupor of rejection for twenty-four hours. He loved Mattie. If she didn't love him back, he might crawl into a ditch and die there.

His gut told him to give Mattie more time. Mattie liked him well enough. He didn't doubt that. But he had sprung the "I love you" thing on her out of the blue, and she probably felt as if she was being attacked instead of courted. Freeman frowned to himself. Unfortunately, the longer he waited, the more room he left for Caleb to sidle into Mattie's heart. Maybe Caleb was over there right now, singing love songs or helping Mattie finish a puzzle or taking stitches on one of Esther's quilts.

Freeman would have hitched up the buggy and ridden over there on the forbidden roads, just to get there sooner, but he had no idea what to do once he got there. Was there a gift he could bring that she wouldn't reject? Was there something he could say that wouldn't make her mad? Could he do anything to convince her to love him? And could he do it without Caleb peeking over his shoulder?

Sadie strolled into the barn with Sarah, Cathy Larsen, and Dewey close behind. "See, I told you. He's just standing there, not doing nothing. He's been like that all morning."

Freeman pushed off the wall and pretended like he'd just finished with the nearest stall. "What do you mean I'm not doing anything? I've been mucking out for an hour."

Sadie propped her fists on her hips. "You have not. I peeked in not ten minutes ago, and you were standing right there staring at the wall."

"Aren't I allowed to take a little rest? Mucking out is hard work."

"Not that hard," Sadie said. "I do it all the time."

Freeman gave up arguing with her. What did it matter anyway?

Dewey pulled his phone out of his back pocket. "My mom wanted us to show you Bill's new video on YouTube. It's already got fifty-seven views."

Freeman shook his head. "I already told my sisters. Mattie quit the race. Bill's videos don't matter."

"Just watch," Dewey said, holding up his phone. "I promised my mom I'd show you."

Dewey tapped the screen. "Riot in Byler," the headline read. The next frame showed a photo of dozens of angry people holding torches and pitchforks. "This isn't . . ." Freeman said.

Cathy registered her disgust with a grunt. "We know. This is a scene from 'Beauty and the Beast' that Bill downloaded off the Internet. He came too late to get photos, remember?"

Freeman drew his lips into a tight line. "Why would anyone believe this?"

Next came a video of Bill talking about the "riot," and how some of Mattie's voters had started attacking people. Bill gave his voice an ominous tone. "Gunshots were heard," he said. Then there was an interview with the girl who had knocked Sarah down. She accused Mattie of encouraging her voters to attack Bill supporters. The video ended with a smiling Bill, asking people for their votes and the words *Bill Isom for ALL of Byler* as the video faded to darkness.

"His production value isn't very good," Cathy said, "but he sure knows how to tell a convincing lie."

Sadie took Dewey's phone and narrowed her eyes as she studied the screen. "That's why we've got to tell the truth. Dewey, can you help us make our own YouTube video about what really happened?"

Dewey shrugged. "I guess, but Mom says I can't work on the campaign until I clean my room. And that's going to take like three days."

Cathy waved her hand in Dewey's direction. "This is no time to clean your room. Tell your mom it will have to wait. The election is less than two weeks away."

They talked as if there was still an election to win. Freeman tried not to get testy—*ach*, *vell*, testier than he already was about the lies Bill was spreading. "Cathy, it doesn't matter what Bill puts on YouTube. It's over."

Cathy peered at Freeman as if he'd gone crazy. "Of course it matters. Bill shouldn't be allowed to get away with this."

The familiar sensation of helplessness settled into the pit of his stomach. "There's nothing we can do about it now."

Freeman didn't deserve the glare Sadie gave him. "Just stop it, Freeman."

He glared right back at her. "Why are you so mad at me?"

"Because you're giving up," Sadie said, "and I don't like quitters."

Freeman felt a growl bubbling up from his throat. He swallowed it back down and mustered an exceptional amount of patience for his undeserving *schwester*. "Mattie is the one who quit. And it's better for everyone this way."

All four of them stared at Freeman as if he'd grown antlers on his head. "It's not better for everyone," Sarah said. "It's only better for Bill."

"Look, Sarah. I'm just as mad about Bill as you are, but that's why this needs to stop. If we had stayed out of it, we wouldn't be so angry now. Gotte commanded us not to be angry. We believe in being peacemakers, not in stirring up trouble."

Cathy shook her head. "I'd say Jesus stirred up a lot of trouble in His day."

"That's right. He did," Sarah said.

Freeman folded his arms across his chest. "Do I need to remind you that you cut your knee open?"

Sarah acted as if she couldn't care less about her four stitches. "In a few weeks, you won't even be able to see the scar."

"Most of *die youngie* were scared out of their minds, Sadie almost got hit by a firecracker, and Mattie broke her ankle. People got hurt." Freeman reached out and fingered Sarah's *kapp* string. "My heart stopped when that girl knocked you over. I don't want anyone else to get hurt, and neither does Mattie. It's for the best."

Sarah lifted her chin. "I'm not sorry I got hurt."

Sadie linked arms with Sarah. "And I'm not sorry about the firecrackers." The twins nodded to each other, their lips pulled stubbornly across their faces. "Sarah got hurt standing up for what is right," Sadie said, "just like one of the blessed martyrs."

Freeman stopped himself before he rolled his eyes. "You two are nothing like the blessed martyrs." He glanced at Sarah. "And you weren't so happy about it when blood was running down your leg."

Sarah turned up her nose. "*Ach, vell,* I'm happy about it now."

There was no arguing with a stubborn teenager, and it was useless to try. He shut his mouth. The campaign was over, and Sadie and Sarah could debate about it all they wanted. It wouldn't change anything.

Sadie narrowed her eyes. "Aren't you willing to fight for what you believe is right? Aren't you willing to fight for Mattie? You're such a chicken."

Now they were being unfair. "Mattie made the decision to quit. There's nothing to fight for anymore."

Cathy swatted away his excuse. "Mattie is just being

noble. She came to town and then turned everything upside down. She feels responsible for all the bad things that have happened, even though the blame is squarely on Bill."

Freeman pressed his lips together. Mattie *did* blame herself. She said everyone would have been better off if she hadn't come to Colorado. Well, Freeman knew for sure and certain that he wouldn't be better off. He didn't realize how empty his life had been until Mattie had filled it.

Cathy stuffed her hands into the pockets of her pink parka. "You're her closest friend in the Amish community. You need to reassure her that it's okay to run, even though people got hurt—or maybe *because* people got hurt. You can't let Bill get away with this."

"But it's Mattie's decision. Not mine." Freeman took off his hat and ran his fingers through his hair. "Why would I convince her to keep going with the election? I think it's better that she quits."

The wrinkles around Cathy's mouth bunched together. "That's why she quit."

"What do you mean by that?"

"She quit because you wanted her to quit," Cathy said.

Freeman's patience was razor thin. Now it was his fault? "Mattie knew exactly how I felt from the very first day. If she had quit when I wanted her to quit, she wouldn't have even started."

Sadie pinched her lips into a sour expression. "*Ach*, Freeman, you're so *dumm*."

"You may think that hurts my feelings, Sadie, but you tell me I'm *dumm* when I eat more than my share of corn at dinner. And when I sing too loud in church."

Sadie backed away sheepishly. "I do not."

Sarah put her arm around Sadie and pulled her back into their circle. "Freeman, we know that you and Mattie haven't always agreed about the campaign, and we know that she hasn't always listened to your advice, but we know she'll get back in the race if you ask her to."

His heart sank. "She won't do anything I ask. She doesn't even like me anymore."

"Of course she likes you," Sarah said.

Would they leave him alone if he told them the truth? "I told her I love her." He slumped his shoulders. "And she kicked me out of the house."

Sadie and Sarah looked like twin trout, their mouths wide open as if gasping for air. Cathy's frown sank deep into her face. Dewey had no reaction. He was looking at his phone.

"What did you do?" Sadie asked, her tone sharp with accusation.

"I told you. I said 'Mattie, I love you,' and she ordered me to leave."

A scold flashed in Sarah's eyes. "But how did you say it? You must have really messed it up if she kicked you out of the house."

Freeman didn't need to be discussing his love life with his two little sisters and an old lady. He propped the stall fork against the wall and headed out of the barn. "Thanks for your sympathy," he tossed over his shoulder. A pair of hands were thrown around his neck from behind, and he stopped in his tracks before he choked to death. He turned his head. Sadie hung on his back as if she wanted a piggy-back ride. "Let go of me," he grunted, hooking his fingers around Sadie's arms in an attempt to pry her away from him.

Sadie giggled and released him. "*Ach*, Freeman, you're so *dumm*. Just stop for a minute and talk to us. We want to help."

He smoothed his hand down the front of his shirt. "Sure, you want to help. You want to help me right off a cliff."

"We do not," Sadie said. "We know more about girls than you do, and we can help you figure out why Mattie threw you out of the house."

Sarah wrapped her arm around Freeman's elbow. "It must have been the way you said it, because she loves you something wonderful."

Freeman's heart nearly leaped out of his chest. "Did she tell you that?"

"No, but everybody can see it." Cathy seemed quite sure of herself. "When you're together, she rotates around you like the moon does to Earth."

Sadie huffed out a breath. "Don't get a big head about it. You're bound to mess it up."

Sarah nodded. "It sounds like you already have."

Freeman didn't know whether to be insulted or ecstatic. Ecstasy won out. Did Mattie love him? *Could* Mattie love him? "But . . . then . . . okay, tell me what I did wrong."

"Tell us what happened."

He drew his brows together. "She started crying about quitting the race. I reassured her she was doing the right thing."

"*Ach, bruder*, how could you?"

Sarah hushed Sadie. "Just let him tell it. We can sort it out later."

"I brought her flowers."

Sarah smiled encouragingly. "Did she like them?"

"Caleb sat on them. Then he told her he loved her."

Sarah's face turned red. "Caleb loves Mattie?"

Freeman scrubbed his hand down the side of his face. "I panicked because I love her too, and I didn't want her to think that Caleb was the only one. So I told her that I love her, and Caleb got mad at me. We argued about who loved Mattie more, and then Mattie got mad at both of us. She ordered us to leave."

Dewey was still gazing at his phone, but the other three stared at Freeman as if his story was the most interesting thing they'd ever heard.

Cathy shrugged. "Well, that explains it."

"How does that explain anything?" Why could Cathy understand what he still couldn't grasp?

Sadie raised her eyebrows. "You made about four mistakes."

"I counted five." Sarah's expression overflowed with pity. "You didn't think things through very well, but I'm not going to fault you for that. You're in love. We can't expect you to be sensible."

"Do you girls even like me? You can't seem to find one good thing to say about me."

Sadie waved her hand in the air. "*Ach*, Freeman. We like you well enough, but if you want our help, you have to be able to bear some chastisement. You have many flaws."

Freeman bit his tongue. He did have many flaws, but how would this help him with Mattie?

Sadie tapped her finger to her lips. "First of all: Caleb."

"Caleb is a definite problem," Cathy said. "Mattie has been very kind to him, and she's pretty. We can forgive him for believing he's in love." Her glare was so sharp, Freeman took a step back. "What were you thinking, arguing with Caleb about who loves Mattie the most? If Mattie believes that you love her the way Caleb loves her, no wonder she's irritated. She doesn't want young love. She wants true love."

"I love her with all my heart."

Sarah winced. "Mattie might have thought you were just trying to make her feel better when you told her you love her. If a boy did that to me, I'd be mad at him for toying with my emotions."

Cathy nodded. "It's manipulative."

Freeman couldn't help but feel defensive. "That's not what I was trying to do. Caleb blurted it out. I couldn't let Mattie think he was the only one."

Sadie never passed up a chance to make Freeman feel worse about himself. "You told her you love her after she quit the race. That's the worst thing you did."

"Why does that matter?"

Sadie rolled her eyes as if it was obvious. "Would you have told her you love her if she'd decided to stay in the race?"

"Of course." He thought about that for a minute. "Eventually. I still don't understand why that makes a difference."

Sadie and Sarah shared a knowing look.

"You only love her because she did what you wanted her to do," Sadie said.

"That's not true." But the truth didn't matter if Mattie didn't believe it. Freeman's heart lodged in his throat. "She thinks my love is tied to what she does."

Sadie hooted. "That sounds about right."

Freeman narrowed his eyes in Sadie's direction and then decided he should probably listen to what she was trying to tell him. "I don't always approve of you, but you know I love you, don't you?"

"You don't ever approve of me, *bruder*."

"Of course I do." But as soon as he said it, he wasn't so sure. More than once, Mattie had lectured him about his tendency to share his opinion too freely. Maybe he used honesty as an excuse to be critical and sometimes downright rude. And he *was* hard on Sadie. She just had so many shortcomings. How could he simply look past them? How would she improve if he didn't point out where she fell short?

It felt as if a firecracker exploded right next to his ear as a sudden rush of realization and understanding hit him right between the eyes. *Ach.* He hated it that Sadie was the one to make him see sense. "But . . . but do you know I love you?"

She shrugged. "I suppose so, even though you don't like me very much."

Her admission didn't make Freeman feel any better. "Of course I like you, Sadie. You have many good qualities. Sometimes you do your chores without complaining, and you are a very good artist. You're brave and kind to everyone. Everyone but me, that is."

Sadie didn't seem impressed. "You said three good things about me and two bad ones." She counted on her fingers. "I'm brave, kind, and artistic. I also complain about chores, and you think I'm mean to you. No wonder Mattie kicked you out of the house."

Sarah's eyes flashed with annoyance. "That's not nice, Sadie. He's clumsy about showing it, but Freeman is a good boy with a good heart."

Freeman felt lower than a worm. If Sadie was that irritated with him, Mattie was probably livid. "I'm sorry, Sadie."

Sadie sighed. "I know. You think you have to boss me around or I won't turn out well. You can't help yourself. But you can't do that to Mattie if you want her to love you."

"You can't put conditions on your love," Cathy said.

"I don't. I truly don't."

Sadie wasn't convinced. "Then you've got to make sure she knows that."

Cathy patted him on the shoulder. "How much do you really love Mattie?"

"More than I love myself."

"Do you love her enough to do what's best for her?"

"For sure and certain."

"Good," Cathy said. "Because finishing this race is what's best for her. You need to convince her that running for office is what's best for everybody, Amish and English alike. Because it is. Bill Isom has got to go, quietly, if possible, but I don't mind if he goes out with a bang. A man with that moral turpitude and that chest hair should not be in government. Mattie needs to know that you support her, that staying in the race is the best choice."

Freeman didn't know if that was true. He didn't want it to be true. Mattie would be safer if she didn't finish the race. But safe or not, she was miserable, and Freeman wasn't going to ignore it any longer. Mattie would only be truly happy if she saw this campaign through to the end, and Freeman had been a fool to think he could convince her to stop being herself, to think he could change her into someone other than who she was. His heart beat like a drum playing a wild rock song. "Do you really think she'll listen to me?"

Cathy nodded. "You're the only one she'll listen to. Use that power wisely."

"And don't mess up," Sadie said.

It wasn't exactly a vote of confidence, but it was *gute* advice. He was determined to do it right this time. For Mattie.

But should he bring flowers?

Chapter 15

Mattie stiffened as Uncle Levi strolled into the kitchen and set a puzzle box on the table. *Ach*. A new puzzle could only mean one thing: Caleb was coming over. She stopped herself from growling out loud. Caleb was the second-to-last person she wanted to see right now. She didn't know what had prompted him to declare his love for her yesterday, but she *did* know that she had to put a stop to his affection immediately. Caleb was a sweet boy. He was also seventeen years old, immature, and not her image of the ideal boyfriend.

She didn't know who her ideal boyfriend was, but it wasn't Caleb, and it certainly wasn't Freeman Sensenig, who had conveniently decided to love her the minute she quit the campaign. Freeman wanted a nice, normal Amish *fraa*, and since there weren't any girls his age in Byler, he had been exceptionally lucky that Mattie had come to town. He must have found it annoying that Mattie hadn't behaved like a *gute* Amish girl. But now her "wild" days were over, and he was free to profess his love and get on with marriage and life.

Aunt Esther bustled into the kitchen with a binky precariously hanging by its handle from her ear. She'd just put the *buplie* to bed, and sometimes she misplaced Junior's binky, so she often carried an extra one around her ear. "I'm going to mix up a quick batch of cookies." She glanced doubtfully at Mattie. "Levi asked Caleb to come over to cheer you up."

Levi smiled as if it was the least he could do for his poor, pathetic niece. "I borrowed a puzzle from Ben and Linda. I thought you might like to work on a new one tonight."

If she didn't want Caleb to grow old doing puzzles at Esther's kitchen table, Mattie was going to have to be completely honest with Esther, Levi, *and* Caleb. She smoothed her hand over the top of the puzzle box. It was a picture of a house on a lake with ducks swimming in the water. "I don't think Caleb should come over anymore."

Esther's frown seemed to go all the way to her toes. "What? Why not? You two have gotten along so well together. Caleb has been very *gute* for you."

"He's a teenager, Aunt Esther. A nice boy, but not someone I want to spend three nights a week with."

"But you have to admit that you're less lonely than when you first came to town. That's all Caleb's doing."

Ach, vell. It was mostly Freeman's doing, but she was finished with him too. "Aunt Esther, I like Caleb. I don't mind doing the occasional puzzle with him, but yesterday he told me he loves me."

Esther drew her brows together. "That can't be right. Caleb is too young for you."

"*Jah.* He's too young, and I don't want to encourage him. He needs to spend time with girls his own age."

Esther looked more puzzled than ever. Wasn't she upset that her brother-in-law was going to get his heart broken? "I can't believe he loves you. Are you sure that's what he said?"

"*Jah.* He told me he loved me so much that he'd crawl

to Denver to prove it. I said I didn't want to hear it and told him to go home."

"He did leave in quite a hurry yesterday. I wondered why." Aunt Esther lifted her hand to her mouth. "Oh, dear. What have I done?"

"I don't understand what Caleb is thinking," Levi said. "You're five years older. He knows better than that."

Esther paced the floor. "This is all my fault. Caleb's a typical teenage boy. Of course he would fall in love with Mattie. She's kind and pretty, and they've spent so much time together. *Ach,* Levi, I'm so sorry." She pressed her fingers to her forehead and glanced at Mattie. "I asked him to distract you from the campaign, not fall in love with you."

Mattie acted surprised, though Caleb had told her as much months ago. "'Oh, what a tangled web we weave when first we practice to deceive,'" she recited. She didn't want Esther to feel too badly about it, but Esther should be a little embarrassed for scheming to keep Mattie away from her own campaign.

Aunt Esther gave her an arch look. "And what have you and Caleb been doing for the last few months? Not watching the sunset, that's for sure and certain."

Esther's expression made Mattie want to giggle. She raised her hands in surrender. "*Ach*, Aunt Esther, we have been doing our best to hinder each other. And look where it's gotten us. Caleb is in love, and my ankle is broken."

"You wouldn't be talked out of it. I had to be sneaky."

Mattie cocked her eyebrow. "So did I."

Esther huffed out a frustrated breath. "I suppose I shouldn't have interfered."

Levi widened his gaze. "That's a surprising admission."

"What's so surprising about it?" Esther said.

"You don't like to be wrong."

Esther looked at Mattie and pointed to Uncle Levi. "See what I have to put up with?"

Uncle Levi grinned and pointed at Esther. "See what I have to put up with?"

Esther grabbed a kitchen towel and snapped it in Levi's direction. "Watch yourself, or you won't get any cookies."

It felt so *gute* to laugh. Mattie hadn't laughed for two days.

Esther propped her hands on her hips. "There's a welcome sight. I've missed your smile."

Mattie slumped her shoulders. "I don't have a lot to smile about."

Levi rubbed his arm even though Esther's towel had completely missed him. "Ouch. That hurt something wonderful," he said, with a twinkle in his eye. He turned and tramped down the back hall. "I'm getting out of here before you give me a bigger welt." He let himself out and closed the back door.

Mattie loved how easygoing Levi was and how much he and Esther seemed to adore each other. "I'm sorry about sneaking around with Caleb, Aunt Esther. If it makes you feel any better, he nearly threw up every time I got in his buggy."

"It doesn't make me feel better, but I knew it was your idea. Caleb would never step one toe out of line on his own. You've corrupted him," Esther said, but she tempered her words with a smile, so Mattie knew she was forgiven.

"Caleb didn't want to deceive you, so sometimes we would go watch the sunset before going to Cathy's. Sometimes he would drop me off at my meeting and watch the sunset by himself. Sometimes we glanced at the sunset when we passed out flyers. I can assure you that there was a lot of sunset watching going on."

"*Ach, vell*, I can't be mad at Caleb. He's my brother-in-law, he's seventeen, and he was trying to please me."

"You can be mad at me. I shouldn't have dragged Caleb into my campaign."

Esther shook her head. "I don't blame you. You were completely honest with me, and I used Caleb to try to sidetrack you. Besides, you're my niece, and you're in *rumschpringe*. I should have accepted your decision, but I was just so worried about you."

"I know. I'm sorry."

Esther hung the towel on the hook behind the sink. "That's neither here nor there anymore. What's to be done about Caleb?"

Mattie smoothed her hand across the table. "I hate that he's going to be hurt again."

"Again?" Esther asked.

Mattie eyed Esther skeptically. "Was there ever really a girl named Lily who broke Caleb's heart?"

Esther turned red, but she soon recovered from whatever temporary embarrassment she felt. She shoved the air away with her hand. "*Ach*. Of course there was a Lily. She was his second-grade sweetheart."

Mattie groaned and rolled her eyes. "Well, you didn't lie, but you certainly stretched the truth as far as it would go."

Esther giggled. "I can't see that it's against the commandments."

"I had my suspicions." Mattie blew a puff of air from between her lips. "I'm just going to have to tell Caleb the truth, though I'm not looking forward to it." She gave Esther the stink eye. "And you are going to have to stop inviting him over for puzzle night."

"Okay, okay. No more inviting Caleb for puzzles or sunsets. But there's nothing we can do about tonight. Levi asked him to come over."

Mattie had been dreading the conversation ever since Caleb had told her he loved her yesterday. "*Ach*, *vell*. It can't be helped. When he comes, you send him into the kitchen alone, and I'll rip off the Band-Aid. Quicker is better."

Aunt Esther nodded. "I agree. I will leave you two alone for a few minutes and then I'll come in and give Caleb a whole plate of cookies and a glass of milk. That will make him feel better."

"I hope so."

Someone knocked on the door. Mattie's heart thumped against her chest. She hated awkward conversations. She hated the thought of hurting Caleb's feelings. Despite his nausea, he had been a faithful and dependable campaign worker. She didn't love him, but she was very grateful for his support.

Mattie couldn't jump up and get the door because of her foot. Esther disappeared down the hall, while Mattie waited with her cast propped on the nearest kitchen chair. "Mattie," Esther called. "Can you come out here? Put on a coat."

Did Esther think it was better if Mattie broke the news to Caleb outside so he wouldn't even have to come into the house? It would make for an easier getaway. She grabbed her crutches, which were propped against the table, and hobbled down the hall. Esther stood with her hand on the doorknob, and all Mattie could see in the doorway were a pair of legs and a pair of hands wrapped around a monstrous vase of flowers.

The sight of flowers momentarily stole her breath. Only one person had ever brought her flowers, and the hands wrapped around that vase looked suspiciously like Freeman's. She didn't know whether to be annoyed that he had the nerve to show up or thrilled that he was trying again. She swallowed her annoyance. He'd been kind enough to spend all that money on flowers. She might as well hear what he had to say for himself.

Freeman leaned to the side and peeked out from behind the bouquet. The tentative and dazzling smile he gave her made her heart pitter-patter like rain against the window— rare San Luis Valley rain. "I brought you flowers," he said.

His smile momentarily struck her mute. She swallowed hard. "Again?" was all she could think to say.

His smile got even wider. "Caleb sat on the last ones."

"They're beautiful."

"Not as pretty as you."

The way he looked at her made her knees feel like Jell-O. "*Denki*. That's very nice." The flowers didn't make up for his many flaws, but she could be convinced that he wasn't beyond all hope.

His eyes flashed with a secret delight. "I also brought you two hundred other things."

"Two . . . two hundred other things?"

Freeman handed the unwieldy bouquet to Esther and stepped back and off the porch. Mattie gasped when she saw a huge crowd of people standing in Aunt Esther's front yard—two hundred, if Freeman had counted right. Freeman helped Mattie put on her coat, and then she limped out the door on her crutches. As soon as people saw her, they clapped and cheered and made an impressive amount of noise. Lord willing, they wouldn't wake Winnie or the baby.

Sarah and Sadie stood right up front, beaming like two propane lanterns. Over a dozen Amish *youngie* congregated around them, including Caleb, who was clapping so hard, Mattie could hear his individual claps amidst the hullaballoo. Cathy Larsen and Dewey stood in the crowd with Tami Moore, the mayor, and Margaret, the woman who took notes and was tasked with throwing unruly citizens out of council meetings. Mattie's heart took flight at the sight of two posters held up by the same person in the back. MATTIE FOR TOWN COUNCIL one said. WE STAND WITH MATTIE said the other.

Mattie recognized many of the people she had met and talked to while passing out flyers and eating hot dogs around a bonfire. There were farmers and retirees, teenagers and mothers with small children. It was a slice of Byler itself. And Mattie felt as if she were floating five inches off the ground.

"Mattie," Cathy called. "You can't quit. Byler needs you."

"We need you," someone else yelled.

"Mattie, Mattie, Mattie," the crowd chanted. The sound reverberated through Mattie's entire body. Hearing two hundred or so people yell her name was quite a heady experience, but nothing was as dizzying as looking into Freeman's eyes and seeing herself reflected there. For a brief moment, they were the only two people in the world. The campaign didn't matter, her ankle didn't matter, and his many faults didn't matter. In fact, staring at him, she couldn't remember a single flaw. He gazed at her as if she was the only person who mattered to him. But . . . surely, he didn't want her to get back in the race. He wanted her to quit. He'd told her dozens of times.

He must have sensed her hesitation. Stepping onto the porch, he sidled close to her. "They're in love with you, Mattie."

Her pulse raced out of control. "I thought you didn't approve," she said, breathlessly hopeful.

"This is something you want to do, Mattie. This is something you need to do. Forgive me for not realizing it sooner. The thought of you getting hurt made me ill, but I was only thinking of myself. The decision to quit made you miserable, and I can't bear to see you so unhappy."

"But what about Sarah and Sadie and the others?"

"As Sadie reminds me daily, she is old enough to make her own choices. My *schwesteren* are squarely behind you." He leaned in closer. "And so am I."

Mattie trembled, and it wasn't because of the cold.

He motioned toward the crowd. "Bill has been a scab on this town for far too long. You've given people something to hope for. You can't abandon them, even if you think it's for the best." He grinned sheepishly. "Even if I used to think it was for the best. You were brave enough to run in the first place. You're brave enough to see it through."

Being timid wasn't Mattie's weakness. But she could be selfish and reckless at times, and she didn't want to make those mistakes again, especially not when other people were counting on her to do the right thing.

Dat would disapprove no matter what she decided. Bill Isom would think of more ways to make trouble. Aunt Esther would insist that Mattie watch the sunset every night. But all these people, including Freeman, thought she should run. Nobody here believed she was selfish or foolish or even impulsive.

Aunt Esther had deposited the vase inside, and she came out onto the porch with Uncle Levi, still with the binky hanging from her ear. Uncle Levi puckered his lips, obviously trying to hide a grin. He looked at Esther. "I think your plan has gone horribly wrong."

Esther sighed in resignation. "I think it has."

Mattie burst into laughter. So did Esther and Levi. "It's too late to register to vote," Mattie said.

Esther growled and shook her finger in Mattie's direction. "Just be grateful I don't find you a widower who likes to do puzzles."

Mattie widened her eyes in mock horror. "Please. No more puzzles."

People laughed and cheered and chatted, and the impromptu campaign rally was obviously too disorganized for ·Cathy. Taking matters into her own hands, she stepped up on the porch next to Mattie. "So, Mandy, are you back in the race or not?"

"It's Mattie," Freeman said, trying to be helpful.

Cathy turned on Freeman and puckered her whole face. "Has it ever occurred to you that maybe I have a speech impediment? Or maybe I'm just a huge Barry Manilow fan." She spent her ire on Freeman then turned to Mattie. "Are you back in the race or not?"

Mattie curled her lips and nodded. "For sure and certain."

Cathy's "I'm happy" expression was slightly cheerier than her "I don't like you" expression, but Mattie knew her well enough to recognize the difference. Cathy put her fingers to her mouth and whistled loudly enough to get everyone's attention. "You can all go home now," she shouted. "But make sure you tell all your neighbors. Write in Mattie Zook for *all* of Byler. Don't let Bill fool you. That is not his slogan, and I'm thinking of suing him for patent violation. And be sure to spell it correctly—with two *T*'s."

More cheering and smiling. "Vote for Mattie," the mayor yelled.

Freeman held up his hand. "Before you leave, be sure to step inside and take a look at Esther Kiem's quilt shop. She's got authentic Amish quilts, baby quilts, and wedding quilts. Quilts for every occasion."

"*Ach, du lieva*, Freeman," Esther said, flustered at being the center of attention. "What do you think you're doing?"

Freeman winked at Mattie. He truly was the smartest

boy Mattie had ever met. A few quilt sales would soften Esther up like a butter on a warm day.

A dozen or so people strolled into the house to take a look at Esther's quilts. Esther rushed in behind them, excitedly shushing them so they wouldn't wake *die kinner*. Others got in line for a chance to shake Mattie's hand and wish her well. Many people handed her money. Freeman pulled out a tiny notepad from his pocket and wrote down names and amounts.

After the crowd had thinned out, Sadie and Sarah ran up the porch steps and caught Mattie in a three-way hug. "*Ach*, Mattie, isn't it exciting?" Sadie said. "I have a *gute* feeling you're going to win."

Sarah could never resist correcting Sadie. "Lord willing."

"Lord willing," Sadie repeated. She reached across Sarah and poked Freeman in the chest. "And I guess I shouldn't call you a chicken anymore, though I'm going to anyway."

Freeman rolled his eyes and pointed to the spot where she'd poked him. "I'm going to get a bruise."

Sadie giggled. "It serves you right."

"Freeman has been a great help to me," Mattie said. "In too many ways to count." His grateful smile took her breath away.

Sadie would probably die before she gave Freeman any credit. "He hasn't hardly done nothing except show up places. What kind of help is that?" She pulled a cell phone from her coat pocket. "Sarah and I did better than that. Look what Dewey helped us make."

She tapped on the screen, and a video started playing. Sadie and Sarah appeared first, talking about what had really happened at the debate two nights ago. They smiled and laughed, and Sadie told how she batted away a whole string of firecrackers. Cathy was even in the video, showing her photo of Bill's nephew in a "Vote for Maddie" T-shirt. Finally, words in bold red letters scrolled up the screen. "Her ankle is broken, but she's still in the race. Write in Mattie Zook for ALL of Byler. Be sure to spell it right."

Mattie grinned. "*Ach*, that is very nice. You both look so pretty. But how did you know I would decide to get back in the race?"

Sadie giggled. "We knew Freeman would be able to talk you into it. I'm not sure what you see in him, but it's obvious you like him something wonderful."

Freeman crossed his arms over his chest and frowned, but his eyes flashed with affection. "Thanks a lot."

Mattie thought her face might burst into flames. As much as she'd tried to talk herself out of it, she truly did adore Freeman, even though he was the most irritating boy she'd ever met. Her heart did seven cartwheels. *Ach*, she loved Freeman to the moon and back, and the feeling made her dizzy.

Someone cleared his throat behind her. Caleb stood next to the porch. "Um, Mattie, can I talk to you?"

The breath whooshed out of her like a popped balloon. Though she'd rather break her other ankle, now was as *gute* a time as any to break Caleb's heart. She pressed her lips together and remembered the Band-Aid. Quick and relatively painless was the way to do it.

Freeman gave her a doubtful glance, but she couldn't do anything about his feelings right now. She awkwardly maneuvered her crutches then her foot off the porch. Would Caleb be more or less likely to cry with or without an audience? "Maybe we should go to the side of the house where we can have some privacy."

He stuffed his hands in his pockets. "Okay. Do you need help?"

"*Nae*. I'm fine." She limped around the corner of the

house where silver-white frost covered the lawn. This side of the house was in shade most of the day. "Caleb," she began.

He obviously wanted to speak first. "Mattie, I think we should break up."

She felt her eyebrows inch up her forehead. "Break up?"

He tried to take her hand, but her fingers were wrapped around her crutch handles. He ended up awkwardly clasping her wrist between his thumb and fingers. "I know I told you I love you, but I'm taking it back. I just don't think a relationship with you is going to work. The last thing I want is to hurt you. Can you ever forgive me?"

Mattie bit her tongue to keep from smiling. "Forgive you?"

He released her wrist and paced back and forth in front of her, leaving a path where his boots trampled the frost. His breath came out in shallow puffs, and he looked truly upset. "I know how much you depend on me to help with the campaign, but I just can't do it anymore. I'm pretty sure I have an ulcer, and I'm too young to have an ulcer, and I just think that as long as you are a candidate for town council, it's best that we don't date anymore."

Caleb thought they'd been dating? *Ach*, *vell*, he was pouring his heart out to her. She wasn't going to argue. "I see," she said.

He stopped pacing and pinned her with an intense and compassionate gaze. "This is all my fault. Blame everything on me. Please don't be mad at me forever."

She tried to hide her relief and at the same time show a certain level of disappointment. "*Denki* for your honesty. It's better to do it this way, just like ripping off a Band-Aid."

"*Jah*. Like a Band-Aid." He nodded thoughtfully. "I hope I said the right things. This is the first time I've broken someone's heart." He glanced behind him. "I need to go.

Sarah wants to show me the video she and Dewey made, and she's invited me to her house for pumpkin muffins."

"Sounds *appeditlich*."

He turned to leave then stopped. "I just want you to know that if I were old enough to vote, I would vote for you, even if I got in trouble with my *dat*."

"*Denki*, Caleb. That means a lot to me."

Now that he'd delivered his message, it seemed he couldn't leave fast enough. "Okay, then. See you at *gmay*." He turned and practically ran around the corner of the house.

Mattie exhaled deeply. That had gone better than she could have possibly imagined. She smiled to herself. Caleb had given a wonderful *gute* break-up speech. She was impressed. That boy would do well in life.

Freeman came strolling around the corner of the house, concern saturating his features. "Caleb said you're upset. Is everything okay?"

"Oh, Freeman," she exclaimed. She clapped her hand over her mouth to keep the laughter from escaping.

He must have mistaken the sudden movement for distress, because he ran to her side and wrapped his strong arms all the way around her. Mattie thought she had died and gone to heaven. Melting into his warm embrace was the best feeling in the whole world. Ever. She'd be perfectly happy to stand like this all evening until she had to go to the bathroom or needed to break for a snack.

"What's the matter, *heartzley*?" he cooed. "How can I help?"

Her body shook with laughter, and her happiness soon exploded from between her lips. "*Ach*, Freeman. I'm fine. I'm fine. Boys are just so *dumm*."

He nudged her away from him, looking mildly amused, curiously puzzled, and acutely irritated all at the same time.

"*Dumm?* I don't see what's so *dumm* about it. I just wanted to see if you were okay."

She pulled out of his arms and laughed until the irritation overtook every other emotion on his face. "I'm sorry," she said, the words tripping from her lips like a babbling brook. "I'm not laughing at you, even though you are aggravating at times."

"I'm not *that* aggravating," he muttered.

She took a deep breath and tried to regain her composure. "Caleb just broke up with me."

One eyebrow quirked upward. "You were dating?"

The laughter bubbled up again. "Nope. Not dating. And apparently, he doesn't love me anymore."

Freeman's face relaxed into something less cross. "*Vell,* that was quick."

"The sneaking around has been hard on him, he thinks he has an ulcer, and not even the force of his love can withstand an election."

Freeman sidled close to her and slid his arms around her waist. She thought she might faint. "We've been through bonfires, police cars, broken ankles, firecrackers, and smashed roses together. I would never let an ulcer come between us." His soft, low tone caressed her skin. "My love can withstand anything."

"I suppose it can," she murmured.

"Don't suppose, Mattie. Count on it. You can always be sure of me." He bent his head and brought his mouth heart-stoppingly close to hers before pausing for a breathless moment. "Are you still mad at me? Because I really want to kiss you."

"*Ach,* I'm mildly irritated and also fairly certain I love you."

His lips twitched in amusement. "Are you irritated because you love me or because I'm so irritating?"

"*Jah.*"

He chuckled. "The perfect reason to kiss."

He tightened his arms around her and brought his lips down on hers, sending an electric shockwave all the way to her toes. This was even better than his embrace, and if she didn't need to breathe, she'd be perfectly happy to stand like this with her lips attached to his forever.

She dropped her crutches, snaked her arms around his neck, and pulled him closer. She'd kissed boys during games of Please or Displease, but kissing Freeman was like nothing she'd ever experienced before. It was better than peanut butter chocolate pie, better than brilliant orange sunsets, better than a bonfire on a crisp fall evening. For sure and certain it was even better than winning an election, even though Mattie didn't know what that felt like yet.

After several blissful seconds, Freeman pulled away and held tightly to her elbow while he picked up her crutches. "Just so we're clear," he said, smiling as if he couldn't help himself, "you and I are a couple now, right? Because I don't want to jump to conclusions like Caleb did."

She giggled and nodded enthusiastically. "We are, even though you're too blunt and spend way too much money on flowers."

"I had to make a big impression and an even bigger apology." His look was so full of love, Mattie's heart nearly burst from her chest. "And I didn't want you falling in love with Caleb first. I had to be reckless."

Mattie laughed. "*Ach, vell*, not much danger of that. Even if I loved Caleb, he isn't likely to fall in love with me again. I'm not exactly the girl any boy wants for a *fraa*."

"You're the girl *I* want for a *fraa*."

Her heart tried to pound its way out of her chest. The wind was knocked out of her for the second time in a week. "I . . . I . . . am?" she managed to ask.

"*Jah*, you are." He kissed her swiftly then searched her face, his lips twitching with amusement. "But maybe it's too early to lay it all out there like that. You and Caleb just broke up."

Mattie giggled and cuffed him on the arm. "Don't blame me for Caleb's wild imagination. I'm just a nice Amish girl minding my own business."

"*Ach*, I don't know if you've ever minded your own business."

She gawked at him in mock indignation. "Can I help it if other people are constantly stepping on my toes. I can't just stand there and let my toes get smashed, though Cathy says I'd be more interesting with eight toes."

"I don't think you could get more interesting, but it might be a *gute* way to get voters to feel sorry for you. Voters like an underdog. That's what Cathy says."

"*Vell*, then voters should love me."

Freeman gazed at her as if she were a chocolate peanut butter truffle. "They do. And so do I."

He had to stop looking at her like that or she'd forget her own name. "Okay," she groaned. "Enough of that. Flirting will have to wait until after the election."

He pasted a serious, no-nonsense expression on his face and straightened his spine. "Election first, then romance. Got it."

Mattie couldn't help but laugh at the teasingly earnest look on his face. "You have no intention of being sensible, do you?"

He wiped a grin from his face. "I'm always sensible, but you'll have to forgive me because I've never been irrationally in love before. I might irritate you without meaning to."

It was breathtaking to think that Freeman loved her like that. "You irritate me all the time. I've learned to live with it."

His eyes grew round and pitiful. "You're so long-suffering, Mattie. I don't deserve you."

She laughed. "I've never heard one boy pile so much manure on one girl."

He reached out and slid his strong arms around her again, pulling her close enough so she could feel his warm breath on her cheek. "Every word I said is true, Mattie. I'm wildly in love with you, and I can't begin to deserve you. But that doesn't mean I won't try."

She pressed her palm to his warm cheek. "I certainly hope you'll never stop trying."

"I won't. Before or after the election." He bent over to kiss her again, and she wedged her index finger between their lips. He drew back in surprise. "No more kissing?"

"I don't know what your bishop says, but mine is pretty strict about kissing before marriage. I try to be obedient when I can."

Exasperation danced with affection on his face. "If you ask me, it's an inconvenient time to be obedient."

"To paraphrase Caleb, *there is no convenient time for obedience*. Besides, I already told you, no romance until after the election. I don't need more distractions."

"Is that all I am, a distraction?"

She gave him her brightest smile. "*Ach*, Freeman, you're much more than a distraction. Since you're going to make me say it, you mean everything to me—the moon, the sun, and the stars. Does that make you feel better?"

His eyes sparkled. "I've never felt better in my life."

"*Gute*, but you have to admit that kissing is a distraction. I mean, even now, you won't quit staring at my lips."

He turned a light shade of red, nudged his gaze upward to meet hers, and chuckled. "Okay. I suppose you're right."

She puckered her lips teasingly. "I usually am."

"Well, I won't argue with that. I don't want to distract

you, but is it okay if I give you a congratulations kiss when you win the election?"

"What if I lose?"

"Then I can try to make you feel better with a kiss." He pumped his eyebrows up and down.

Mattie hadn't thought it was possible to be this happy. "My bishop won't approve."

"How much disapproval can he send from Pennsylvania?"

"My *dat* manages to send a whole bucketful of disapproval in every letter."

Cathy stuck her head around the corner of the house. "There you are." She hobbled toward them, a look of annoyance etched into her face. "I hate to break up the party, but you still have a campaign to run. We're two days behind, and Bill has already posted three more videos on YouTube. Am I the only one with a sense of urgency?"

Freeman winked at Mattie. "You're right, Cathy. It's time to finish what we started."

"Good," Cathy said. "Because Dewey has his phone ready." She motioned toward Mattie. "We need you to come inside and make a statement."

"I don't know if Aunt Esther will like me making a campaign video in her home."

"The video was Esther's idea. She sold sixteen quilts after the rally so she's in a good mood. Let's get in there before she changes her mind."

Nothing could soften Aunt Esther's heart like a *gute* day of quilt sales. Lord willing, Mattie's days of running a secret campaign had come to an end.

Chapter 16

Mattie's arms felt like jelly, and her back was so sore, she wanted to lie down on Cathy's kitchen table and take a nap. At this point, she didn't even care who had won the election. She just wanted to sleep.

Instead of stretching across Cathy's table, Mattie opted to sit in one of Cathy's uncomfortable kitchen chairs, prop her crutches against the table, and slip her boot off her good foot. The toes on her other foot were wrapped six inches thick in blankets. After pulling the blankets away from her cast, she set them on the chair next to her. Then she shrugged off her coat, retrieved a tissue from her apron pocket, and dabbed at the thick layer of zinc oxide sunscreen on her nose. Cathy had insisted on the sunscreen. November in Byler was cold, but it was also wonderful sunny, and Cathy didn't want Mattie's nose to be beet-red for her acceptance speech. Not that most people would be interested in an acceptance or a concession speech. Mattie could count on two hands the number of people who cared enough about the election to gather at Cathy's house after the polls closed. Most Englischers didn't want to venture into the cold when they could hear election results on the evening news.

Cathy handed Mattie a cup of something warm and

chocolaty. "Sugar-free cocoa," she said. "It's not very good, but I'm off sugar, and this is all I have in the house."

Mattie took a sip. Cathy was right. It wasn't very *gute*, but at least it was warm, and Mattie thought she might never be warm again. She and about twenty other people had spent all day standing on street corners in Byler waving signs that read: WRITE IN MATTIE ZOOK FOR TOWN COUNCIL. VOTE TODAY. If there was anyone in Byler who didn't know she was running, it wasn't her fault. She, Cathy, and Freeman had done everything they knew to do. If she didn't win, she had to believe it was Gotte's will. She would accept that, even though it would have been nice to know sooner so she wouldn't have gone to all this work. But she really couldn't regret running for town council. The campaign had brought her and Freeman together, and if that was the only *gute* thing that came out of it, that would be more than enough. Her cup was full to overflowing.

Someone knocked on Cathy's front door, but before she could open it, Dewey marched into the kitchen carrying a white box and a boyish grin. "Hey, Grandma. Hey, Mattie. I brought a cake."

"Well, that's real nice of you," Cathy said. "We can celebrate even if Mattie doesn't win."

"It's got raspberry jelly and vanilla cream filling." Dewey lifted the lid to reveal a quarter sheet cake with white icing and blue and yellow frosting flowers. In big blue letters it read, "Congratulations, Dewey."

Cathy's face puckered with a thousand wrinkles. "Uh, they got the name wrong."

Dewey's neck turned red and splotchy. "We didn't know if Mattie would win, so we didn't want to jinx it. But I got extra credit in my Careers and Technology class and my Colorado History class for working on Mattie's campaign.

I got a 3.9 GPA for the term. Mom was so happy, she ordered this cake."

Cathy slapped her knee and winced. "Well, Dewey, you're about the smartest boy I ever met. You need a haircut, but other than that, I couldn't be prouder."

Putting Dewey's name on the cake had been a wonderful *gute* idea. That way, no matter if she won or lost, no one would feel bad about eating it.

Sadie and her Englisch friend Kirsten arrived next. "*Ach*," Sadie sighed, unwrapping the baby-blue scarf from around her neck. "It is so cold out there. I thought my nose was going to freeze off." She grinned at Mattie. "But it was worth the shivering. We had at least twenty people honk and wave at us, and one lady stopped and told us she was voting for you for sure and certain. And the family in the house on the corner gave us doughnuts and milk for lunch."

"*Denki* for helping me, Sadie and Kirsten. I couldn't have done any of this without you."

Kirsten grinned, her face red with the cold. "It got me out of school for the day. Totally worth it."

Sadie grabbed Mattie's hand. "You're going to win for sure and certain. Everybody I know voted for you." Sadie and Kirsten oohed and aahed over the cake, took one sip of cocoa, and poured it down the drain when Cathy wasn't looking.

Sarah and Caleb arrived shortly after Sadie and Kirsten, along with half a dozen others who had stood on street corners. Sarah had volunteered to stand on the corner closest to the school where the voting was taking place, and she had somehow convinced Caleb to go with her. Caleb helped Sarah off with her coat, and Mattie smiled to herself. Sarah was a much more suitable girl for Caleb than Mattie would ever be. Mattie was unpredictable, stubborn, and fearless. Sarah was pretty, obedient, and sensible. She would never give Caleb a reason to throw up ever again. They were perfect for each other.

Freeman was the last to arrive, almost an hour after the polls had closed. He walked through the door and immediately scanned the room for Mattie. She knew that because she had been watching for him, and when he finally caught sight of her, his smile nearly blinded her. In three long strides he was at her side. He removed his hat, coat, and gloves and took her hand in his. She immediately pulled from his grasp. "*Ach*, your hands are like ice."

She could get lost in that clear blue gaze of his. "I ran out of hand warmers at about four o'clock."

"I should have given you more this morning. Cathy has a whole case in her van."

He grinned. "I have to confess, I helped Marion Whittaker fix his truck. He lives just down the road from my assigned corner, and he asked me to take a look at it. I hope that was okay. His wife duct-taped the campaign sign to the telephone pole until we were finished."

Mattie loved Freeman for so many reasons, but his unselfishness and *gute* heart were right at the top of the list. "Of course you had to help him. Did you get it to work?"

"*Jah*. It's an old truck, and it's going to die soon enough, but the fix should give him a few thousand more miles." He gave her a tentative smile. "Lord willing, you didn't lose any votes because of me."

"*Ach*, helping a neighbor is more important than winning an election. You did the right thing."

Mischief sparkled in his eyes. "But I really want that congratulations kiss."

Mattie gave him a wry smile. "You'll only have yourself to blame if you don't get it."

He slumped his shoulders in mock dejection. "That's what I'm afraid of."

Another knock at the door. Aunt Esther and Uncle Levi bustled into the kitchen and out of the cold. A ribbon of warmth traveled up Mattie's spine. "*Ach*, I didn't know you were coming."

Aunt Esther took off her coat and bonnet and gave Mattie a sensible smile. A rolled-up dollar bill was tucked behind her ear. "Heaven knows we tried to talk you out of this, but it's an important night for you. We wanted to be here. Levi's *mamm* is watching Winnie and Junior." She scrunched her lips to one side of her face. "Besides, because of your campaign, I've sold twenty-three quilts in less than two weeks. I would be ungrateful indeed if I didn't give you a little credit." She reached out and pulled Mattie into a hug. "I never would have been brave enough and stubborn enough to do what you did. The others are grateful too, though they'll never thank you."

"I don't need their thanks."

"But you deserve it. So I will say *denki* for all of us. If we get to drive our buggies on the main roads, it will be because of you." Aunt Esther reached into her apron pocket and pulled out a letter. "This came for you today. It looked important, so I brought it over."

Mattie glanced at the return address. It was from her lawyer in Leola. Since she'd decided to run for town council, Mattie had barely thought about the garbage their neighbor had been dumping on their property. Her lawsuit was the reason Dat had banished her to Colorado. She tore open the envelope and scanned the letter. Her heart skipped a beat. She handed the letter to Freeman. "Does this say what I think it says?"

Freeman read the letter, his eyes getting bigger with every line.

"What does it say?" Uncle Levi asked.

Mattie glanced through it again. "I think it means that my lawyer is going to make a lot of money."

Freeman looked as surprised as she felt. "It turns out the people who were dumping garbage on your *dat*'s property were also dumping garbage and chemicals on other farms in the area. They're being fined by the government, and they have to pay to have it cleaned up." He read the last line again. "They want to give Mattie a special award for filing that lawsuit and bringing the problem to their attention."

Mattie grabbed her crutches and stood up. "My lawyer says I get some money in the settlement, but as the Amish aren't supposed to sue people, I suppose I'll let the lawyer keep it."

Dewey had been listening in to their conversation. "You should donate it to a charity, like the Dewey Markham College Fund." He grinned when they all looked at him as if he had a cat sitting on his head. "I'm just kidding—about my college fund, I mean. There's a food bank in Monte Vista that likes it when you give them money."

"That's a wonderful *gute* idea," Aunt Esther said. She glanced at Mattie. "Your *dat* is going to be very happy that there won't be any more trash dumped on his farm."

"Dat *will* be glad." But he'd never admit to being glad about it, because then he'd have to acknowledge that he'd been wrong about Mattie, and he'd probably rather die.

Dewey's phone rang. He answered it and motioned for everyone to be quiet. "Mom says we need to turn on the TV. They're reporting on local races."

The whole group seemed to move as one into Cathy's living room where her massive television set was already on. A pretty woman dressed in pink was talking about one of the races in Colorado Springs while pictures of the candidates and the number of votes flashed behind her. Mattie's stomach lodged in her throat as the report focused on towns in the southwest part of the state. The feeling was much like standing on the edge of the rocks at the lake about to jump in—exhilarating and terrifying. Freeman sidled close to her and took her hand. She didn't pull away this time. She didn't care who saw them clasping hands in the middle of Cathy's living room. If there ever was a time she needed some physical support, this was it.

"And now," the woman said, "here are the results from the San Luis Valley area."

Mattie's heart did a belly flop.

Byler was small enough that the reporter didn't even say it by name, but a list of small towns and the results of their races scrolled along the screen. Mattie held her breath. Freeman held his breath. It seemed there was no breathing going on in the whole room.

Then she saw it.

Byler Town Council Race—Mattie Zook 847.
Bill Isom 232.

Everyone but Caleb erupted into cheers. Caleb had been drinking his second mug of sugar-free cocoa and had missed reading the tally. He soon caught on and cheered as if the win had been his doing. Freeman squeezed Mattie's hand, which was as much affection as either of them dared show surrounded by so many people. Mattie didn't realize she'd started crying until she felt a tear plop on her hand. It was over. And now she could stop dreading firecrackers and YouTube videos.

She and everyone there had done something big and amazing. A Pennsylvanian Amish girl had beat the Byler incumbent with a write-in campaign, and she'd done it without the support of most of the *gmayna*. Was this Gotte's will? She didn't know, but she was going to use the victory for the *gute* of everybody. The thought of being able to get rid of that buggy ordinance made her giddy.

Freeman looked at her, all the things he couldn't say shining in his eyes. She caught her breath. The results of the election were stunning, but the most important and astonishing thing she'd done this year was win Freeman's heart.

Everybody lined up to congratulate Mattie on her victory, and Freeman led her to a chair so she could sit and rest her leg while she talked to her friends. Dewey's phone rang, and he handed it to Mattie. It was Tami Moore to report that her sister had just given birth to a ten-pound baby girl and to tell Mattie how excited she was to work with her on the town council. "Fred will be outnumbered. Maybe he'll figure out how to get along."

They ate Dewey's cake and drank plain old water, because sugar-free cocoa isn't any way to celebrate. Most people left after the cake, leaving Mattie, Freeman, Dewey, and Cathy standing in the kitchen savoring the victory, or in Mattie's case, wishing for her bed. Her ankle and armpits and smile ached from overuse. All she wanted to do was sleep for three days straight. She barely had enough energy to sit upright in Cathy's uncomfortable kitchen chair.

Freeman cleared the used paper plates and cups, and Cathy swiped a dishrag over the tabletop. "Okay, then. That was a very nice party. Now it's time to get to work," Cathy said.

Mattie felt like a wilted dandelion. "Time to work on what?"

Cathy pulled a notebook from a drawer and set it on the table. "There is a piece of property south of town owned by the Bureau of Land Management. If we could convince them to give it to us, we could build a huge pickleball complex. The people are wild for pickleball, and I think we should give the people what they want."

Freeman eyed Mattie, his eyes glowing with sympathy and maybe a touch of anticipation. He had promised her a congratulations kiss. "It's been a long day. Let me take Mattie home, and you two can talk about this next week."

Cathy was eighty-four. How could she not be exhausted? "As your chief of staff, I strongly recommend that we get started on this. Who knows if someone else with deeper pockets will beat us to that land?"

"We all need to go home, Grandma," Dewey said. "Mattie won't even be sworn in until January. We have time."

Cathy tilted her head in Dewey's direction. "I forgot to tell you, Mattie. I made Dewey your deputy chief of staff. He's going to get you on social media."

Mattie wasn't sure that she needed a deputy chief of staff, especially since she didn't know what a deputy chief of staff was. "That sounds like a great idea." Everything could be sorted out tomorrow or the next day or, if Cathy had mercy on her, next month.

Freeman handed Mattie her crutches. "Come. I'll take you home."

Mattie stood and positioned her crutches under her arms. The doctor said she could have a walking cast in a few weeks. That was *gute*. Her underarms had scabs.

Freeman must have seen her wince. "Do you want me to carry you? It would be less painful."

She stifled a smile. "And much more exciting, I'm sure."

He raised his hands and backed away, chuckling softly. "I'm just trying to be helpful."

Freeman ran outside and hitched up his horse while Mattie gathered her things and said goodbye to Cathy and Dewey. Cathy wouldn't accept her thanks because she insisted she was only doing her civic duty. Mattie would definitely have to make her a cake. *Ach*, *vell*, maybe not a cake, since Cathy was off gluten, sugar, and dairy. As far as

Mattie knew, the only things Cathy could eat were vegetables and potato chips. Maybe Aunt Esther could help Mattie make a thank-you quilt. Mattie didn't quilt, but she could hold the baby while Esther quilted.

Freeman returned to the house to fetch Mattie. He stayed right beside her as she hobbled to the buggy; then he helped her climb inside. Freeman spread a blanket over her legs and made Mattie tremble when his fingers brushed against hers.

When they'd settled into the buggy, they sighed in unison, as if they'd both decided to be relieved at the same time. Mattie glanced at Freeman and laughed. "I think we're both ready for this day to be over."

"I'm not quite ready. I've got one more thing I have to do." Even in the dimness, she could see his white teeth flash in a grin.

Could he hear her heart beating? Because *she* could. "Something you *have* to do? You really don't *have* to do anything if you don't want to."

"I've never wanted anything more. I've always wanted to kiss a town councilor."

She giggled. "Always?"

"Oh, *jah*. And by *always,* I mean since about half an hour ago." He slid his arms around her and pulled her close.

Mattie didn't mean to ruin the moment, but a wide, involuntary yawn escaped her lips. She'd been up since four this morning, and even her hair was tired. Several strands had escaped her *kapp* and tickled her cheek and neck, begging her to go to bed and let them rest.

Freeman sighed and moved back to his side of the seat. "No matter how badly I want to kiss you, you need your sleep, and I'd rather have your full attention. I have a feeling Cathy will be knocking on your door at six tomorrow morning with a proposal for a whole slew of lampposts."

Freeman was right. Mattie wouldn't fully appreciate his kiss in her drowsy state. She leaned back against the seat. "Okay, then. I won't get all huffy about it, but I don't want to hear any excuses tomorrow."

He laughed. "No more excuses. Not even if the bishop watches over my shoulder."

She folded her arms. "*Ach, vell*, I don't know about that. I won't invite him over if you won't."

Freeman jiggled the reins, and the horse started moving. "Now that you don't need a campaign manager, I was thinking that maybe I could be your driver. Every town councilor needs a driver."

"I suppose that would work, but I was thinking of asking Caleb to drive me around. He enjoys it so much."

"I don't wonder but he does."

Bright red and blue lights flashed behind them, and Mattie turned to look. "Um, Freeman?"

"I see it." He growled and pulled over to the side of the road.

The police car pulled behind them. A police officer shined a light into the buggy. This particular policewoman was starting to feel like an old friend. "Sir, I'm sorry, but there's a town ordinance prohibiting buggies on this road. I'm afraid I'm going to have to write you a ticket." She wrote down Freeman's information and strolled back to her car.

Freeman glanced at Mattie, the irritation oozing from his pores. "Someday we're going to laugh about this." But at least for Freeman, it didn't look like someday was going to be anytime soon.

Mattie, on the other hand, couldn't contain her laughter. She laughed until tears rolled down her cheeks. Not even Freeman's annoyed expression could dampen her mirth.

Bill Isom might have lost the election, but he'd just gotten his revenge.

Chapter 17

Eight months later

"Are you sure about this?" Tami asked.

Mattie nodded. "It's been my plan all along."

"But I had hoped that maybe you'd have so much fun that you wouldn't want to quit."

Standing in the elementary school foyer, Mattie felt the familiar twinge of regret at the base of her throat, but she'd made her decision over a year ago, and she wasn't going to back down now. What she would be getting more than made up for what she was leaving behind. Being on the town council paled in comparison to being Freeman Sensenig's *fraa*. "I have had fun. Working on the town council hasn't been like anything I expected. But we re-pealed the buggy ordinance and did a lot of other good things. It's time to let someone else more qualified take over."

"The only qualification you need is that you have to care deeply. You're overqualified." Tami wasn't really trying to talk Mattie out of anything. They'd had this conversation several times over the months.

"There are many people who care about Byler. And it's

time for an Englischer to take over. The Amish still flash me suspicious looks in church."

Tami shrugged. "Well, at least Bill has moved away. He's not likely to come back just to run for town council again. Especially not when he has the chance to be mayor of a much bigger place."

Four weeks after the election, Bill and his wife had moved to Alamosa, and Bill was running for mayor. Lord willing, the people in Alamosa would be able to see right through Bill's flashy photos and fancy YouTube videos. He'd posted a video last week with the title, "Bill Isom Rescues Local Resident." It was a video of Bill—with his shirt off—pulling a cat out of a tree, which would have been heroic if it hadn't been Bill's cat and the tree hadn't been a mere six feet tall. But mercifully, he had shaved his chest hair for the video.

Tami's features softened into something like regret. "I wish you'd stay on just until the next election."

"I want to be baptized something wonderful."

"I know." Tami gave her an affectionate smile. "You and Freeman can't get married until you're baptized, and you can't be baptized until you quit the town council. I'm not blaming you. This is all Freeman's doing."

"Indeed, it is. If I didn't adore him so much, I'd stay. But I love Freeman way more than I like being on the council. A thousand times more. I'll survive."

"I don't know if *I* will."

Mattie grinned. "You'll be fine. You'll be better than fine. Like Cathy always says, you've got girl power."

Tami didn't like that description. "Girl power. It sounds like a teenage superhero movie."

Freeman opened the swinging glass door and strode into the school, grinning like he'd never felt sad a day in his life. His smile made Mattie's heart beat a little faster. He was practically glowing. He clapped his hands together. "So is everything ready?"

Tami scolded him with her eyes. "You've got a lot of nerve, coming in here looking so smug. Don't you even feel a little bit sorry for me?"

Freeman looked as if he could float off the ground with only a slight nudge. "Sorry, Tami, but I can't even pretend to feel bad for you today." He gazed at Mattie, and his eyes flashed with affection so deep, she could have dived into it. "Tami, you know I have no tact, and I'm not even going to try to be sensitive to your feelings. I'm happier than I have a right to be, and that's the honest truth."

Tami gave Mattie a sideways glance. "I don't know how you put up with him."

"I don't either. He's my burden to bear, for sure and certain."

Freeman's jaw dropped in mock indignation. "I'm not a burden. I'm more of a plague."

Mattie giggled. "Yep. I was trying to spare your feelings."

Tami pulled out her phone. "It's almost time. I'm going to take a seat." She threw her arms around Mattie. "You're still allowed to come to town council meetings, aren't you?"

"I'm sure I am."

"Well, then, come and see me occasionally. I'll miss you." Tami squared her shoulders and huffed out a breath. "It's going to be fine, but I certainly have enjoyed serving with you on the council."

"Me too." Mattie was doing exactly what she wanted to do, but most every choice was accompanied with a little regret. She would miss Tami. She would miss the mayor and Margaret, the enforcer. She'd even miss Fred, who wasn't a bad guy when Bill wasn't egging him on. She sniffed back her tears. "Is she in there?"

"Yes. Everything's ready."

"Okay. Thanks, Tami. I'll be right in."

Tami slipped into the lunchroom, leaving Freeman and Mattie alone in the lobby. Freeman looked behind him and took Mattie's hand. "Are you sure?"

Mattie raised her eyebrows. "That's what Tami asked. Do I look like I'm torn about this?"

"*Ach, vell.* I know you enjoy being on the council, and I know you hate the thought of another Bill getting elected."

"I do, but there's no danger of that for at least three years. And if the voters are foolish enough to vote for another man like Bill, then I guess they get what they deserve."

Freeman's lips twitched. "That's a very unforgiving speech."

Mattie laughed. "A little too honest?"

"Maybe just a little."

She took a step closer to him and squeezed his hand. "I'm not going to put my life on hold for the *gute* of Byler. I'm going to be a little selfish this time."

"I, for one, am grateful for that, even though I feel like I'm the one who's being selfish." He sidled even closer and hooked his arm around her waist. Lord willing, nobody would come out of the lunchroom and see them standing like this. The bishop was sure to hear about it. "I'm willing to wait three more years if you want to serve out your term. I'll hate every minute of it, but I'll do whatever it takes to make you happy."

"We've already talked about this. Being with you makes me happy. Being your *fraa* is all I could ever wish for. Stop trying to talk me out of it."

He pulled her close until his arms were wrapped all the way around her. "I would never try to talk you out of this," he whispered, right before he leaned in and planted a tender and breathtaking kiss on her lips.

When they finally pulled apart, Mattie cuffed him on

the shoulder. "Why did you do that? Now I'm going to be completely worthless for the presentation."

He chuckled. "I couldn't resist, and you'll be fine. You don't even have to say anything tonight. All you have to do is look pretty, and that's never been hard for you."

Her heart did a little dance. She would thank Gotte every day for blessing her with the best man in the whole world. "Then let's go."

They walked into the lunchroom together just as the mayor stood up to the microphone. "Friends and neighbors, as you know, Mattie Zook has resigned from the town council, leaving me to appoint another council member to take her spot."

Along with the customary seven or eight regulars at the council meeting, there were probably thirty other people there to witness the swearing-in. Mattie and Freeman opted not to sit on the uncomfortable round stools and stood instead against the back wall. Since the audience was sitting in darkness, and everyone was facing the other way, Freeman took Mattie's hand and tucked her arm beneath his. She smiled at him. He smiled at her. This was where she wanted to spend the rest of her life, tucked closely next to his heart.

"We appreciate all the work Councilwoman Zook has done for the town, and we know that the new member of the council will carry on Mattie's legacy. I'm pleased to announce that I have appointed Cathy Larsen to the council. Congratulations, Cathy."

Freeman clapped louder than anyone in the room.